# the Mystery at Lilac Inn

## Eileen Haavik McIntire

Fourth in the Series

Amanita Books
Columbia, Maryland

Library of Congress Control Number:2019910949
ISBN: 978-0-9991565-5-1
Cover design by www.selfpubbookcovers.com/RLSather

Published by Amanita Books, an imprint of Summit Crossroads Press, Columbia, MD, USA.

The author welcomes your comments. E-mail her at eileenmcintire@aol.com. Also visit her website at www.secretpanels.net.

**Books By Eileen Haavik McIntire**

**The 90s Club Series**
*The 90s Club & the Hidden Staircase*
*The 90s Club & the Whispering Statue*
*The 90s Club & the Secret of the Old Clock*
*The 90s Club & the Mystery at Lilac Inn*

**Historical Adventures**
*Shadow of the Rock*
*In Rembrandt's Shadow*

**Suspense**
*The Two-Sided Set-Up*

**Visit Eileen's website at
www.SecretPanels.net**

# Table of Contents

# 1. Saturday

Nancy gripped the steering wheel and peered through the late morning fog shrouding the deserted country road ahead. She looked out at ghostly shapes of trees and shrubs. Drips from oppressive low-hanging branches overhead tapped like bony fingers on the car top.

"Are you sure we're going the right way?" she asked.

Sitting next to Nancy in the shotgun seat, Louise shook her head. "Never been here before. I don't know."

A wraith clothed in a flowing white gown leaped across the road in front of the car. Behind her trailed a small black cat. Nancy slammed on the brakes and screeched to a stop. As she caught her breath, she watched the woman disappear through the roadside shrubs into the fog.

"Shades of Wilkie Collins' woman in white," gasped Louise, referring to an early mystery writer, "and her familiar, the cat." She clutched at her heart in mock terror. "What was that?"

"Not an apparition. Was she fleeing something?" Nancy uneasily scanned the woods for a pursuer. "I almost hit her." She felt as if her white, curly hair stood on end. She glanced in the rearview mirror. No traffic behind her on this back road in West Virginia. Visions of zombies, escaped killers, and deranged hillbillies crossed her mind. No one knew where they were. Nancy erased those nightmares but stayed in place to calm down. Her hands still trembled on the wheel.

She glanced at Louise. "Are you okay? You didn't hurt your wrist when I braked, did you?" Nancy bit her lip. It was her fault Louise's wrist was broken in the first place. She'd been knocked down when they confronted dangerous criminals at Whisperwood Retirement Village, their home in central West Virginia. They were both ninety and founders of Whisperwood's able, alert, and active 90s Club.

"It's fine." Louise flexed her wrist. "I've been working out and swimming. I'm in great shape." She winked at Nancy. "Bring on the bad guys."

"Okay," Nancy said, still feeling shaken and tense. Where did that woman come from? The quiet stillness and the fog surrounding them felt creepy. Again she conjured up the horrors of a B movie. "You saw her too, didn't you?" Nancy asked

"Don't start getting weird on me," Louise said. "Sure. I saw that woman. She wasn't a spook." Her chuckle reassured Nancy. "You ever see a ghost lugging some kind of bag?" asked Louise. "Looked like a suitcase."

"It was a wheeled carry-on," said Nancy. "Can't imagine why she was pulling it through the woods if someone was after her."

"Maybe the bag is full of diamonds," Louise quipped with a sideways grin at Nancy. "Maybe they're stolen, and she knows you're coming." She shrugged. "Or it could be drugs."

Nancy shook her head. "Probably underwear." Her gaze swept across the dense foliage on both sides of the blacktop. Heavy branches of oak and hickory hung out over the road, adding to the hint of menace. "This is only a narrow country lane. Are you sure we're going the right way?"

Louise looked back at the road behind them. "We turned left at the old wooden church on the corner, like they said." She tossed her long gray braid over her shoulder. "Anyway, I saw a Lilac Inn sign a quarter-mile back pointing this way." She scanned the woods behind them. "I don't see our ghost or her white dress now. Nobody else around."

"So no one was chasing her." Nancy drove cautiously forward, watching for any more wayward pedestrians who might suddenly materialize.

"That we could see, anyway," added Louise.

Around the next bend, Nancy spotted a large sign, "Lilac Inn, Restaurant & Country Resort." An arrow pointed down a paved drive. Through the trees, a palatial white mansion gleamed in the sunlight breaking through the fog.

"Looks like Tara," Louise said as Nancy parked in the designated area. Nancy smiled, not up to a laugh yet after the close call. A whiff of fragrance from the inn's namesake in full spring bloom wafted by. What a lovely way to welcome guests, Nancy thought.

They strolled along a shady mulched path through oaks, hickories, and mountain laurel, then they passed rustic wooden cabins to reach the hotel verandah. Nancy was glad she'd worn slacks and walking shoes. This West Virginia resort emphasized hiking, canoeing, golf, tennis, and other outdoor activities. She glanced at Louise's khaki shirt, shorts, and leather hiking boots. She had replaced the cane she used at Whisperwood with a hiking stick. Louise called it a trekking pole. "Better than a cane," she insisted, "because I can stand upright." That outfit would fit in well with the resort's outdoorsy ambiance. As always, Louise wore a social action button on her shirt. This time she had dredged up an old and rusty "Give a Hoot, Don't Pollute."

They walked up the steps to the verandah. Nancy glanced at the other guests lounging in rocking chairs and a porch swing, who idly watched their ascent. The verandah was about twelve feet deep and stretched the width of the building. The gray floor decking set off two groups of white wicker chairs around coffee tables. At the far end, servers had set up four-top tables to extend the restaurant into the outdoors. Everything appeared freshly painted and well-maintained.

"Look there." Louise pointed at a ramp alongside the steps. "Help for people with disabilities. Good." She tossed her long braid over her shoulder.

Nancy nodded. Louise never gave activism a rest, but accommodations like the ramp were important and required by law for public places. Someone had to be the watchdog, especially in West Virginia, whose residents fought zoning laws and any other perceived assault on their rights.

The two women stepped through a set of double doors into a spacious lobby with varnished oak floors and old-fashioned, lilac-flowered wallpaper. In the center of the room, a crystal punch bowl held clusters of lilac blossoms on a marble pedestal. Their scent drifted across the foyer. Nancy finally relaxed as she took in the cool and calming quietness. "Charming atmosphere."

But then the charm was broken. A tall, overweight man in a white chef's jacket exploded out of a door down the hall. "I'm not going to stand for this," he said. "All those supplies cost money, and I need them. I can't do my job if I don't have them." He slammed the door shut behind him and stalked down the hall to disappear through another door.

Nancy looked at Louise.

"Trouble in River City," Louise mumbled. "Anyway, the food is supposed to be great." She headed for the dining room where a young woman in a lavender T-shirt and black jeans was opening the doors. "Good timing," Louise said. "Dining room is now open for lunch."

Nancy cast an approving eye at the light green and beige decor. White tablecloths with dark-green napkins covered the inside tables. It felt cool and relaxing to enter this pleasant room—quite a change from the spooky drive through the fog to reach the inn.

"I will seat you, ja?" said the hostess in an accent Nancy couldn't place.

"The verandah, please," said Louise.

The hostess led them through French doors to a table on the veranda alongside the back railing. Here, the tables were bare with a green paper mat at each place held down by flatware. The scent of lilacs was even more pronounced, floating in on the shrubs surrounding the hotel.

Nancy took a seat against the rail with the woods behind her, always more comfortable with her back to the wall—or railing in this case—where she could watch the other diners. It was a police officer's habit she had acquired in working with them. Louise snatched up the menu and eagerly pored over it.

"Good to have a change from Whisperwood," Nancy said. *And a friend so enthusiastic.*

"You bet," Louise agreed. "I'm getting the trout. Caught locally, it says."

Nancy inspected the menu, decided on the curried chicken salad and turned her attention to the other diners. Guests were arriving in twos and threes, most of them choosing to sit outside on the verandah. The sun had come out in earnest, quickly dispelling the lingering fog.

"Tell me about this place," Nancy said. "It's beautiful. I wouldn't mind spending a week here."

"It's a resort," said Louise, "with a meal package. Restaurant is open to the public for lunch and dinner. Most people come here to relax and don't want to leave to find a meal somewhere else." She folded her arms on the table. "Anyway, nearest town is five miles away."

"Lovely spot, quiet," said Nancy. "Are you going to tell me now how you found it?"

"My great-niece Julie and her husband Will bought it." Louise radiated pride. "Saved for years, studied hotel management, worked in other resorts, found investors. They know what they're doing."

Nancy surveyed the clean, pleasant surroundings. "I hope I can meet them."

Louise glanced toward the doors. "I don't know where they are. We should have seen at least one of them when we came in." She leaned toward Nancy and spoke softly. "I'm a little worried about them. When I talked to Julie on the phone a few days ago, she asked me about you."

Nancy sat back. "Me?"

"They'd heard about your exploits, know you're a retired detective, and they found out I pal around with you. She asked me to bring you along."

Nancy's eyes brightened. She missed detective work. Then she thought of the crimes they'd solved in the last year. Maybe not so retired, but she could do without the pain and the terror. Still, they had escaped with their lives, and they'd brought the criminals to justice. Nancy grinned at Louise. "Definitely sounds like a mystery. They must be busy running this place."

Louise nodded. "We'll look for them after lunch."

Their food arrived as Nancy watched the hostess escort a slightly overweight woman of average height to a table for two. She wore jeans, a short-sleeved white cotton shirt, and sandals, and she carried a book. She had curly brunette hair and appeared to be in her thirties. Unless she changed her clothes and dyed her hair in the last fifteen minutes, Nancy didn't think she was the woman in white, but her reddened eyes and frown gave her a sad look. There was buried anger, too, in the grim set of her mouth. After a cursory glance at the other diners and a quick peek at the menu, the woman opened her book.

Then an African-American family bounced in with two young children, a boy and a girl. The two kids ran to the railing and looked over it, while their parents selected a nearby table. The boy pointed down onto the lawn. "There's a turtle," he said excitedly.

"That's not a turtle," the girl answered scornfully. "It's just an old stump." Their parents hushed them and insisted they sit properly at the table.

The next person to be seated was a tall, thin, gray-haired man wearing khaki cargo shorts and a tan vest covered with pockets. He carried a small backpack that clunked when he set it on the floor. He barely acknowledged the hostess, showed no interest in the other diners, took his seat, and studied the menu.

Nancy continued watching the new arrivals, hoping the woman in white would appear. They hadn't passed any houses for more than a mile, so she had to be staying at the resort.

Louise pointed her fork at Nancy. "I know what you're doing," she said. "You're looking for that woman we almost ran down." She glanced around the room. "And you're trying to see which of these people are crooks. That's why you took that seat."

Nancy laughed. "You know me so well." Her eye caught a movement outside the dining room door, then a woman wearing a white dress walked in. Nancy studied her for a moment. "Is that her?" Nancy asked. "Doesn't quite look like the same dress, but I only had a glimpse."

Louise casually turned to stare at the woman. She shrugged. "Could be. Go ask her." Then she took another look. "No carry-on bag, but she's probably already checked in as a guest here."

"A little too much on the stout side, too," added Nancy. She ate her salad thoughtfully. What would she ask the woman? Did I almost run you down this afternoon? Why weren't you watching? Who were you running away from? Why?

She glanced at Louise who was observing her. "I'll go," Nancy said. Curiosity was her middle name. Everybody knew that about her. It's what got her into trouble but made her life interesting. She walked over to the woman in white who had been eyeing the door and recoiled in surprise to see Nancy standing over her.

"Pardon me," said Nancy politely and introduced herself. "Are you all right?"

"Of course," the woman said, appraising Nancy with gray, interested eyes. "Why wouldn't I be?" She sounded more like a New Yorker than a West Virginian. Her blonde hair was cut short in a shaggy style, and her tanned face was bland and unremarkable.

"Did I almost run you down on the drive this morning?" Nancy asked. The woman looked blank. "When you ran across the road in front of my car."

"It must have been someone else," the woman replied. "Say, are you alone? I am. Why don't you join me? My name is Marilyn."

"We've finished our lunch, but we can chat." Nancy waved at Louise to join them as she took a seat at Marilyn's table. Louise spoke to the server as she picked up her water glass to move to the third place at the other table. "I'm Louise," she said. "So are you our woman in white?"

Marilyn laughed. "No, I'm not, but I did read the mystery by Wilkie Collins. How about that?"

"Whoever it was ran across the road in front of my car and then disappeared into the woods. She seemed scared," said Nancy. "We hope she's all right."

"How strange," said Marilyn. "I didn't see anyone walking alongside when I drove here although I suppose some local farm kid . . ."

"Surprised us," said Louise. Nancy nodded.

"If nobody was hurt, forget about it," Marilyn added. "How long are you staying? I'm here for the week. I got laid off from my job. Registered nurse." For a moment something like anger flashed across her face, then she added, "Pretty upsetting, so I decided to go somewhere else. Try something different." She looked out at the woods surrounding the hotel and laughed. "And this hotel certainly has that."

"Tough break. When I was laid off years ago, I had panic attacks," said Nancy with a shudder.

Marilyn looked at her hands and didn't reply.

"My great-niece and her husband own Lilac Inn," explained Louise. "We're here for lunch, and then she's supposed to show us around." Her eyes darted to the door. "Haven't bumped into her yet. We live about an hour away."

"You live in the area? What's it like?" asked Marilyn. "I can't imagine being so far away from stores and theaters."

"You're a nurse, you said?" Louise winked at Nancy. "I worked for various unions and for a lot of social causes." She tossed her braid. "Some of them could probably use your skills."

Marilyn cast her an appraising look. "Can you fill me in about what's going on in this county? Social services, that is." She surveyed the surrounding woods. "Maybe I'd like to move here. Certainly won't do any harm to learn about how the services function in a rural area like this one. I'm looking for possibilities."

"Way to go!" Louise said, raising her hand to high-five Marilyn. "That's right up my alley. I can take you around. I'll show you how to get to Whisperwood, and we can go from there. You're here for the week?"

Nancy smiled at Louise's enthusiasm. She'd love to take on Marilyn as a project and find her a new job, especially if it helped one of her social causes. Nancy wasn't so sure about Marilyn and what her true motivation might be.

"Whisperwood?" Marilyn asked.

"Sure. That's where we live." Louise patted Nancy's arm. "Retirement community. We have all kinds of things going for the residents there, but also for the community around Whisperwood."

"Louise is shaping up our little village," added Nancy. "She got them to plant only noninvasive, native species, reduce pesticide use, and bring in a speaker on consumer fraud." Nancy smiled fondly at her friend.

"And I got them to OK my beehive near the garden." Louise nodded with satisfaction. "And Whisperwood has a college scholarship for the local high school kids who work there."

"It's a nice place to live and work," added Nancy, "and they do hire nurses, too."

Marilyn clasped her hands and chewed her lip as if she were thinking. "It sounds ideal," she said. "I'd like to visit Whisperwood and learn more about the social services in town."

Louise beamed. "Okay. We can probably do that later this week. I'll check my calendar."

Nancy watched them quietly, pleased that Louise had found a like-minded spirit. They finished their meals, paid the tab, and waved goodbye to Marilyn as she left for a yoga class.

"Now let's go find my niece," said Louise.

"Good," Nancy said. The chef's complaints and the missing hosts made her think all was not well at Lilac Inn.

***

## Ad in Travel Magazines
## Lilac Inn Resort: Wild and Wonderful

Spend a week or a weekend at beautiful Lilac Inn Resort, Spa, and Restaurant. Golf, tennis, hiking trails, canoeing, all in an elegant resort with a fine restaurant open to the public for lunch and dinner. The beautiful surroundings adjoin a Wildlife Management Area. Lilac Inn has the best West Virginia offers. Book your carefree vacation now! Call 304-555-5529.

# 2. Saturday Afternoon

Nancy and Louise ambled back to the lobby, then Louise led the way down a hall of what appeared to be meeting rooms. "I could swear this is the room the chef ran out of," whispered Nancy.

"Let's ask Julie what it was all about." Louise wasn't shy. She tapped on the door labeled "Manager."

"Come in," said a woman's voice inside. As they entered the office, she glanced up from a stack of papers and shrieked, "Aunt Louise!" She leaped out of her chair to hug Louise. Nancy stood by. She'd seen the troubled look on the niece's face, and her greeting was too emotional. Something was wrong.

Louise broke the hug. "Julie, this is my friend Nancy Dickenson."

"Yes, the detective. I'm so glad to meet you," she said, gesturing to the chairs in front of her desk, but she cast a doubtful glance at Nancy. Nancy knew what that was about. *My age.*

"Both of you," Julie amended. "Have you had lunch?"

They nodded. Nancy took a closer look at Julie's face and saw tension and worry. Her lips trembled, but she shook her head, pressing her lips together into a tight line as she reached to a hook on the wall and picked off a ring of keys. "Then let me show you around," she said but stopped to peek under her desk. "Come on, girl," she coaxed. "Meet the public."

A golden retriever with soulful eyes crawled out and took cover behind Julie. "It's okay, Tilly," Julie said. "They're nice people." She looked at Louise and Nancy. "She's a bit timid, I'm afraid, but she's a good girl. She doesn't know what to do since we won't let her bark at the guests." The dog followed Julie as she ushered them out of the office, locked the door, and led them down the hall. "Will drove to town for supplies. He'll be sorry he missed you."

"I'm sorry to miss him, too," said Louise. "How does he like working here?"

"You know how he is," Julie said with a shrug. "Loves tinkering and fixing things, so he's made this place look good."

"It's beautiful," said Nancy, noting the luster on the varnished floors. "You've got to be proud."

Julie smiled. "Thank you. We've worked hard. I'm so glad you came by, so I can show it off to you." She opened the door to a large room with floor to ceiling shelves along one wall. "Library and Game Room," Julie said. Books filled several shelves; games and puzzles were stacked on other shelves; and three card tables were set up in the center of the room. A half-completed puzzle spread across one

"We call ourselves a resort," said Julie, "and most of our guests usually come for a week. We did build a tennis court and a pool, and we have an agreement with the golf course owners to let our guests use their course. It abuts our property."

The next room was a TV room. "We show movies here

three nights a week. Usually old classics." Then Julie took them through the gym and out a rear door to the pool, tennis court, and golf course. "We have everything here for a relaxing stay. And we're next to a Wildlife Management Area with hiking trails. We even have a bird blind overlooking the pond."

"Quite a full-service resort, in fact," said Louise.

Julie nodded. "We mostly have hotel rooms in the main building, but we also offer several cabins for families or people who want to be really on their own."

"I'm impressed," said Louise.

"So am I," added Nancy. Judging from the cars in the parking lot, the resort had a number of guests even this early in the season. "How are the bookings?"

"We really opened about a month ago," Julie said, "and school's not out yet, but our chef is drawing local residents in for lunch and dinner. Right now, we have eight sleeping rooms and one cabin booked, so it's a good beginning. Bookings for the summer have been coming in steadily."

The business seems to be doing well, Nancy thought. Why does she want a private detective?

"Okay," said Louise. "We've seen the set-up, and it looks great. Now tell us what the problem is. Why did you want me to bring Nancy?"

Julie looked from Louise to Nancy, doubt in her eyes. Nancy stood tall and folded her arms as she gazed back. *She thinks we're too old for what she needs.* Julie's next words confirmed it.

"We're fine," she said, staring at her hands. "A few bugs in the system, that's all. And I'd heard so much about your friend Nancy from you, Louise, I wanted to meet her,."

Louise snorted. "Then why did the chef storm out of here before lunch, yelling about supplies being taken?"

Julie sighed. "I'm sorry you heard that. Everybody's nerves have been a little tight lately. That's part of the problem." She reached down to pet the dog who crept to her side and leaned against her.

Louise folded her arms and stood tall with Nancy. "Is that so? Then why do you seem so worried? What's wrong, Julie, and don't give me any bull hockey. Nobody messes with us."

"We're racking up quite a reputation at Whisperwood for solving problems and catching crooks," said Nancy. "You can trust us."

"Very well, then." Julie took a deep breath. "Someone here is a thief, and if that isn't enough, people say monsters are prowling our property." She smiled grimly at the shock on their faces. "Let's go back to my office."

***

### Item in a West Virginia Tourism Magazine

The latest star in West Virginia's fine resorts is Lilac Inn, located 15 miles north of Charleston. Owners Julie and Will Harris renovated the stately southern mansion once owned by coal magnate Tyrone Calhoun. It later became a plush bed and breakfast operated by the Cook family. The resort offers comfortable bedrooms, each with magnificent views of the surrounding countryside, a fine restaurant rapidly gaining fame in the Charleston area, an idyllic country setting next to the Wildlife Management Area, tennis courts, pool, and an 18-hole golf course.

# 3. Saturday Afternoon

Nancy and Louise followed Julie back to her office. Despite the worried frown on Julie's face, Nancy could see nothing wrong with the hotel. The restaurant, still serving lunch, was crowded and delicious aromas of sizzling hamburgers and barbecue wafted by. Thieves? Monsters? In this idyllic setting?

Julie was obviously troubled and dubious about any help she and Louise could provide. Ageism in action, no doubt. Able, alert, and active at ninety, Nancy scoffed at the assumptions made about older people and thought of herself as a perennial. She knew she had to fight the people who bought into the media images of walker-bound decrepit elderly. Bigoted people were easily manipulated by those same stereotypes. Sometimes Nancy exploited them to solve crimes. She could play innocent little old lady with the best of them.

Julie would probably hide any personal difficulties she and her husband were having. Anyway, domestic problems weren't Nancy's department. She was a detective, not a psychologist. She and Louise took the chairs facing Julie who sat behind the desk. Tilly padded past them to lie at Julie's feet.

"Your resort is lovely," said Nancy.

Julie nodded an acknowledgement. "Would you like tea? Coffee? Coke?"

A delaying tactic. Nancy could see Julie clench her jaw, doubt marking her face as she twisted and untwisted her hands contemplating them.

"I'm fine, thank you," said Nancy.

"Already had lunch," Louise muttered. Never one to prevaricate, she added, "What's wrong?"

"Something strange is going on here, and I don't like it." Julie picked up a couple of paper clips and rubbed them against each other. "I want our guests to feel comfortable and safe here. It's a family resort, not a mystery weekend."

"Is someone making trouble?" asked Louise, always ready for a fight.

Julie leaned back in her chair and shook her head before she spoke. "Someone on my staff seems to be a thief." She picked up a tissue, brushed it across her eyes, and blew her nose. "I'm not crying," she added, "allergies."

Nancy didn't think it was allergies.

Louise pursed her lips and folded her arms. "What's been stolen?"

Julie rapped on the desk. "High-quality supplies from the restaurant pantries and housekeeping closets."

Nancy studied the reddened, puffy eyes, the tension in Julie's body, and the grim look on her face. *She's close to the breaking point with worry and stress. This resort is a mammoth undertaking. They're probably operating on a thin margin with a heavy dose of borrowed money.*

"Why do you think it's someone on staff and not a guest?" she asked.

"Guests don't have access, and they leave after a week,

but the thefts continue. Has to be someone on staff." She looked at them through troubled eyes. "That's what the chef was yelling about this morning. I know you heard that. We can't afford the losses. We opened only a month ago, and let me tell you, things are pretty skinny right now."

"Do the staff go home when their shift is over?" asked Louise.

Julie shrugged. "Most do. They have their own cars and live nearby. Two interns from abroad are staying here. They're in an exchange program to learn how Americans manage hotels and restaurants. One of them also teaches yoga. Nice kids. I'd hate to think either one was the culprit."

"Nothing was stolen from the guests?" asked Nancy. Restaurant and housekeeping supplies wouldn't be too profitable.

"Not so far." Julie clenched her hand. "I'm afraid it's only a matter of time before they get hit, too."

"How long do guests usually stay?" asked Louise.

Julie fiddled with the paper clip. "This is a resort. People book for a week. Saturday to Saturday. Most don't bring their fancy clothes and jewelry, but some could, and a thief on staff would find that out quickly. I worry our supplies won't be enough, so he'll start after the guests."

"We could check out the situation, conduct background checks," said Nancy, "and talk to the staff . . ."

"Be careful how you talk to the staff. I don't want them suspicious of each other or feel they're not trusted. The atmosphere will turn ugly. We depend on a friendly attitude among our employees."

"Let me think for a minute," said Nancy.

"While you're thinking, we have another concern we need help on." Tilly growled as if she knew what Julie was going to say. Julie reached down to pet her.

"What else is going on around here?" asked Louise.

Julie sighed. "Have you ever heard of the Green Monster?" Tilly growled again.

Louise leaned back and waved her hand as if to push something away. "Totally debunked. Years ago."

"I've never heard of it," said Nancy. "What Green Monster?"

"I'll tell you the story." Julie sat up in her chair and eyed Nancy. "In 1952, two brothers at a farm near here watched a bright object cross the sky and land on a local man's pasture. They raced home and told their mother they'd seen a UFO crash in the hills." Julie paused and picked up another paper clip.

"She got together a group to try to find whatever the boys had seen. According to the newspaper articles, it was a large pulsating 'ball of fire' that left a pungent mist making their eyes water and noses burn. The group of observers reported that a creature bounded towards them and then headed off. The group returned home and called the sheriff who investigated the area. Others arrived and before you knew it, the news media were full of stories about a flying saucer setting down in a field."

"Yeah, all a bunch of hogwash," said Louise. "The boys saw a meteor land. That's all."

Julie glanced at Louise and nodded. "I'm sure that's right, but the media made a big deal out of it and despite the so-called UFO and aliens being explained away and debunked, the locals put on a Green Monster Festival around here for years. Probably some people still believe a flying saucer landed."

"It sounds like a movie I saw a long time ago." Nancy leaned back and stared at the ceiling. Then she snapped her fingers. "*Invaders from Mars.* About a boy who saw a flying saucer land. In the movie, everyone who went to the site to investigate came back with some kind of dart in their neck that put them under the control of malevolent aliens."

"I wish I'd never heard of it," said Julie vehemently. "That and the Mothman."

"Mothman?" Nancy wanted to laugh at the name, but instead she raised an inquiring eyebrow. "Another monster?"

"Wow," added Louise. "You got two monsters here?"

Julie waved her hand. "Another local legend."

"More hogwash, no doubt," Louise said.

Julie glanced at Louise and nodded. "Like you said. Years ago, some people in this area thought they saw a huge monster with red eyes flying around at night. They immediately told everyone they'd seen a Martian or some such. Investigators came in, studied the reports, and decided it was only a large sandhill crane. Those cranes can be taller than a human being, and at night in the light of a flashlight their eyes reflect a red glow."

"Has somebody been seeing a Green Monster or Mothman around here recently?" asked Nancy.

"Yes," said Julie, frowning with narrowed eyes. "At least, a rumor is floating around that a monster was seen, but the rumor can't be pinned down. Why would someone spread a rumor like that? People in town are accusing us of trying to revive the Green Monster rumor to rev up our business. It's all ridiculous."

"Of course," drawled Louise, "it could be good for business. Draw curiosity seekers."

"The locals are afraid it would bring in the wrong kind, people who'd tramp across their lawns and flower beds but not spend a dime here. They're blaming us for starting the rumors."

"Unbridled sightseers." Nancy nodded. "I've seen that kind of destruction."

Julie reached down to stroke Tilly. "So have I. What's worse is that a couple of our guests told me they'd been frightened by some kind of monster in the woods. They've seen the red eyes peering at them and a large hulk coming after them. I'm sure it's all nonsense, too, but those guests left early. They'll tell their friends. We need good word-of-mouth, not scary monster stories."

Nancy tapped her lips. "What do you think they saw?" she asked. A revival of stories about a mythical Green Monster and a Mothman could be a nuisance or it could attract more business, but it might seem catastrophic to someone already under heavy stress exacerbated by the thefts.

"Who knows?" Julie replied. "Our guests come from urban areas like Washington or Baltimore or even Pittsburgh. A deer could come running at them in the dark and terrify our city folk. Or an owl or, like the UFO investigators reported, a sandhill crane."

"Wouldn't Tilly make a ruckus?" asked Louise.

Nancy smiled at the thought of timid Tilly making a ruckus about anything.

Julie glanced down at the dog who gazed soulfully back at her. "She's a sweetie pie, but not up to a ruckus, I'm afraid. Not even much of a watchdog." She reached down to scratch behind Tilly's ears. "We don't need Green Monsters or Mothmen or mysterious thefts wrecking our plans."

"Could someone be using the thefts and monster sightings to sabotage your business?" asked Nancy.

Julie gasped. "Sabotage?" She frowned. "Sabotage? I never thought of that." She shook her head. "I can't believe anyone would try to wreck our business. Why? We're no threat to anyone, and we provide good jobs. We don't even have much competition out here. If we did, and they tried to buy us out, all they'd get would be a bundle of debts and a business yet to prove itself." She shook her head. "Anyway, the thefts are minor but persistent. The monsters don't really have anything to do with us. I don't think sabotage is the reason."

The three looked at each other. Finally, Nancy nodded, hiding the quiver of fear and uncertainty that she felt, but she knew they, that is, the 90s Club, could help Julie. "To investigate this," she said slowly, "we'd need to stay here."

Louise sat up, grinning with enthusiasm. "I'm for that."

Julie raised her hands. "Wait a minute. I don't mean for you to take this on. I thought you might have some ideas about how to handle these problems."

"You need help," argued Louise, "and we've got a proven track record."

"We do," said Nancy. "We'll track down the culprits and deflate those monsters."

"Piece of cake," added Louise, flexing her muscles.

Julie looked from one to the other, smiling at Louise's enthusiasm. She paused to stare out the window. "I'm afraid you'll get hurt, your age, you know . . ."

"Us?" Louise snorted with a glance at Nancy. "We've bested the worst, and we're still here, but they're not."

Nancy nodded but she thought again of Louise's wrist, broken in their first case. *That was my fault.* They'd almost been killed in their last one. Now they were landing in the middle of a new situation, but missing supplies and UFOs didn't seem too dangerous or difficult, more like pranks.

Julie wrung her hands. "You know, I can't afford to pay you."

"Are you kidding?" Nancy waved the thought away. "We'll pay you for a lovely, restful week at a beautiful resort and enjoy ourselves while we find the thief and what's going on with the monsters."

"It will be fun," said Louise.

"You two are something," said Julie, shaking her head. "All right. You're on, but you'll stay here as our guests, free of charge."

Nancy glanced at Louise. Julie would feel bad about taking their money while asking them to work for her, but this arrangement would be a win-win for all of them.

Louise chuckled as she glanced at Nancy. "Sounds great to me. And while we're enjoying ourselves, we'll keep our eyes open for the thief, detecting. What do you think, Nancy?"

She'd love to take on Julie's concerns and stay in this luxury resort, but what if they failed? She refused to believe age could limit her ability as a detective, but she was confronted with negative beliefs about aging wherever she went.

Louise saw Nancy's hesitation. "What? Are you getting timid and scared in your old age?" she taunted. "My wrist is fine, and anyway, that was an accident." She shook her hand to demonstrate, and Nancy watched her cover her wince. "These thieves are penny ante, not big-time criminals and murderers. I vote for helping Julie out."

Nancy chewed her lip. She'd been an investigator all her life and only hesitated to protect her friend and, she supposed, her reputation as an investigator, but Louise was raring to go. They would have to start right away to catch the thief. Then she looked into Julie's face and saw the desperation in her eyes. "Of course, we'll help," she said. "In fact, we've already begun to sort out the guests. Don't worry. We're on the job as of now."

"And you can call on us to help out however we can in other ways, too," added Louise. "You're family!"

"A week's stay at this beautiful resort is an excellent return on our work for you," said Nancy. "We can't guarantee results, but we'll do the best we can."

"Okay, then." Julie nodded toward Nancy as if making up her mind. You'll stay here with access to everything, even the golf course. Anything you need or want, you can have, but you have to promise me that if your investigation turns dangerous, you will tell me, and we'll notify the police."

Louise beamed. "Lovely idea. And we won't be taking up rooms you could use for paying guests because it's still a bit early in the season."

"We aren't fully booked yet, so it won't be an issue." Julie chewed her lip as she studied Nancy.

Nancy smiled reassuringly. Julie had seen her hesitation, but the more Nancy thought about it, the more she liked the idea. This place was only an hour from Whisperwood. Living there was like being on a cruise ship. She certainly didn't need a resort vacation. Still, Lilac Inn would offer a change of scenery and the challenge of a new investigation. She and Louise could easily go home anytime if necessary. As she realized how simply this week could be arranged, glee seemed to swell up inside. Undercover work. Real detective work. She could do this, and it would be fun. Amateur thieves, it sounded like. Not dangerous at all. She shivered as she thought again of the past year when thieves and murderers almost killed her and Louise and their friends, George and Fitz, too.

"One thing," Julie said. "I don't want to believe it's a staff person who's responsible. And I don't want them suspicious of each other or upset because they think I think they're guilty. You'll have to be subtle. Watch for anything that seems odd or wrong to you, then tell me."

"Of course," said Nancy. "I understand that. Bad for morale. Makes people nervous even if their conscience is clear."

"That's right." Julie looked from Nancy to Louise. "The staff are as upset as I am about the thefts."

Louise reached over and tapped Nancy's hand. "Did you hear me? What do you think? I'm ready. We can start tomorrow, which is Sunday. We'll join the other guests for the week and keep our eyes open."

Nancy nodded, a smile growing on her face. "I think so. Yes, we can start tomorrow." She looked at Julie. "That is, if it's okay with you."

"Perfect." Julie beamed at them. "I can't tell you what a relief this is. Louise has told me all about you, Nancy. I know you're excellent at this kind of work despite. . ."

*Despite our age she was going to say.* Nancy drew herself up. "Not only me," said Nancy. "Louise, too, and our able assistants, George and Fitz."

Louise nodded with a grin. "We're a good team."

"I'll introduce you to our security guards," said Julie, heading for the door. We have three on duty here, each taking eight-hour shifts, so we're covered 24 hours a day."

Nancy reached out a hand to restrain her. "I don't think so. It will be better if no one knows who we are and why we're here."

Julie looked at her doubtfully. "You really think so?"

Nancy nodded with lips set firmly. "Yes, I do. We don't know who's stealing, or who's reviving the monsters, and we don't know why. They think they're safe and can operate with impunity. We don't want them to be on the alert."

***

### E-Mail to Upcoming Guests
### Reservation Confirmed

Thank you for choosing Lilac Inn. You will find everything here for your comfort and convenience. Be sure to pack your swimsuit but most of your needs from golf clubs and tennis rackets to water floats can be borrowed, rented, or bought at Lilac Inn. A daily schedule of events will be posted in the lobby each day. If a tour or activity interests you, be sure to put your name in early at the reception desk. Tours book up fast. We wish you a pleasant stay.

*Julie and Will Harris, Owner/Managers*
*Lilac Inn Resort and Restaurant*

# 4. Saturday Evening

"Golf, you say?" George Burroughs rubbed his hands eagerly. He sat with Nancy, Louise, and their friend, Fitz Connelly, in the ballroom-sized dining room at Whisperwood Retirement Village. White tablecloths graced the tables in the peach-aqua color scheme of the room. The four friends, all over ninety, had formed the 90s Club at Whisperwood the preceding year. Their investigations into shady happenings at the village had saved it, protected its residents, and given the 90s Club its crime-solving reputation.

Nancy stared at George's tie. Did it really have red and gold sequins sewn on it? He usually wore bright colors, but sequins on a tie? She sneaked another look. Yep. Sequins on his tie.

"Tennis?" said Fitz Connelly. He no longer wore the ubiquitous tool belt he'd affected the first several months after he'd arrived at Whisperwood but kept the polo shirt and jeans. His full head of tight white curls and neatly trimmed beard contrasted nicely with his darker skin and gave him a distinguished look underlined by a vaguely British-Jamaican accent, acquired while growing up in Jamaica and modified by working around the world. He was a widower with no children. "Where is this resort exactly?" he asked.

"Only an hour away," said Louise. "It's about fifteen miles from Charleston and five miles from a small town, and it's next to a wilderness management area."

Fitz gazed at them with pursed lips. "Wilderness area?"

"And a pond," Nancy added. "There will be a lot of birds, and Julie says they have a bird blind." She knew Fitz was an ardent birder. What if Fitz and George joined them? The four of them made a great team. "The hotel doesn't have many guests right now."

"Can we come, too?" Fitz and George both added simultaneously. They looked at each other sheepishly and laughed.

Nancy smiled, pleased they would want to help. Of course they would. "I'm sure the hotel can accommodate you," Nancy said.

Their server, an African-American teenager named Taneesha, arrived and filled their water glasses. Then she stood with pen and pad in hand ready to take their orders. "What hotel is that?" she asked, her expression alert and interested as usual.

Nancy looked up at her. "Lilac Inn. It's about an hour from here."

Taneesha nodded. "I know it. My cousin Daquon works there. The owner is teaching him hotel maintenance."

Nancy tucked this nugget into her memory. Daquon might be useful. "Does he like working there?" she asked.

"I haven't heard any complaints." Taneesha glanced at the hostess desk. "Uh oh. I've got to get your orders, or they'll start checking on me."

Nancy doubted that. Taneesha was efficient and hard-working. She was observant, too, and had helped Nancy solve two cases at Whisperwood. She was also a short-timer, heading off to college in August.

"I'll have the tilapia and shrimp sauce," Nancy said. "And please send the manager over so we can order wine." Whisperwood was strict about alcohol and its underage staff.

The others gave their orders, and Taneesha disappeared into the kitchen. The manager arrived at their table and took four orders for chardonnay, everyone's choice this evening.

"Great minds think alike," quipped George. "Tell us about the case."

"Don't know much," said Louise. "There's a thief at the hotel. Julie thinks it's someone on staff." She twirled her water glass and leaned back in the chair.

"Someone's also spreading rumors," added Nancy, "They're saying the Green Monster and Mothman are alive and well and hanging around the resort."

"Whoa," George sat up. "Green Monster? Mothman?"

Nancy laughed. "I'd never heard of them, either." She explained the story.

"Kind of like Sasquatch," said Fitz.

"Abominable snowman," added George. "This is getting interesting."

"So our job is to squelch the stories and find the thief," Nancy summed up. "But we need to be careful in talking with the staff. Mainly keep our eyes open. And also listen for anyone, probably a guest, spreading monster stories."

"Piece of cake," said Louise.

Nancy hoped, as Louise said, it would be a piece of cake. She watched Taneesha move among the tables. "Cousin Daquon is a bonus we didn't expect. He might come in handy."

Louise looked at Nancy and laughed. "I caught that, too."

George pushed his lips back and forth. "What if Fitz and me show up for the week?" he said, glancing at Fitz. "Paying resort guests, pure and simple."

"I think they'd love to have you," said Nancy.

Louise reached over and squeezed George's hand. "That'd be wonderful." They looked into each other's eyes.

Oh, brother, thought Nancy. Everyone knew Louise and George were an "item," but she hoped they'd play it cool at Lilac Inn to avoid attracting undue notice. The thought led her to Fitz. Dear Fitz. She had known him since her college days, and they'd kept in touch through marriages, deaths, career moves, and so on even if it was only an exchange of holiday cards and letters. He moved to Whisperwood shortly after she did, but it was only a few weeks ago that he told her about the tragic loss of his son. She saw how difficult it was for him to talk about it, and his sharing, his vulnerability, touched her heart. Her eyes softened now when she looked at him.

Fitz caught Nancy's eye, inclined his head toward Louise and George, and winked. Nancy smiled. They were in perfect accord, but then wistfulness and sad memories of her first two husbands clouded her thoughts, and she looked away.

As if he read her mind, Fitz cleared his throat to bring her back from that dark place. "I'd enjoy a week at a resort," he said, "especially if I can get some tennis in."

"That's great," said Louise. She was grinning at George. He was grinning back.

"The 90s Club strikes again, but wait a minute," put in Nancy. "Let's think about this. What's the best strategy here? Should we know each other," she explained, "or would it be better to act like strangers, fellow hotel guests?"

All of them stared at the table. The manager brought their wine, and they toasted each other. Then their dinners came. Halfway through the tilapia, Nancy broke the silence. "If we pretend we don't know each other, we can investigate separately and develop friendships as the week progresses. Best of both worlds."

"I don't know about that," said George. "We ought to be old friends meeting again by coincidence. I want to be able to pal around with you gals."

"I don't think it will help to pretend we don't know each other," said Fitz. "People are bound to ask us where we live, and once we all share that, they'll put two and two together. But let's play it by ear. George and I will make reservations tonight. I'll cancel out whatever appointments I have for next week."

"I already have," said Louise.

"Me, too," added Nancy

George sat back, patting his lips with his napkin. "Don't have any. Not a social butterfly like the rest of you."

"Why don't you two rent one of the cabins?" suggested Nancy. They're nice, all modern facilities and will be more private if we have to get together and talk. They have two bedrooms, I believe."

"They better," muttered George. "Is it easy to walk around that place? I've got my cane, you know."

"I use trekking poles," said Louise. "Maybe not the cabin, then. The rest of the hotel has accommodations for people with disabilities."

"They got golf carts, don't they?" George asked suspiciously. "If they don't, I'm not going."

"Of course they do," said Nancy, remembering her first case at Whisperwood and the golf cart ride that ended one life but saved hers.

Fitz was getting bored with the haggling. "So what's our strategy? How are we going to conduct this investigation?"

"Carefully," said Louise. "I don't want to get tied up and almost killed this time."

"Neither do we," the others said in chorus. None of them laughed. Nancy knew they were all remembering the close calls that almost killed them in previous cases at Whisperwood and during their trip to Fort Lauderdale. She felt responsible for the danger she'd put them in and wanted nothing like that to happen again.

She nodded at Louise. "You start. Tell them about your niece and nephew and how they turned an old building into a resort."

Louise filled them in on the hotel. "It's only been open for a month. They've sunk a lot of money into it themselves and acquired additional investors. They need good publicity, not notoriety with stories about monsters and thefts." She glanced at Nancy. "Your turn."

Nancy laid down her fork and rested her elbows on the table. "Julie gave me a list of the guests and the staff. After dinner, we can return to my apartment and go over them. We might spot something."

"Okay." George rummaged in his pocket and pulled out a small bottle of pills. "Allergies. If we're going to Nancy's place, I gotta take these."

"We've talked with one guest already at lunch today," said Louise. "I don't see how she could be involved in anything illegal."

"But I have questions about the other guests we saw," added Nancy, "and the woman we almost ran down."

"The woman in white," said Louise.

Nancy nodded. "The woman in white."

***

**Notice to Arriving Guests**

Upon arrival, pull up in front of the hotel. Our staff will unload your bags and take them to your room for you. Hand them your car keys, and they'll park your car in the parking area. You may leave your car in any available space there.

*Will and Julie Harris, Managers/Co-Owners*
*Lilac Inn Resort and Restaurant*

# 5. Saturday Night

After dinner, the foursome trooped down the hall to Nancy's apartment. They stayed outside while Nancy shooed Malone, her overgrown cat with a savage temper and a grumpy disposition into the bedroom. He was known to nibble on ankles and apparently saw Nancy's guests as tasty delicacies.

Piles of papers were spread out on the sofa and dining room table. Nancy cleared the table and waved at the chairs around it. The others were used to Nancy's lack of housekeeping skills and took their places.

Nancy brought her purse to the table and pulled a sheaf of papers out of it as she sat. "Here's the list of staff and guests for the week. Two of the staff are interns; one from Ireland, one from Norway. They're here in an exchange program to study American methods. I copied the list for each of you. It would be good to memorize it." She passed the lists around. "I'll read the names out, and if anything occurs to you about these people, share it. Most of the other staff live in the area." She began to read.

"We've told you about the owners, Julie and Will Harris. Julie oversees the reservations, restaurant, and housekeeping staff while Will oversees maintenance and grounds along with Taneesha's cousin, Daquon. They've only been in business a month and are stretched tight financially.

"Head of housekeeping is Carola Crain. Local. Father was a miner. She has two grown kids, one of them works with her, Missy Crain. Missy is part-time but will move to full-time when the season gets going.

"The groundskeepers are an outside company on contract with no access to the guest rooms or other facilities. The restaurant chef is Tom Boysie, usually called Chef Pierre by the staff. The two servers, as I said, are interns from other countries here for six months. They live on the property in a house with Julie and Will." Nancy paused and looked at the others over her glasses. "Neither one drives, and they have to rely on hitching a ride with the hotel van if they want to go to town."

Louise nodded. "Can't see them stealing hotel supplies. Where would they hide them? What would they do with them? Besides, they probably have to fill out all kinds of forms to come here, and their future careers ride on doing well and getting good recommendations."

"Humph," said George, adjusting his seat. "I say we rule out Daquon and the groundskeepers. Taneesha vouches for Daquon and that's enough for me. The groundskeepers are outside contractors and wouldn't have access to culinary and housekeeping supplies."

"Yeah," added Louise. "And why would anyone risk his job by stealing supplies or spreading rumors about the Green Monster? Doesn't make sense."

"What about the guests? We need a list of them, too," Fitz said, laying aside the staff list. "One of them could be the rumor-monger, might even be intent on sabotaging the operation for some competing company."

"I've got the guest list here," said Nancy. She passed out copies of the list. "Fortunately, there aren't too many right now."

"I'm wondering who or what frightened the woman in white," added Louise.

Fitz viewed the list through squinted eyes. "What is this about a woman in white?" he asked.

"She ran across the road in front of me like a scared rabbit," Nancy explained, shuddering at the memory. "I almost ran her down."

"She was wearing a long white dress," added Louise. "Reminded us of the woman in that Wilkie Collins' mystery. I'd like to know what she was running from."

"Read the list," said George, drumming his fingers.

Nancy scanned down the list. "Here's a surprise. Harvey Smithson is staying there. Remember him?"

The faces around the table looked blank.

"He lives here at Whisperwood. He's a jeweler. He gives talks on how to buy precious stones and the history of jewelry." She looked at their puzzled faces. "He's the one who spread those plastic ants all over the buffet table in the dining room," she added.

"Oh. That guy," said Louise, shaking her head. "He almost gave the dining room manager a heart attack with those ants."

A faint smile crossed Nancy's face. Harvey had made a name for himself that time.

"Don't care for him much," said George.

"If the thief only stole jewels," Louise said, "instead of

housekeeping supplies, then we'd know where to search."

Nancy continued with the list. "Here's a Malcolm Smithson." She looked up. "That must be Harvey Smithson's brother. . .I guess. Maybe a son. Harvey seemed like a confirmed bachelor to me, but people can be surprising.

"Then there's Aysha and Cole Robinson with their two kids, Kimberly and Kai." Nancy glanced at Louise. "They must be the family having lunch when we were there. Maybe the kids are home-schooled."

"They were cute," added Louise.

"Cute. Yeah, I guess." Nancy never had children of her own and tended to keep her distance or treat them like small adults.

"Kaye Anderson, alone."

"Could she be the 'woman in white'?" asked Louise.

Nancy shook her head. "We saw her at lunch, remember?" She turned back to the list. "Lew Cookson, also alone. Evan Lester. Ann Bashaw and Lula Beall. Sarah and Gary Lochowsky. Marilyn Jackson."

"Six women possibles for the woman in white," grumbled Louise.

"We can rule out Marilyn Jackson," said Nancy. "We talked to her at lunch. She knew nothing about it and didn't resemble the woman at all."

"Are we showing up there tomorrow?" asked George, shifting his body in the chair.

Nancy nodded. "You and Fitz go separately and make your own reservations. Rates will be down since it's not the season, yet. You can see by the list, the hotel isn't even half full. Plenty of rooms available. Louise and I will leave early tomorrow morning." This reminded her that she needed to arrange for someone to take care of Malone. Her kitty would not be pleased at the change. *I'll have to talk with him. Give him extra treats.* He'd punish her if she didn't.

Fortunately, Whisperwood's Home Support Team offered pet sitting services. The support staff would still be at peril from Malone, who was not a nice kitty, but one person had made special efforts to gain his trust and was allowed to serve him.

"One more thing," Nancy said as they rose from the table. "This is Saturday. We have until next Saturday, when this crop of guests goes home, to find out what's happening at Lilac Inn. That's one week. Seven days."

George whistled. "That's not much time. We'll have to work fast."

***

### Note to Guests at Lilac Inn

We strive to make your visit as comfortable as possible. Please let the staff know if you have a problem or concern. We will endeavor to fix it as quickly as possible. We also keep common toiletry items on hand such as toothpaste, toothbrushes, shampoo, combs, etc. If you forgot to pack such items, drop by the front desk. Also, Sam Johnston in the Pro Shop will be happy to schedule your tee times and supply whatever equipment you need.

> *Your hosts,*
> *Julie and Will Harris, Owner/Managers*
> *Lilac Inn Resort and Restaurant*

# 6. Sunday Morning
## SEVEN DAYS TO GO

"When Julie and Will were planning Lilac Inn," Louise said as they packed Nancy's car the next morning, "they decided to make it an ecotourism site, you know, where they try to protect the environment as much as they can. Recycling. Native plants. Composting. Elimination of pesticide use. You know the drill."

Nancy wasn't sure how golf courses fit into sustainability, but the ecotourism idea was laudable. "Sounds good," she said. "Julie didn't mention that at all."

"Too worried, I guess, so I'm gonna help. I've got my collection of honey in this box, and I'll get Julie to let me offer honey tastings to the guests." Obviously proud of this unique idea, Louise grinned at Nancy. "Friends have been sending me honey from around the world for years. I've got honey the bees made from tupelo tree blossoms in Mississippi, lemon tree blossoms in Israel, white waxy honey from Ethiopia, avocado honey from Florida, heather honey from Scotland, and I forget where the others are from . . ."

Louise had taken up beekeeping that spring and enthusiastically talked about it to anyone who showed even the faintest whiff of interest. "I can tell them about bees, too. People ought to know their bees and honey. That's an ecotourism subject, for sure. It's important."

"Excellent idea," Nancy said, hiding a smile. She stowed their suitcases and the box of honeys in her car trunk. Then Louise laid her beekeeping suit and hat on the box with other beehive paraphernalia.

By ten-thirty that morning, they'd received their room keys and were settled in at the resort. "We're not booked up," Julie said, waving her hand from behind the reception counter, "as you can see, so you can get into your rooms early. Usually, check-in time is three p.m."

"All right," said Louise. "Let me show you my idea." She set the cardboard box on the counter and donned the hat.

Nancy wandered into the library, thinking there must be a local book or pamphlet about this property. The Internet only offered the resort's website. She found an entire shelf of books about the region by local authors, including a pamphlet on the Green Monster and a brochure on the ghost-hunting services of a local woman who also offered palm and tarot readings. At the end of the shelf were three slim, leather-bound books entitled, *The History, Times, and Lives of Lilac Inn, 1830-Present*. The book was copyrighted 1950. Nancy smiled. Not quite the present. She picked up one of the copies and leafed through it.

Then Louise called her from the hall. "Come meet my great-nephew." Nancy slipped the book into her purse and joined Louise to greet a middle-aged, brown-haired man in baggy plaid shorts and blue polo shirt, standing with one elbow on the reception counter. He had roaming heavy-lidded eyes like a lizard and beaked nose like a hawk. Nancy refused to go by appearances, but his strong features drew her interest.

"Hello, Ms. Dickenson, ma'am," he said with exaggerated deference.

Nancy revised her opinion. Maybe not interesting at all. Just banal. He'd treat her with kid gloves, too, Nancy thought. Another case of ageism in action, but she was courteous. "Call me Nancy. I'm pleased to meet you."

Will wiped his hands on his pants. He glanced down at them. "Sorry. Working in the shop. Hands are greasy." His eyes turned toward the side wall, then the door, but never once looked at her. Nancy found it disturbing, but she had exploited the hasty assumptions others made about her enough times to avoid that trap herself. She glanced at Louise. What did she think of her great-nephew?

Whatever she thought, she wasn't showing anything but a friendly excitement at seeing Will again. Nancy followed her lead, and Julie looked pleased. He must be all right, she thought, since Julie married him, and they've been together almost ten years. Nothing seemed off about their relationship. So far.

"I'm interested in what you're doing to promote ecotourism here in West Virginia," Nancy said.

"Julie's idea." Will cast a fond glance toward his wife. "We're listed on several ecotourism sites." He chuckled. "Don't you worry, though, we don't go overboard, like with composting toilets and stuff like that."

Nancy saw fleeting annoyance cross Julie's face. She was the driving force here and had the vision. What role did Will play? She supposed the golf course was his idea.

"Nancy and I support ecotourism and want to know all about it," said Louise. "Climate change is real. We have to protect our environment, and right now, we're filling it with poison, covering the land with asphalt and concrete and producing way too many people."

Louise was ready to begin lecturing, but Will interrupted her. "Of course." He laughed. "All for that. Have you heard about our aliens from outer space?"

Julie frowned. "We agreed not to bring up those rumors."

"Oh, but honey," said Will, "they add to the interest of this place." He turned to Nancy. "Don't you think?"

Julie glanced at Nancy and Louise. "We had two guests leave early," she said, "because they saw red-eyed monsters in the woods."

Will brushed that off. "They'd leave if they saw a snake in the woods, too. I wouldn't worry about it."

Julie bit her lip. Nancy saw Louise's eyes spark as she narrowed them in Will's direction. Nancy wasn't too impressed with Will either. They were saved from Louise's angry rebuttal when Will turned to the door. "Now if you'll excuse me. . ." He winked at Nancy. "I'm an inventor, too," he said, "besides an innkeeper."

"Wait a minute, Will," said Julie, "we need to discuss some landscaping details. . ."

He waved as he hurried away. "Later, later."

Nancy watched Julie stare down at her hands. At that moment, a woman in a light and filmy white caftan hurried by lugging a wheeled carry-on bag. Nancy glanced at her, then took a second look as she recognized her as the "woman in white." Nancy grabbed Julie's arm. "That woman." Nancy nodded toward her as she trotted down the hall. "Who is she?"

Julie glanced at the retreating figure. "That's Patty

Hovermale. She's a neighbor and our local spirit guide and fortuneteller." She grinned. "So she says. Why?"

"She's the woman I almost ran down."

"She was in the road?"

"Ran across it in front of me, wearing that white dress. Ghostlike." Nancy shuddered. "Scared me to death."

Julie shrugged. "She calls herself a ghost hunter, palm reader, you name it. Anything to make a dime." Julie folded her arms. "Hangs around here looking for business. She's poor and desperate and probably also lonely." Julie squared her shoulders and added, "But she's good for recreation on a rainy day and likes to dress the part. Adds interest."

If she hangs around the hotel, thought Nancy, and she's looking for money, she might also have sticky fingers. Someone worth watching. "So what does she do here?"

"I guess you could call her part of the entertainment," Julie said with an arched eyebrow. "If you can believe it in this day and age, she'll be holding a séance here every week—if there's any interest—and show up at teatime and after dinner to read palms and the tarot cards. Actually, she has quite an amusing act. I'm not sure if she takes it all seriously or not, but the guests like her. I'm not into that stuff myself."

"She carries her tarot cards and séance stuff around with her?" asked Nancy. It brought back memories of her second husband, the magician. A séance. He would have loved that, loved figuring out the medium's tricks. But Julie was talking, and Nancy shook off the memories.

"She's never without that carry-on," Julie said. "Maybe it's some sort of security blanket for her. She's a recent widow and has a hard life. It does make it convenient to lug her secret paraphernalia around, whatever that is."

"You never hear of anyone holding a séance anymore," Louise said, arms folded and skepticism in her voice. "Bunkum, like the Green Monster."

"Sure, but on a rainy night. . ." Julie replied. "Here's an interesting thing about Patty. She loves to read true crime stories. Get her talking about that subject, and you'll be there till Saturday." She smiled at Nancy. "Up your alley. Anyway, the séance and fortunetelling are all in fun. This place is supposed to be haunted, you know."

Louise snickered. "Every huge old house is supposed to be haunted."

"Speaking of that," Nancy put in, "I borrowed one of the histories from the library."

Julie smiled and the worry lines disappeared. "Good. The house goes back before the Civil War. It was built by a wealthy family as a hunting lodge and summer retreat. Union soldiers camped here and afterward, it was sold to another wealthy family who enlarged it. In fact, every successive owner added rooms and more features. The last one before us turned it into a bed and breakfast. We were lucky it came on the market when it did."

"It's beautiful, and you've worked hard renovating and maintaining it," said Nancy.

A brief smile crossed Julie's face. "Thank you. Tomorrow you'll have to walk the trail to the pond and the birdwatching blind. We don't allow hunting on our land, but we're next to the state Wildlife Management Area, which is open to hunters during hunting season." She hastened to add, "Don't worry. It's not hunting season now, though."

"When Louise hears about the birdwatching blind, she'll get me up early," said Nancy. Fitz was a birdwatcher, too. *He'll love this place.*

"Speaking of the outdoors," said Louise, "let's take a look around."

She and Nancy walked out to the lobby as Fitz and George arrived. Fitz had binoculars around his neck, and George labored under a bag of golf clubs.

"Hey, Nancy," Fitz called as he walked in, "I've already seen a red-tailed hawk—flew right in front of us."

"Almost gave me a heart attack," grumbled George, dropping the golf bag on the polished wooden floor. "What's a bird like that doing out here, anyway?"

Nancy caught Louise's eye. So much for appearing to be strangers to George and Fitz. They laughed as a young African-American man wearing blue overalls hurried forward and picked up the golf clubs. "I'll hold the clubs till you check in and get a room number, then I'll take them over to the Pro Shop." The name over the breast pocket said "Daquon."

Taneesha's cousin. Nancy nodded approvingly. "I'm Nancy Dickenson," she said to Daquon, extending her hand. "I know Taneesha."

His grin lit up his face. "She told you about me?"

"All good things. We like Taneesha a lot," Louise chimed in.

"Yeah. Whisperwood's a great place. You guys even gave her a scholarship for college." Daquon shifted the golf bag. "They don't offer that here." He held up a hand. "Don't get me wrong. I like working here, and I'm learning a lot. I'm fine with that."

George stepped over to Daquon and peered at his name badge. "Daquon, is it? Would you take my clubs over to the Pro Shop now? I'll drop by later and take care of any paperwork."

"No paperwork to do at the Pro Shop," said Julie, joining Nancy and Louise. "The shop will take care of your clubs and has most everything you might need. We'll e-mail you your receipts." She smiled at George. "I'm Julie Harris, Louise's niece. You and the other gentleman are friends of Louise and Nancy?"

"Good friends," said Louise. Nancy caught the secret smile Louise threw at George.

"Yep. Me and Fitz are here to show these two gals a good time," said George, winking at Louise.

"The other way around, more like." Louise snorted and tossed her long, gray braid.

"Hey, isn't it time for a nosh?" asked Fitz, nodding at Julie. "I have a reservation, too. Fitz Connelly."

Julie smiled at him. "Pleased to meet you. I hope you have a pleasant stay. Let me get you registered and give you your keys." She spent a moment on the computer, presented each of them with a paper to sign, and then gave them their keys. She glanced at her watch. "And, yes, it's lunch time. The restaurant is open. Go on in. I can't join you, I'm afraid." She waved toward the restaurant.

Nancy took Fitz's arm, pleased that he was booked for the week. The four of them made a good team. They called themselves the 90s Club, but few would guess they were all over ninety. They exemplified the "able, alert, and active" new paradigm for the perennial decades.

She hoped that this time they could solve the mystery without almost getting themselves killed.

***

**Notice to Guests**

The woods to the west of Lilac Inn belong to the West Virginia Wildlife Management Area. You are free to walk the many hiking trails there, but take care not to get lost. Also, it is a wildlife area, so watch out for ticks, snakes and bears.

*Julie and Will Harris, Owner/Managers*
*Lilac Inn Resort and Restaurant*

# 7. Sunday Lunch

Nancy, Louise, George, and Fitz followed the dining room hostess out to the verandah. Restaurant tables were filling up. It looked like the locals might be finding this a nice place to go after church. Nancy hoped so. Which ones were staying at the inn? Most of them had probably shown up for lunch yesterday, too, and she recognized a couple of them. This would be a good place to observe and perhaps meet the other guests. Nancy resolved to stay there until the dining room closed to prepare for dinner when she'd have another opportunity to observe guests.

Marilyn stopped by their table, and Louise introduced her to George and Fitz.

"So you've decided to spend the week?" asked Marilyn. Although she seemed vivacious and attractive in light blue slacks and black T-shirt, she walked with a brooding sense of purpose.

"They had space, so we decided to take a vacation," said Louise.

Nancy slid her chair sideways and gestured at the empty space. "Join us for lunch?"

"Thanks," Marilyn said, "but I promised Ann and Lula I'd sit with them." She turned to Louise. "When are you taking me to Whisperwood?" she asked.

"Can you drive?" asked Louise. "I don't have a car."

"Sure. It's not a Cadillac, but it runs."

Louise hemmed and hawed, obviously torn. Nancy smiled to herself. Louise didn't want to miss a thing going on here. Finally, Louise said, "How about tomorrow morning? We'll go to Whisperwood and have lunch. It's like a cruise ship, you know. Pub, library, dining room, gym, swimming pool. Even entertainment most nights." She snapped her fingers, picking up enthusiasm. "Hey, I can show you my bee hive, then I'll take you into town, and you can meet people in the local social service agencies."

"Perfect," said Marilyn. "Maybe we can skip the bee hive, though." She winked at Nancy. "Not into bees, bugs, or insects of any kind. Tomorrow it is. Now I'll go join Lula and Ann. They're waving at me."

Nancy nodded and smiled at the other two women as Marilyn walked to their table.

"It'll be fun showing her around," said Louise defensively to the other three, but she frowned at Nancy. "Nothing better happen while I'm gone."

"I'll make sure it doesn't." Nancy hid a smile as she picked up the menu.

After the dining room cleared, she spent the afternoon exploring the hotel and looking for opportunities to speak with the guests. This wasn't too successful. Those who weren't out on excursions disappeared after lunch, probably for an afternoon nap. George and Louise were walking on the grounds somewhere, and Fitz took his binoculars and meandered down one of the hiking trails.

The two kids in navy blue T-shirts and shorts tossed a ball back and forth in front of the hotel while their parents sat together reading on the verandah. They looked up as Nancy took a chair nearby.

The man reached over to shake Nancy's hand. "Aysha and Cole Robinson," he said in a deep baritone and nodded toward the kids. "The girl's Kimberly and the boy's Kai. Here for the week." He fanned himself with his hat. "Glad to get out of D.C.," he added. He wore a yellow polo shirt and green plaid Bermuda shorts. His wife was similarly dressed in a pink polo and white Bermuda shorts.

"Nice to meet you," said Nancy, giving her name. "School out so early?" As soon as she said the words, she regretted them. Did she appear judgmental? It was only an idle comment.

Aysha laughed. "Private school. Not a problem. It accommodates all kinds of schedules."

"We're both military," said Cole. "Travel a lot. Glad to spend time together when we can."

"Great place to relax," said Nancy. "Kids can run around on their own." She thought of the lake. "Do they like to swim?"

Aysha laughed. "Of course. Basic survival skill." She glanced at Cole who nodded.

"What brings you here?" he asked.

Nancy settled back in her chair. "Wanted a change of scene, and I know the owners. They invited me and my friend to spend a few days. So you live in D.C.?"

"Close enough," said Cole. "Fort Meade, Maryland." He leaned back and tipped his cap down to cover his eyes.

Fort Meade, Maryland. Nancy knew people who rattled off Fort Meade as their workplace. It was an army base, but it was also a euphemism for the National Security Agency. NSA. Did Cole and Aysha work for the NSA? Were they spies or code breakers? Her eyes flitted toward the couple. They were sitting back, eyes closed, doing what they said they wanted to do. Relaxing. Their kids had wandered off into the woods. She supposed they were safe enough. The pond was the major hazard, but the kids knew how to swim. She closed her eyes in the warm sunlight, felt the lilac-scented breeze wafting by, and listened drowsily to the buzzing insects.

She felt a gentle shake and opened her eyes.

"Have a good nap?" asked Fitz, smiling down at her.

Nancy sat up and looked around. Cole and Aysha had left. Fitz sank into a chair they'd vacated.

"Up for a round of tennis?" he asked, swinging a tennis racket in front of him.

Nancy stretched and glanced at her watch. Three-thirty. Good heavens! I've been asleep more than two hours! "Let me find a bottle of water and a racket," she said. "I'll meet you at the court."

Nancy followed the path to the tennis court behind the hotel. As they batted the ball back and forth, her eyes were continually drawn to a barn that stood behind the hotel and on the far side of the court. A broad meadow extended beyond the barn toward a copse which she guessed was part of the Wildlife Management Area.

The barn was about the size of a three-car garage and sturdily built. The outside was painted white like the main building, and the roof was in good repair. A double-wide sliding garage door spread across most of one side, and a dirt road from there led to a door behind the main hotel building. Will could also enter the barn through a standard-sized door on the side.

After their game, they walked toward the barn. Nancy was curious. They tried the standard door at the side, but it was locked. She heard nothing from inside. She was ready to dismiss it as a place to store tools and a mowing tractor when Will showed up.

"Can I help you?" he asked, his roaming eyes not once looking at Nancy straight on. He had donned gray overalls covered with dark stains, and he carried a ladder.

Distracted by his eyes, Nancy took a moment to respond as she wondered whether his gaze was a quirk, a physical ailment, or the result of some emotional tic. The last person she'd met with that habit turned out to be a serial killer. You're not Miss Marple, Nancy chided herself. No village parallels, please.

"You do a great job maintaining the property," Fitz said. "Is this where you keep your tools?"

"Sure it is, along with all the other stuff I'm working on." He hesitated as if he wanted to say more.

"Other stuff?" Nancy prompted, forcing herself back to the present.

"Like I said before, I'm an inventor." He leaned the ladder against the wall. "Even if I look like the hired hand here."

Nancy heard the snarky tone. Did he resent the role he played as a maintenance man? She ignored his tone and replied with enthusiasm. "How interesting! What are you working on?"

"A couple of things." He pulled a ring of keys out of his pocket. "Gotta get back to work. Enjoy the resort!"

"We'd like to see your inventions sometime," Fitz said.

"Sure. Some other day, okay?" He stood at the door. Nancy could see he wouldn't open it while they were there. Why not? Afraid they'd steal his ideas?

On the way back, they encountered the two kids, heads together cooing to something in their hands. Nancy stopped as they passed. "What have you got there?" she asked.

"It's a baby bird," said Kai in an awed tone.

"It sure is," said Fitz, studying it. "A robin. You should put it back where you found it."

Marilyn walked over from the verandah. "A baby bird?" She looked at the bird a moment. "I know what to do with it," she said. "Give it to me."

Kai was too well-mannered to refuse an adult. Marilyn took the bird and walked toward the woods by the barn.

The kids ran away, and Nancy and Fitz climbed the verandah steps. Later, they joined Louise and George in the lobby for the cocktail hour. Most of the guests had showered and changed into dressier attire, which the hotel brochure suggested for Sunday evening. Other nights, it explained, were more casual. Nancy wore black slacks, a silver top with blue sequins, and sandals. Louise had made an effort, changing into a clean khaki shirt, jeans, and black running shoes. The men wore sports jackets and ties. George, as usual, outshone them all with sky blue slacks, lemon yellow, long-sleeved shirt, and navy blue bow tie with yellow polka dots. The other three were used to George's unusual taste and didn't comment. As he'd told them before, he liked color.

The cocktail hour gave Nancy a chance to chat with the other guests. Cole nodded and Aysha waved a cocktail glass in her direction. Sarah and Gary Lochowsky, a sixtyish couple from Cleveland, stopped to introduce themselves and chat with Nancy on their way to the bar. He wore a dark navy jacket and tie. Her outfit, a long ivory dress with a sparkling necklace and earrings of diamonds and emeralds, seemed way too formal, even for this dressy occasion. She turned to Gary. "Dear, please, may I have my shawl?"

Gary picked up the shawl, slung over his arm, and draped it across her shoulders.

Nancy introduced herself with a smile, but she longed to take a close look at the jewelry. Could those stones be genuine?

"I'm retired," Sarah said in a high titter. She nodded Gary's way. "He hasn't retired, yet. Insurance. Gary's had health problems, so we're here to relax and have a good time." Sarah spotted Julie behind the bar serving drinks and patted Nancy's arm. "Excuse me, dear. I need to have a word with our hostess." Gary had already turned to a tall, thin man with gray hair who seemed a bit lost in this crowd. Nancy recognized him as the lone diner with a backpack at Saturday lunch.

Louise stood in a corner chatting with Marilyn. Nancy stopped to ask Marilyn about the bird.

"It's better now, poor thing," said Marilyn. "It's been dispatched."

Dispatched? The meaning dawned on Nancy. "You what?" Nancy gaped at her. There was no need to kill it.

"Don't get upset." Marilyn sipped her wine. "It wasn't going to make it, not with foxes and hawks in the woods. No mama bird around. Probably abandoned because it was sick. I took it out of its misery, that's all." She turned back to Louise, and Nancy walked away. Maybe Marilyn was right. Maybe the bird was sick. She hadn't looked closely.

She noticed Fitz leaning on one elbow at the bar, gazing in her direction. George was regaling two women with some tall tale. The women listened politely, laughing as required. Both of them looked about forty.

Nancy continued to survey the room. Her eyes stopped at another lone man who seemed to be Aysha and Cole's age. Mid-forties maybe. He was slightly overweight and balding, and he appeared to be listening to George's story, but Nancy saw he was more interested in assessing the two women. He held a can of Budweiser in one hand although Nancy noticed beer being served in frosted mugs. He must have spurned the nicety. Parading himself as a "man's man" was Nancy's take.

She drifted in his direction. He didn't notice her until she pretended to trip and grabbed his arm.

"Oh, I am sorry," she said. "I slipped on the floor."

"That's all right." His eyes swept over her in a quick perusal and immediate dismissal. He turned back to the two other women, seeing them as more suitable prey, but Nancy wasn't about to be ignored. She batted his arm to draw back his attention. "I'm Nancy Dickenson. I arrived today." She looked at him for his response, knowing full well that her age put her out of contention for any interest from him.

He nodded perfunctorily. "Lew Cookson." He turned his back to intrude on the other two women. "Pardon me, ladies," he said. "I didn't get your names. Are you here for the week, too?"

"Ann Bashaw." She reached over and took the other woman's hand. "This is Lula Beall. First time here, but I'm loving it." Ann was box-shaped and wore jeans with a blue plaid shirt under a Navy sweatshirt. Lula wore a flowered knee-length dress with white Nikes. They smiled at each other.

"And I'm here to be with her," Lula giggled.

"We're birders," Ann said. "I plan to add ten birds to my life list. My goal this week. And improve my golf strokes, too."

"She's the birder," Lula giggled again. "I'm here for the golf."

Nancy saw Lew assess the situation, then look over at the elevator as it opened and decanted the forlorn woman Nancy had noticed at lunch the day before. She stood on the edge of the crowd, brows drawn together in an angry frown tinged with sadness. Nancy thought over the list of guests. This could be Kaye Anderson. Her ultra-feminine full-skirted blue dress with a low neckline drew Lew's interest. He muttered something to Ann and Lula and strode confidently toward Kaye like a male boss gorilla. *So predictable.*

Nancy smiled at Ann and Lula. "You're birders?" The two women nodded. "Then perhaps you can tell me what you should do if you find an abandoned baby bird on the ground?"

"That's easy," said Ann. "Leave it alone. Or if you think it fell out of a nest and can get to the nest, try putting it back. It'll be all right."

"The kids found a baby robin," said Nancy.

"Baby robins often spend two to five days on the ground before they can fly. Just leave it alone," said Ann, reaching for a mushroom appetizer as the server passed by.

"Leave it alone," repeated Lula.

Marilyn probably knew nothing about birds and thought she acted for the best, Nancy decided. Another human bumbler in the animal world. She sipped her wine and stood next to the reception desk. She wondered where Harvey Smithson was and what his brother was like. Then she noticed the taciturn loner she'd spotted before, leaning, arms folded, against the wall, beer gripped in one hand, surveying the group with distaste. He was probably Evan Lester, the other single man on the list. He seemed uncomfortable in this social situation.

As she watched the guests mingle, she felt anxious undercurrents. From Evan? He certainly wasn't mixing in this crowd. Kaye looked tense and wary as she received Lew's attention. Nancy turned and saw Julie standing back against the wall behind the bar. Like Nancy, she was observing and assessing the guests.

***

**Notice to Guests**
**Movie Tonight: The African Queen**
Join us in the library at 8 p.m. for popcorn and a showing of the classic film, *The African Queen*, starring Humphrey Bogart and Katherine Hepburn. This is an adventure the entire family can enjoy.

*Julie and Will Harris, Owner/Managers*
*Lilac Inn Resort and Restaurant*

# 8. Sunday Dinner

When Lew left Kaye to return to the bar, Nancy casually meandered toward her. Kaye managed a tentative smile.

"May my friend Louise and I join you for dinner?" Nancy asked. She hadn't talked to Louise about this yet, but Louise would see the opportunity at once. And if she didn't, Nancy was quite capable of pumping Kaye on her own.

Kaye looked at her uncertainly. "I'm not much company."

"That's all right," said Nancy. "Something troubling you?"

"No," said Kaye. "I'm fine."

She seemed miserable. "Isn't this a nice place to vacation?" Nancy asked.

Kaye's eyes darted around the room. "I-I guess so," she said. "That is, it certainly is."

Nancy took her into dinner with a hard stare at Louise who understood and relayed Nancy's unspoken message to Fitz and George before joining Nancy. Kaye was unhappy about something. Her face showed the strain with clenched jaw and tense frown. What had happened to her? Nancy wondered if it were an unhappy love affair. Was there any connection to the happenings at Lilac Inn or had she brought her unhappiness with her?

The hostess led Nancy, Louise, and Kaye to a square table inside the dining room instead of out on the verandah. "Gets a bit cool in the evenings," she explained.

"Please ask the manager to take our wine orders," Nancy said to the hostess. A little wine might help Kaye loosen up.

"Your server can take your order," the hostess said with a puzzled look.

Nancy realized her mistake. This wasn't Whisperwood with its high school servers. The servers here were over the age limit and could serve alcohol. She'd only lived at Whisperwood a year. How quickly she'd taken up the life-style there.

Nancy smiled at Kaye as they seated themselves. "You're here by yourself?" Nancy asked.

Shifting emotions crossed Kaye's face before she replied. "I am. I needed a vacation. I can get away like anyone else, can't I?" she said, her tone defensive and petulant.

"Of course," Nancy responded soothingly as the server approached and asked for their drink order. "Chardonnay," she said. "Wine for you?" she asked Kaye.

"I'm not sure . . ." Kaye began.

Louise stepped in. "We'll both have Chardonnay, too." She turned to Kaye. "I take trips by myself all the time."

"You do?" Kaye asked, astonishment on her face. "By yourself?"

"Can't be bothered to wait around for someone else to make up their mind. Don't have to cater to anyone that way, either."

Kaye gazed at Louise in wonder. "Coming here by myself was a real stretch for me."

*Oh, brother. Was Kaye really such a hothouse plant?* Nancy changed the subject before Louise embarked on a lecture about feminism. Nancy wholeheartedly agreed with Louise on that, but time was precious, and she wanted to learn more about Kaye.

"Are you from Washington?" Nancy asked.

Kaye nodded. "I work for the U.S. Treasury. Only an administrative assistant, I'm afraid. Saved up for this trip."

"Working for the Treasury has got to be interesting, though," said Nancy, hoping to draw her out.

"Not really," she sniffed and changed the subject. "What do you plan to do tomorrow?"

The conversation continued in that vein. Kaye derailed any more questions about her private life, leaving Nancy to wonder exactly what she did for the Treasury and why she really came to Lilac Inn. Nancy settled back, let go of prying, and worked instead on establishing a friendly relationship. She could fill in details about Kaye more casually in the days to come.

Dessert arrived, strawberries and shortcake, and they duly enjoyed it. Kaye refused coffee and stood, excusing herself. As she left, Nancy glanced at Louise, who shrugged. "Guess she didn't like our conversation."

Fitz and George left their table to join Nancy and Louise, and the foursome wandered to the lobby. Louise and George moved on to the card room. "There's got to be somebody here who plays bridge," George grumbled.

Nancy and Fitz walked out to the verandah. She spotted Harvey Smithson immediately, sitting in a wicker chair across from another man who resembled him except for the added pounds and bloated face. *He must be Harvey's brother.* Harvey looked fussy in a black-checked, short-sleeved, buttoned-up shirt tucked into loosely fitting slacks. His grey tie had a discreet pattern in burgundy. The other man wore a pale yellow polo shirt and gray slacks.

They were talking to each other in hard, low voices, but Harvey happened to see Nancy. He rose, replacing the angry look with a welcoming one. "Ms. Dickenson. Mr. Connolly." Harvey smiled at Nancy and nodded at Fitz. "A surprise to see you two here. Come meet my brother,"

The other guests turned curiously at the loud voice. "My brother Malcolm." Harvey waved a hand in Malcolm's direction. "This is Nancy Dickenson. I've told you about her." He added in a voice loaded with meaning, "The private detective."

"Long retired," Nancy murmured and added for Malcolm's sake, "This is my friend, Fitz Connolly." Fitz smiled benignly at the two men.

"Pull up a chair," said Harvey.

Fitz dragged two wicker chairs toward the Smithson brothers. Nancy took one as Fitz settled into the other.

Harvey watched from his own comfortable chair. "What brings you to this luxurious outpost?" he asked.

Nancy had her cover story ready. "I was feeling claustrophobic at Whisperwood. I needed a change of scenery."

"I came to brush up on my tennis," said Fitz. "And I like birding."

Harvey laughed. "We're here for our annual brother-bonding week." His voice turned bitter. "So called."

"We choose a different place every year," added Malcolm, twirling his brandy snifter. "Try to beat each other at golf, tennis, and whatever other game we come up with." He sneaked a glance at Harvey and then pretended to study his fingernails. "Whatever it is, I'm much the better player. I'm the winner in our family."

Harvey snorted. "You wish."

Malcolm turned to Nancy. "He only beats me if I don't see him move his ball out of a sand trap. Have to watch him like a hawk."

"I never cheat," said Harvey, his mouth set in a grim straight line, his eyes angry.

"Sure," said Malcolm with a side grin to Nancy and Fitz. "We bet on who wins our games. I got twenty bucks off him today."

Harvey stood and repeated through gritted teeth, "I never cheat, and I've had as much of this braggart as I can stand for one day. Good evening." He marched stiffly away.

Malcolm sipped his brandy. "Don't mind him. A sore loser, that's all. It'll blow over by tomorrow. It always does." He grinned at them. "I apologize for his bad manners. You may consider me the better brother." He took another sip and added with a smug twist, "Most people do."

Nancy heard the malice. Brotherly bonding, indeed. "Are you a jeweler, too?" she asked to dispel the ugly tone of Malcolm's words.

"Sure. Practically born to it. Me and Harvey." He took another sip of brandy. "I design jewelry, too. A hobby, you know. Real stuff. Gold, silver, semiprecious stones. No glass or plastic beads."

She wondered what the two men were arguing about when she arrived. They seemed intent and serious, but it was probably their golf scores. "What other games do you play?" she asked.

He waved his hand. "Mostly we make bets. Little things, you know. Inconsequential. How many flowers in a vase? How many minutes till the coffee comes out? That sort of thing. Twenty bucks to the winner on every bet," added Malcolm. He glanced at his watch. "So far on this trip, Harvey's down nine hundred dollars." He laughed. "But who's counting?"

A young woman in a lavender uniform carrying a tray approached their table. "It's complimentary Irish coffee we serve on Sunday evenings. Would you be liking one?"

"I would," said Fitz, taking the cup as it was handed to him. "Splendid."

Malcolm put aside the now-empty snifter. "Me, too." The server handed him a cup.

As Nancy took the cup, she read the server's name badge. "Bridie Callahan." "Are you one of the interns?" she asked.

Bridie nodded. "Yes, Miss. I'm from Dublin. It's hotel management I'm studying."

"How do you like working here?" Nancy watched the young woman as she spoke. Would she be a likely ally or was she a thief?

Bridie hesitated. "A lovely hotel it is, Miss. A bit of the green, I like to say, with the forest all around. I am learning so much here, new ideas I will take back to home when I begin me career."

"I imagine so," replied Nancy with a smile. "Wonderful opportunity for you."

"That it is, Miss." The now-empty tray rested on Bridie's hand as she deftly bent down to retrieve a button on the floor. "You must have dropped this."

"Oh. Thank you." Nancy put the button back in her pocket. The girl was observant, too.

Nancy turned to say something to Fitz when a vision in a long gold dress swept in front of them. Her honey-colored hair curled in a halo around her head and a fringed multi-colored shawl covered her shoulders. Several strands of beads hung from her neck. Heavy make-up did nothing to disguise her age, which Nancy judged to be about fifty. The woman posed, standing tall, staring down her nose at them. Nancy recognized her as the "woman in white."

"I am Madam Nuri," she said dramatically, mostly to Fitz and Malcolm but casually including Nancy. "I read fortunes in your palms and in the cards." She pulled a thick, oversized deck of tarot cards out of a pocket and flashed them in front of Nancy and Fitz.

At that moment, Sarah and Gary Lochowsky arrived. "Mind if we join you?" he asked, pulling two more chairs to the group. He smiled at Nancy and turned to the others. "I'm Gary Lochowsky and this is my wife Sarah." She wiggled her fingers at the group. Madam Nuri merely nodded as she returned the cards to a pocket hidden in the folds of her dress.

Nancy tore her eyes off Madam Nuri and greeted the newcomers. "I'm Nancy and this is Fitz Connolly." Fitz shook Gary's hand.

"It's our anniversary today," bubbled Sarah. "You probably think we're way overdressed for a casual dinner, but we're celebrating." She smiled lovingly at her husband. "One year, already."

"Not at all," said Nancy. "That's a beautiful necklace."

She longed to ask if the stones were real. She'd like a closer look. If they were genuine, she hoped Sarah was putting the necklace in the hotel safe at night. It had to be an attractive target for the thieves. And there was a thief at Lilac Inn.

"Thank you. A gift from Gary," she said. "I love it. The only quality jewelry I have." She giggled. "Oops. Shouldn't have said that."

Momentarily upstaged, Madam Nuri took back control. She reached forward to lift the largest emerald, hanging as a pendant, bringing it closer to peer at it.

"Here, what are you doing?" asked Gary, putting an arm in front of the woman to push her away.

She stepped back. "A beautiful stone and only one small fracture, one tiny imperfection no one would ever notice." She curtsied. "I congratulate you, Madam."

Sarah possessively covered the large emerald with her hand. "Thank you. It is beautiful. I love it, and it's mine. To me it is perfect." She drew back to peer at Madam Nuri, lowered her voice and said waspishly in a low undertone, "If anything is fake, you are."

Madam Nuri glanced mildly from Gary to Sarah. "You are right, madam, but it is my nature to expose the pretensions," she paused and stared at Sarah, "the frauds, and even the emeralds with imperfections." She spoke in a deep voice with a foreign accent Nancy couldn't place, but she heard a world of meaning in those words. They sounded almost like a threat. That accent must be put on.

The moment passed. The fortuneteller pulled the shawl closer around her shoulders, shivered, and glanced toward the lobby. Kaye stood inside, nibbling her lower lip as if trying to decide what to do. Nancy watched Nuri focus on

Kaye Anderson's face. Nancy tried to see it from Madam Nuri's perspective. It was a study in conflicting emotions. Sad. Angry. Vulnerable. Strong. Who was the real Kaye Anderson? Did Nuri see a customer there? Or a victim?

Nancy watched a slight, predatory smile cross Nuri's own face. Then she moved swiftly toward the lobby, announcing her wares like a fishwife. "I tell fortunes, I can see into the future, and I give private readings. Ask for me at the front desk. I will come to your room. This week only, I give special prices."

Marilyn appeared as Nuri finished her spiel. They took long looks at each other, then Nuri spoke in a low voice that carried a hint of malice in it. "I know what you do," she said.

"Really," sniffed Marilyn, walking past to brush her off.

"You will answer to much," said Nuri. Marilyn tossed her head and hurried away toward Nancy.

"Julie and Will need to watch that woman," said Marilyn. "It's like she's dropping hints that she knows all about us. Fishing. Doesn't bother me at all, but she could rile the wrong person. Anyway, whatever it is, it's all lies."

Nancy nodded. She'd been thinking the same thing. Nuri was probably looking for tidbits she could use in her fortunetelling act. Nancy didn't think she'd imagined the slight shift in Nuri's speech to a stilted local accent. Bela Lugosi must be part of the act, Nancy supposed, wondering if her real name truly was Patty Hovermale. Nuri was a gypsy, or Roma, name. Nancy had spent some time around real gypsies. She could spot a fake one, gypsy name or not.

Malcolm rose and touched his hand to his brow in a salute. "I'm off. Harvey and I have a rematch golf game tomorrow. Wanna be in top form. Got big money riding on this one, although," he laughed, "anyone can whip Harvey. What a wimp." He meandered through the door into the hotel and down the hall to the elevators.

Fitz watched him and then as the elevator doors closed with Malcolm heading up, he turned to Nancy and cocked an eyebrow. "Quite a specimen."

"Yes," said Nancy absently, her attention caught by Madame Nuri's aggressive pounce on Gary and Sarah. Did Nuri know the couple from somewhere else? Sarah was covering up some emotion. Fear?

***

### Need a Partner?

Sam Johnston at the Pro Shop will be happy to assist you in lining up a golf foursome or a tennis partner. Check with him, too, if you'd like to sign up for the weekly tennis tournament. Bottle of champagne goes to the winners.

*Will and Julie Harris, Owner/Managers*
*Lilac Inn Resort and Restaurant*

# 9. Later Sunday Evening

Nancy glanced at her watch. Almost nine. "Excuse me," she said to Fitz and Malcolm. "I'll be right back."

She walked down the hall, peeking into the dining room as she passed. No diners remained, and Bridie was turning the chairs upside down to hang off tables for mopping the floors. The chef must be finishing up for the night, too.

The kitchen was situated past the dining room. Nancy poked her head in the door. Chef Tom sat at a small desk, totaling a column of figures. Behind him, Ingunn was loading a dishwasher and tidying up. A young woman stood at an open pantry with a clipboard.

The chef looked up as Nancy approached.

"I'd like to compliment you on the meals here," began Nancy. She believed in butter.

"Thank you." He took it as his due, but then he sat back and studied her. "You're Ms. Dickenson, aren't you?"

"I am," said Nancy. "I'm surprised you know my name."

"Don't be. Julie told me about you." He leaned toward her. "Something has got to be done about the thefts around here."

Nancy hid her surprise. Why did Julie tell him about her? If he were the thief, he'd be on his guard.

Chef Tom waved his hand. "Don't get excited. I'm as worried as she is about the thefts. I've been missing eggs, meat, condiments, vegetables. Napkins and paper towels, too, and those napkins were linen. I don't like it, and it wrecks my budget. I want you to find the thief and fast."

Nancy nodded. "That's what I want to do."

He sat back again. "Those thefts put all of us on staff under suspicion. I can't think of one person employed here who would steal from Julie and Will. We know how hard they've worked to get this place up and running. We like our jobs. Good jobs are few and far between around these parts, I can tell you. I like living here, and my kids like living here. If this place goes under, we'll have to move."

"Do you have any idea who is stealing the supplies?"

"I've been thinking and thinking, and Missy and I have been watching the supplies like a hawk, but I can't come up with anyone."

"Missy?" asked Nancy.

He turned around and called out. "Missy, come here a minute." The young woman turned at his voice, saw Nancy, and walked to them. "You're Ms. Dickenson, aren't you?" she asked. "I'm Missy Crain, sous chef, bottle washer, and other duties as assigned." She grinned and held out her hand.

They shook hands. "Looks like you're busy," said Nancy.

"We use the interns, too," said Missy. "Nice to meet you. Let me know if I can fill you in on what we're doing." She returned to the pantry.

"Carola Crain helps me sometimes, too," said the chef. "Missy's Mom. She's in charge of housekeeping, and she's straight arrow. I knew her in grade school. Not a black mark to her name. I'd never believe it was her." The chef stared ahead, chewing his lip. "Anyway," he added, "she's been complaining about her own supplies gone missing. I don't get it, don't get it at all." He looked at Ingunn, now wiping down the work table.

The chef inclined his head towards her. "The interns, Bridie and Ingunn, work hard here," he said. "What would they do with the stuff? No place to hide it. They live with the Harrises, you know. Daquon's a good kid, too, and a hard worker, but I never see him hanging around the dining area or kitchen unless there's some specific job to be done. I'm always around when he's here."

"Can you think of any other possibilities?" asked Nancy. "What about the security guards or the landscaping workers?"

"I keep a water jug and a coffee urn filled for them out on the verandah, and they use that, you know, but. . ." He thought a moment, then shook his head. "The landscaping crew never come into the building. They use the rest room facilities next to the tennis court and bring their own lunches. They're on the grounds when I'm in the kitchen. They'd be so out of place inside they'd be spotted in a minute, and they couldn't carry out the supplies without someone seeing them."

"And the guests turn over every week, so it's not them," said Nancy pensively.

"Can't see it," agreed the chef. "I've thought and thought, but I still have no idea who is stealing the stuff and how they get away with it."

Nancy turned to leave, saying, "I guess you lock everything up now."

"You better believe it," said Chef Tom, "and look here." He gestured for her to follow him back to the freezer case. "Every night before I leave, I sprinkle flour on the floor in here. Anyone who comes in is going to leave footprints. I got a little portable hand vacuum to clean it up in the morning."

Nancy smiled at the chef's use of an old trick. "Great idea," she said.

The chef winked at her. "One way or another, between the two of us, we'll get 'em."

***

**Edible Wild Plant Talk and Walk Tomorrow**
Local Master Naturalist Mark Pather will be here tomorrow to speak on edible wild plants followed by a walk to identify and collect a few specimens to offer for dinner tomorrow night. The talk is at 10 a.m. in the library. The walk will begin immediately afterwards.

Open to everyone. No need to sign up ahead of time. Remember that Mark is an expert with years of experience doing this. Some toxic plants resemble edible ones, so please be extra careful if you try this at home.

*Julie and Will Harris, Owner/Managers*
*Lilac Inn Resort and Restaurant*

# 10. Monday Morning
## SIX DAYS TO GO

Nancy reached across the bed to pet Malone, but her crotchety kitty cat wasn't there. She missed her ferocious feline companion, oddly enough. He was wily and tough, not at all the standard kitty one might want as a pet, but they understood each other, and he had saved her life the year before. She opened her eyes, expecting to see him at the window, salivating over the birds flitting through the hedges. But this window had an antique frame with wavy glass panes. Old glass, not like the casement windows at Whisperwood.

She woke up for sure as she remembered she was at Lilac Inn. It was seven a.m., and she was to meet her friends for breakfast at eight. She showered and dressed and then took the stairs down to the lobby, holding onto the rail as the two kids, Kai and Kimberly, raced ahead of her. Aysha followed them, cautioning them to slow down. "Watch out for the old people," she cried out. Then she caught up with Nancy.

"Oh, Ms. Dickenson, isn't it?" she said. "Do you think you should take the stairs? Wouldn't the elevator be safer?" She reached over to take Nancy's arm.

Nancy stepped away, letting Aysha's arm drop. "Not at

all," said Nancy, gritting her teeth. "I always take the stairs if they're available. More exercise, don't you think?" She picked up her pace. Elevator, indeed.

"Yes, but. . ." Aysha didn't finish the sentence, and Nancy smiled at her as she stepped through the door into the lobby, feeling good about squelching a bit of ageism and glad Aysha hadn't cast her in the role of grandma-babysitter for the kids. Nancy had little interest in small children and low tolerance for teens unless they had social skills and something original to say. Not a given.

The hostess greeted her at the door and led her to the verandah where Louise, George, and Fitz were already seated. Nancy reached down to pet Tilly the dog who wandered from table to table on the verandah where he was allowed. A born panhandler. Then she noticed Fitz and the warmth in his expression. Her heart fluttered.

Louise nudged Nancy as she took a seat. "What's going on, Nancy? Detect any villains yet?" She winked at George and Fitz.

Nancy picked up the menu. "Not yet. Looking, though."

The day was warm and pleasant, and all the tables on the verandah were soon taken. Nancy noticed Aysha, Cole and their two kids also being seated on the verandah. The faces of the other guests were becoming familiar, too, and Nancy tested herself on their names. There was no sign today of Patty Hovermale, also known as Madam Nuri and now pegged as the "woman in white."

The intern Ingunn came by with a teapot for Nancy and then poured coffee for the others. She directed them to the breakfast buffet. After she left, Nancy told Louise and George about her encounters with Madam Nuri and the

Lochowskys the night before.

"Why would Sarah Lochowsky bring a valuable necklace here, of all places?" asked Louise. "Asking for trouble."

"Madam Nuri took a close look at it and pronounced it flawed." Nancy shrugged. "I didn't like the way Nuri said she exposed frauds and stared at Sarah while she said it."

"Right. Sarah acted like a speared kipper at that comment," Fitz added. He stretched his neck toward the buffet as he spoke.

Louise put down the menu. "Doesn't Madame Nuri or whoever that woman is read any mysteries? Any of us might have a guilty secret." She suddenly grinned at them "I'll bet you all do. How far would we go to protect it? Would we murder someone?"

George leaned back and patted his stomach. "I might, you know. I'm not the adorable chum you think I am."

Louise snorted. "Nobody thinks you're adorable, George."

Nancy nodded. "I agree with Louise about the fortune teller. If she hadn't implied Sarah was a fraud, I'd think Nuri aka Patty Hovermale was the resident kook. Harmless. Talking about frauds makes her seem menacing."

"Now what?" asked George, tucking his napkin into his collar. "What's our strategy?"

Nancy rested her chin in her hand and thought a moment.

"George can play golf most of the time he's here," said Louise." Join a foursome, ask questions. He'll be in a good position to hear gossip about the other guests and staff."

George drew himself up. "I beg your pardon. We don't

gossip on the course."

Louise laughed. "Sure. We believe you, George, but in case you do hear any, pass it on to us." She sipped her coffee. Laying a hand on George's arm, she added, "In fact, you could make up gossip and see what people add to it." She nodded to herself. "That could get interesting."

"But what'll I say?" whined George.

"Tell them you saw the Green Monster," suggested Nancy. "Someone else might have seen something like that and have a better description. We might get an idea where the rumors are coming from."

"If I did what you say, they'd be coming from me," grumbled George.

Fitz stared at the ceiling. "I wonder if there's any gossiping going on at the birdwatching blind."

"Maybe. If anyone else shows up." Nancy said. "You've wanted to go there since we arrived. Go ahead. The main thing is to keep our eyes and ears open, talk to the guests and the staff, and try to figure out what's going on here. I'll talk to Daquon, too. He has a reason to go into the guest rooms."

"He could be the culprit," warned Louise.

Nancy nodded. "He could be, but I don't think so. He seems so earnest, and Taneesha recommended him to us."

"And your instincts, eh what?" Fitz grinned at Nancy.

"No. Past experience with Taneesha." She smiled. "We do need an ally among the staff. Bridie Callahan, the intern serving drinks on the verandah last night, is observant and bright. We might use her, too."

Louise spoke up. "I'm spending the day with Marilyn, showing her the sights."

George raised an eyebrow. "You have a perverted sense of the sights, Madam. Social service agencies, the domestic violence center, the animal shelter, and a bunch of other community services. A fun day you'll have."

"Nevertheless, Marilyn has been here a little longer than we have," Nancy said, "and may know something useful. She seems so open and forthright but that's what they said about Ted Bundy. Louise, pick her brains as much as you can." Nancy had doubts about Marilyn. She so easily dispatched the baby robin. What kind of person would or even could do that?

"We'll have to hustle," said Fitz. "We only have six days to nail the culprit."

Nancy nodded. "This will be difficult. All of us need to connect with the staff and the guests here and observe. Note anything that seems odd and share with the rest of us. A lot of bits and pieces of information will begin to form a pattern." She watched as Bridie set a wire stand holding an upright card in the center of the table .

"An announcement for the guests," she explained.

"Pleased to see you again," Nancy said. "They have you on the morning and evening shifts?"

"Sometimes, Miss. I help out in the office, too, during the day." Bridie continued placing the announcements on each table. "Glad I am to work whenever they need me. I learn more."

Nancy picked up the card. "Too bad. The weather report says thunderstorms this evening. The pool, tennis court, and golf course will close at 5 p.m. or when thunder is heard."

"I'll be done by that time," said George.

Nancy held up a hand. "Wait a minute. This is excellent. After dinner, Madam Nuri will be available to read fortunes, and at nine, she will conduct a séance."

"What's so great about that?" asked Fitz. "We already heard her pitch last night, and I didn't think much of it."

"Didn't impress me either," added George.

"The séance will bring all of us together, so we can see how the guests react," said Nancy. "And it's going to be done the way we've seen it in a 1930s movie where the men are in tuxes and the women in glamorous evening gowns. We're all supposed to dress like film stars or as close as we can considering it's spur of the moment." She glanced around the dining room. "I guess with this hotel's history and the rumor of ghosts here, Julie and Will thought a séance would fit right in. Thunder and lightning predicted, too."

"It was a dark and stormy night," intoned Louise.

"Made to order," added Fitz, "with a character like a fake gypsy around. Quite imposing, I'd say."

"Great," grumbled George. "Maybe I can make something look good. I never wear formal. I got rules. Colorful, yes, but formal, no." He glanced down at his vividly purple polo shirt.

Louise grinned. "This'll be fun! We can look for the gimmicks she uses to rock the tables, make the knocks, and conjure up weird voices. Always wanted to do that." A devilish gleam appeared in her eyes. "Maybe we can add noises of our own to mix things up a little."

"This is right up your alley," said Fitz to Nancy. "You were married to a magician. He probably told you all about this séance stuff."

Nancy smiled as she nodded, looking down at the table. Funny and sad memories flooded her mind. Bill used to love going to séances, magic shows, fortunetellers. They were his business. She glanced around the hotel dining room. He would have loved this place.

After breakfast, Louise saw Marilyn gesturing from the lobby. "I brought some resumes," Marilyn told Louise as they walked out the door. "I wouldn't mind a job out here."

The wild and edible plant walk scheduled for the morning tempted Nancy, but she wanted to spend the time looking around the hotel and grounds and seeking out guests for chats. She watched Evan, Aysha, Cole and the kids wander off with the naturalist, then settled on the verandah with the hotel's history book. She selected a chair close to Kaye Anderson, whose face showed the same sad and troubled look Nancy had seen the day before. This morning, Kaye wore navy blue shorts and a white T-shirt. A book lay in her lap, but she stared beyond the verandah into the woods.

Nancy waited for an opportunity to interrupt Kaye's thoughts. Then Julie walked by and noticed Nancy's meaningful glance at Kaye. Julie picked up a coffeepot and stepped to Kaye's table. "More coffee?" she asked.

Kaye looked up, managed a half-hearted smile, and nodded as she reached for her book.

"Have you met our newest guest?" asked Julie. "Nancy, this is Kaye Anderson, visiting here from Washington, D.C. Kaye, this is Nancy Dickenson, who lives in West Virginia and is traveling around the state."

Kaye sent Nancy a perfunctory nod. "We've met," she said.

"I enjoyed having dinner with you last night." Nancy

held up her cup for Julie to refill. "Isn't this hotel gorgeous?" She waved the history book. "I'm learning so much about its background in this book. I happened to find it in the library. Julie is my friend Louise's great-niece. But you're from D.C. How did you learn about Lilac Inn?"

Kaye sighed. "Luck, I guess, surfing the Net. I needed to get away. . ."

"I know what you mean." Nancy glanced at Julie who quietly slid away. "It's good to get a new perspective. I remember . . ." She paused and then took a chance. "Yes, I remember years ago when my fiancé broke up with me. I was broken-hearted, you know. That was the first time I found out how useful it was to get away."

Kaye looked at her with surprise. "Your fiancé broke up with you?"

Nancy almost smiled as Kaye took the bait. Maybe this was a lucky guess. "Oh, yes. I was devastated." Nancy shook her head and glanced at Kaye. "Didn't think I'd ever recover, so I signed up for a two-week bicycle trip in California. I met new people, lived in a different situation with a lot of physical exercise, and by the time I returned, I'd practically forgotten all about him." Nancy laughed. "Not really, of course, but when I met him again, he seemed so shallow and dull to me. I couldn't believe I'd ever seen anything in him."

Kaye's smile had a bitter twist. "Something like that happened to me, but so far, getting away hasn't helped much. I don't think I'll ever get over it—or him."

Nancy was about to say, "Give it time," but bit back the words and glanced at her watch. "How about walking out to the golf course with me. My friend George is playing. Maybe we can see how he's doing, but I warn you, he grumbles a lot."

"Okay," said Kaye, pushing back her chair. "I'm done here, anyway."

They set off down a mulched trail toward the Pro Shop. Nancy spotted a golf cart on the course. As she drew closer, she saw two women standing at the first tee fussing at each other. "We'll be through here in a minute," said one woman in a high, reedy voice. Nancy recognized Lula Beall from the night before. One of Lew Cookson's would-be conquests. She was plump and pretty in a kewpie doll way— pink cheeks, curly bleached blonde hair, soft doe-like eyes. She wore a floral print skirt and plain white blouse.

"You're the hotel manager's friend, aren't you?" she asked. "Nancy something. I'm Lula Beall. This is my wife, Ann Bashaw."

"I'm Nancy Dickenson. You probably already met Kaye yesterday. She's also staying at the hotel."

Kaye nodded.

"Either of you play golf?" asked Ann, the box-shaped woman, wearing the same navy sweatshirt and slacks from the night before.

"Not me," said Kaye as Nancy shook her head.

"Too bad." Lula glanced at Ann. "We were looking for a foursome. Women." Then she smiled. "Guess we'll have to make do with this guy." She waved a club at George as he arrived in a golf cart.

"What do you mean, make do?" said George. "You're lucky to have me."

"Sure we are," laughed Lula. "Get with it, why don't you? Can't stay at this tee all day."

A loud voice called out. "Ho! You need a fourth?" Lew Cookson in a green polo shirt and jeans drove his golf cart towards them. "Got room for another player?" He brought the cart to the group and stopped. "Not too many golfers here this week." He grinned at George and bowed to the women with a long, lingering look at Kaye. "Ladies. Call me Lew. Here by myself. Wife wanted to visit her family, but I've seen enough of them. Too intense, know what I mean?" He laughed, poking George with his elbow.

Nancy raised an eyebrow at Ann and Lula who glanced at each other. Lew Cookson didn't remember meeting them the night before. Because of her age, Nancy knew she was below his radar and of no interest. Did it penetrate his thick skull that Ann and Lula were a couple or was he so smitten by himself or Kaye Anderson he forgot everyone else?

"How's your game?" asked Lula.

"Of course you can join us," said Ann, giving Lula a hard glance. "Glad to have you."

"Kaye and I will get out of here," said Nancy. "We were walking around the grounds, anyway."

"Sorry we don't play golf," added Kaye, leading the way along the edge of the golf course.

Lew stopped in the process of taking a club out of his bag. "You're not playing?"

Kaye shook her head with a smile.

"You can ride along with me. I can show you the game," Lew added.

"I don't think so," said Kaye. "Not today." She led Nancy off the course toward the woods. "There's a path into the woods somewhere along here. Found it yesterday." She glanced back at Lew. "He's one of the few men here not taken, you know. That is, he's here by himself. Him and Evan Lester."

"And the Smithson brothers," added Nancy.

"Oh, yeah. Them," agreed Kaye, frowning in distaste.

Nancy glanced at Kaye, hoping she had no designs on Lew. Nancy had dismissed him quickly as shallow, aggressively macho, and a bully. "Lew is married, though," she said as she followed Kaye. "Hope he takes the hint that Ann and Lula are a couple, but that kind of person is so thick-headed."

Kaye didn't respond. Nancy shaded her eyes and scanned the woods beyond the golf course. "I'd like to find the bird blind. It's supposed to look out over a pond."

Kaye stopped and thought a moment. "We have to go back by the front of the hotel and through the woods beyond the dining room."

They retraced their steps back to the hotel. Kaye again led the way, now indicated by small signs saying "Bird Blind" with a painted cardinal pointing down a wooded path. Dark sunglasses were painted over the bird's eyes.

"Cute," said Nancy.

Kaye managed a short laugh.

They walked about a quarter mile to where the woods cleared and tall grasses took over, giving way in turn to a pond. Nancy stopped to admire the beautiful scene in front of her. "That pond must be at least an acre," she said.

"I think it's larger—probably close to five acres. More of a lake, looks like to me. Most of it's on state land." Kaye walked along the lake. "The state Wildlife Management Area abuts the inn property here."

At Nancy's inquiring look, she added, "I took the tour

for new guests on Saturday. Guess you weren't here then."
She waved at the pond. "I like this place," she said, "and
here's your bird blind."

They walked along a path through the young cattails
growing alongside the pond and surrounding a room-sized
wooden shack. It was painted in camouflage colors to blend
in with the grass and the trees behind it. A side door opened
into the shack. Nancy stepped inside. The room was bare
except for two wooden benches. The wall facing the lake
framed a large cut-out, glassless window, providing an un-
obstructed view of the pond. She blinked as her eyes ad-
justed to the dim light, then she noticed the familiar figure
sitting on the front bench.

"Fitz! This is where you went." she said.

Fitz grinned at her. "Yes, luv, couldn't wait to find this
place." He stooped to peer through the lens finder on his
camera, attached to a tripod to hold it steady.

"You're well-equipped, I see," Kaye said as she entered
the room. "Camera, telephoto lens, tripod. . ."

Nancy introduced them. "Seen anything interesting?"
she asked.

"Pileated woodpecker on my way here through the
woods," he said. "Red-tailed hawk. A couple of wood
ducks, turtles, fish jumping."

"This is lovely," said Kaye. "I'm going to get my binoculars."

"I'll stay a little while longer." Nancy sat beside Fitz
and waved Kaye on her way. "I'm not much of a birder,"
she said, gazing out the wide window, "so point out what
I miss."

"Is she gone?" Fitz whispered, not lifting his eyes

away from the camera lens.

"Yes," Nancy whispered back.

"Good." He turned to her. "I think I saw the Mothman this morning."

"What? The Mothman?" Nancy gaped at him.

"It wasn't a sandhill crane," he said. "It looked like the exoskeleton of an insect, and it was flying. Red eyes, too."

"The Mothman," breathed Nancy.

"It was too far away for a good look, and then it disappeared."

"I wonder what it was, really," said Nancy.

"Whatever it was, it came from someplace close," Fitz looked at her, "and it landed nearby."

"Where, exactly?"

Fitz stepped outside the shack. Nancy followed. He shaded his eyes with one hand and pointed beyond the trees toward the meadow next to the barn.

"You can't see the meadow from here," he said, "but that's where it seemed to land."

Nancy shaded her eyes, too, as she considered the resort's layout. Beyond the meadow was the state Wildlife Management Area. That was government property. Could a giant insect be the result of government testing? Movies from the long ago fifties flashed through her mind, like *Them* with its house-sized ants. Those movies reflected the fears of the new atomic age, but so far, no giant insects or reptiles had ever appeared. Or had they?

***

### Nature Notes for Our Guests

Lilac Inn offers a range of habitats for birds and animals of all kinds. Deer can often be seen grazing the meadow. At night, raccoons and skunks scavenge and owls call out. Hawks and vultures circle over our land, and ducks and geese frequent the pond. These are among the many kinds of wildlife living here. Guide-books are available in the library for your use.

*Will and Julie Harris, Owner/Managers*
*Lilac Inn Resort and Restaurant*

# 11. Monday Afternoon

At five that afternoon, guests straggled in from their various activities to assemble casually in the lobby. Daquon had finished setting up a cash bar and Bridie hovered, holding a tray of hors d'oeuvre.

Daquon saw Nancy and stopped to chat. "Hey! How's your stay so far, Ms. Dickenson?"

"Fine. You all do an excellent job taking care of us," Nancy replied. "I do have a question for you."

"Ask away," he said as he sliced some limes.

"Have you heard any of the guests saying they saw something odd around here?" Nancy asked. "Like maybe a creature resembling the Mothman?"

"That old story?" He laughed. "Not as far as I know." He glanced toward the entrance. "Oops. Gotta get ice and see what the boss man wants." He headed for the door where Will was standing.

Nancy pondered his brush-off and abrupt departure. Could be he still had chores to do for Will. Or it could be he didn't want to discuss the Mothman, but why not?

"Miss?" The young intern, Ingunn, passed by and offered her the tray of hors d'oeuvre.

Nancy took a stuffed mushroom. "You're a long way from home," she said." Are you enjoying your work here?"

She wanted to get a sense of what the young woman was like on the remote chance she was the thief. Her response was a grin and a nod. Her English was punctuated with pauses. "I am learning much here, and I have cousins who live not so very far. Baltimore. You know Baltimore?"

Nancy agreed that she did know Baltimore, charmed by Ingunn's ingenuousness. She and Bridie seemed like two very nice young people. Not thieves.

Louise crossed the verandah pulling a small cart with one hand and clutching her trekking pole with the other. She nodded at Nancy and walked toward the elevator. Marilyn waved at Nancy and the other guests as she followed Louise. They both came down after a few minutes and joined the other guests for cocktails.

Julie acted as hostess and stood at a whiteboard set up in front of the reception desk. She'd written the next day's schedule on it in black. After a moment, she tapped a spoon on a glass for attention. Everyone stopped talking and looked her way.

"We hope you've had a pleasant day," she said, "getting to know each other and exploring the grounds. Any questions?"

The few questions dealt with housekeeping matters. Julie quickly dispensed with those.

"What about the day trips?" asked Aysha. "You talked about a coal mine tour in the brochure." Her face was red and dotted with sweat as if she'd been running, She'd come in from playing with her two kids and still kept an eye on them, chasing each other outside. Juice and cookies were set up on the verandah for them. Her husband Cole was missing. "Taking a nap," Aysha said defensively.

Julie smiled and nodded. "The coal mine tour will leave at nine a.m. on Tuesday morning—that's tomorrow. Meet in front of the hotel at nine if you'd like to go on that trip. On Wednesday, you can go on a canoe trip on West Virginia's famous New River."

"Isn't that the one where people sky dive off a bridge?" asked Marilyn. "Count me out."

Julie laughed. "No sky diving or bungee jumping for you. I promise you that. You'll be on a stretch of the river that's mostly flat water. The shuttle for canoeing leaves from in front of the hotel here at ten a.m. You'll be back in the mid-afternoon, and it includes a picnic lunch." She smiled approvingly as several of the guests applauded.

"On Thursday at one p.m., right after lunch, the van will go into the Charleston historic area for shopping and sightseeing. Please be sure to reserve your space on the tour you choose. This spring, we're not charging extra for any of these activities, so please enjoy them."

In the back, the tall, thin man who usually stood alone, remote from the others, lifted his hand. "Well, now," he drawled. "Any chance you'll take us over to where those kids saw the green monster? Or maybe the red-eyed alien? I know it was a long time ago, but I'm interested."

Nancy took a closer look at him. She'd seen him reading science fiction on the verandah, so of course he'd be interested in aliens and monsters.

Lew turned around and stared at the man. "Say what?"

The other man stared back, arms folded, a frown on his face. Nancy glanced from one man to the other. The science fiction buff had nothing to fear from overweight, out-of-shape Lew.

Julie laughed uneasily. "This is Evan Lester, everyone. He's talking about the two legends of this area. Two boys supposedly sighted the Green or Flatwoods Monster back in the early fifties, and it caused quite a stir." She went on to tell the stories of the two monsters.

"The so-called Green Monster was finally determined to be a meteor that crashed in a field near here. The local people held a Green Monster Festival in this area for years afterwards. The other legend, about a red-eyed giant alien called the Mothman has been debunked as well." She smiled at Evan. "I'm afraid there's nothing to see," she said. "We don't plan tours to those sites, but we can tell you where they are, and you can drive there yourself. Remember the land is privately owned and not open to the public. Anyway, there's nothing to see." She stopped a moment, then repeated, "Both those stories have been thoroughly debunked."

"But I've heard there've been recent sightings of the monsters near here," Evan persisted. "What about that?"

Julie frowned and turned rigid. "Overactive imaginations is my guess," she said stiffly. "I know of no such sightings." Then she recovered her good humor. "However, if you see either of these monsters, come running to tell us. I'm sure we'd all like to meet them."

There was general laughter, and the group set down their cocktail glasses and began drifting down the hall to the dining room. Good for her, thought Nancy.

Julie called out, "Be sure to join us after dinner. Madam Nuri will be in the lobby to tell fortunes at seven and then she will act as our medium for a séance in the library at nine."

Nancy noticed Harvey and Malcolm wandering in.

"Oh, did we miss something?" asked Malcolm.

Julie took them aside and gave them a printed schedule of the tours. "Let me know as soon as you can if you'd like to participate. Please show up on time for the shuttle." She then left them and stepped quickly down the hall to her office while they perused the schedule.

George and Fitz followed Nancy and Louise through the dining room to the verandah. The sun hovered low on the horizon, but only a few slanted rays pushed their way through the gathering storm clouds. Nancy could hear rumbles of thunder in the distance, and the wind had picked up. The weather turned cooler. The storm would hit by the time they finished dinner. Like the other guests, they decided to eat inside. Moonlit walks and drinks outside would also be ruled out. Nancy looked forward to the séance.

The four friends sat at a table inside and quickly ordered their meals.

Louise filled them in on her day with Marilyn. "We enjoyed a day of exploring, and Marilyn dropped her resume at Whisperwood's human resources office. She really likes the place. Then we visited with the social worker." A thoughtful expression crossed her face. "I shoulda been a social worker," she said. "They really make a difference in people's lives."

"You make a difference, too, Louise," said Nancy, "in your work for civil rights and the unions. Organizing, directing, advocating. A lot of people are better off because of you, and you're still involved."

Louise shrugged, "Well, I suppose so, but I was just part of a team. It's a never-ending job."

"Did you get a feeling," Nancy asked, "that she had

some agenda for coming here other than a week's vacation?"

Louise cocked her head. "Funny you should mention it. She's looking for a job, but I think there is something else, something she didn't want to talk about. I didn't press. Nothing to do with the inn's problems, I'm sure." She paused as their meals arrived.

"I know one thing," said Fitz, eyeing the steak on his plate. "Evan Lester is a genuine birder, all right. I walked out to the birdwatching blind with him, and he identified four or five birds I could barely see in the bushes. Knows their vocalizations, too. Whatever else he might be doing here, he knows his birds."

"What do you think of Kaye?" asked Nancy.

"Got something on her mind, and it isn't birds." Fitz speared a piece of steak. "Seems a bit vapid to me and confused." The steak went into his mouth.

Nancy turned to George. "How about your golf game?"

He picked up his glass of wine. "I like those two gals, Ann and Lula, but they're married. Did you know that?"

She nodded. "I'm a detective, George. When one of them called the other her wife, I picked up the clue and drew conclusions." She winked at George. "They seem like nice people. Not into causing trouble."

George frowned. "Oh yeah. Thought I heard wrong. Anyway, they play a good game, and once Lew figured out they were a couple, he pretty much shut up and golfed." George leaned back and patted his stomach. "He's one of those macho competitive guys. Acted like he was the champion golfer of all time, but you know what? Ann ended up with the best score." George laughed. "You shoulda seen his face. I thought he was gonna get ugly, you know? But they picked up their clubs and went into the clubhouse without saying one word to him. I wasn't so lucky, but I got away from him. He's all bluster and brag."

Nancy didn't respond. None of these people seemed like a thief to her. She ruled out Cole and Aysha, too. With their two kids, they appeared to be a charming family with only a vacation on their minds. That left Harvey and Malcolm Smithson, Evan Lester, Marilyn Goldfarb, Kaye Anderson, and Sarah and Gary Lochowsky. None of them seemed likely suspects for anything more than a swiped cookie after dinner.

She'd met the two interns, Ingunn and Bridie, both pleasant, earnest young people. If they did steal anything, where would they hide it? What would they do with it? They'd only been at the inn since it opened a month ago. According to Julie, neither one had a car or a driver's license in this country, and they hadn't been here long enough to make the connections to who might buy what they stole.

It almost had to be someone on the staff. They were here when the thefts started, and they all had ways to transport the stolen goods. They were local, too, so they might know who would buy their stuff.

She couldn't believe Daquon was a thief. The grounds keepers were on a contract and didn't have access to the storage lockers or the hotel interior. The security guards had to pass rigorous tests and background checks. That left the housekeeping and the restaurant staff. Carola Crain, Chef Tom Boysie and Carola's daughter, Missy Crain, the sous chef. She'd have to ask Julie about them. She'd heard what Chef Boysie had to say. What kind of references did they have? Who recommended them? How long had Julie known them?

"Hey, Nancy." Louise snapped her fingers in front of Nancy's face.

"I'm here. Sorry. I was thinking." Nancy looked up to see all of them staring at her. Then she saw that the dining room was almost empty.

"It's seven-thirty," said Fitz, shoving back his chair. "Anyone getting their fortunes told?"

"Not hardly," grumbled George. "I thought that kind of stuff went out in the twenties."

"I'm looking forward to the séance," said Nancy. "Might be better than an old movie."

A clap of thunder deafened them. Fitz grinned. "Atmosphere. Couldn't ask for better."

***

**Notice for our Guests**
**Tonight! A Real Old-Fashioned Séance!**
It will be a rainy, spooky night tonight, so in honor of the weather, we're offering our guests an old-fashioned séance at 9 p.m. in the library. Adults only, please. Remember that it's all in fun. Dress according to your favorite mystery from the Twenties or the Thirties.

*Will and Julie Harris, Owner/Managers*
*Lilac Inn Restaurant and Resort*

# 12. Monday Evening

After dinner, the 90s Club joined the other guests milling around the lobby. This time, Will staffed the bar set up on one side. Madam Nuri sat at a card table by the reception desk, laying out tarot cards as she waited for a customer. She wore a turban and a low-cut, classic black gown with long, full sleeves. A colorful shawl covered her shoulders. It was a calculated costume, Nancy thought. More dignified medium than gypsy girl, but that outfit could hide holes and pockets for magical contrivances as well as the tarot cards. Behind the fortuneteller's chair lay the black carry-on. Nancy studied it. How could she get a look inside? It must hold all Nuri's supplies, her gimmicks and tricks, everything a fortuneteller and medium might need.

Nancy walked over to Sarah and Gary who waited in the center of the foyer, looking lost. Sarah wore an ankle-length black skirt with a shimmering ivory silk blouse along with her emerald and diamond necklace. Gary looked like a pudgy penguin in a black tuxedo and black bow tie. "My wedding suit. Thought it would be appropriate for a séance. Lend a bit of class." He laughed.

"You look lovely tonight," Nancy said to Sarah. "The necklace beautifully enhances you and your dress. Gary has a good eye for jewelry."

Sarah cast a quick glance at him. He was focused on a server and holding up his glass for a refill but turned as he heard his name. "Set me back a pretty penny, I can tell you, and I hadn't even met this lovely lady yet." He winked at her. "Knew I'd meet someone like her, though." He grinned and whispered loudly to Nancy so everyone would hear, "Once I had the ring and the necklace."

Sarah lightly slapped her husband's arm. "Oh, you." She added to Nancy, "And once I saw the necklace, I couldn't say no." She pulled Gary over to the fortuneteller's table and took a seat. Nancy saw cash change hands and disappear in the folds of Madam Nuri's garment. Nuri gathered the cards and spoke to Sarah as she laid them out one by one. Gary stood behind Sarah's chair. Nancy hovered at their side to listen, but Madame Nuri glanced at her with a frown.

"My readings," Nuri said, pausing before laying down another card, "are confidential, you understand?" She was putting on the fake accent and sounded more Hungarian than Zsa Zsa Gabor. Nancy stepped away but walked to a position where she could watch Sarah's face. Nuri spoke softly, her expression intent and hungry. Sarah did not look pleased. Her brows drew down and eyes narrowed in anger, but she pasted a smile on her face. Gary was staring at the bar and did not seem to be paying attention. Sarah kept the smile but her jaw was clamped shut. She rose from the chair, put her arm through Gary's, and they walked stiffly away. She did not offer a thank you, and she did not look back.

What had Madam Nuri told Sarah? Had Gary heard it? He wasn't paying attention, maybe he was hard of hearing.

He hadn't seemed disturbed by it. But then she saw Gary throw a sharp look back at Nuri.

Nancy couldn't help herself. She had to find out what this woman was like and what kind of fortunes she told. Nancy opened her purse, took out a ten-dollar bill, and sat down in front of the fortuneteller.

"I am Madam Nuri," the woman said dramatically, beginning her spiel. "May I have your name, please?" She spoke again in that phony accent.

Nancy looked her in the eye. "Nancy Dickenson."

Nuri took her hand and opened it to study the palm. "And what do you wish to know?"

Nancy hadn't expected a question, but she searched her mind for one that would give her insights into Madam Nuri.

"Please?" said the fortuneteller. "Is simple question, no?"

What Nancy wanted to know was what Nuri told Sarah. "Yes, it is a simple question." Nancy took a deep breath. "Sarah looked pleased when she left you," Nancy lied. "Can you give me a fortune like hers?"

Madam Nuri studied Nancy for a moment. Her hands hovered over the card she had laid down. She raised an eyebrow as she said, "I think not. You would not enjoy a fortune like hers." She swept up the card and stood. "And now I must prepare for the séance. You will excuse me." The skirt of her gown swirled as she walked swiftly away from the lobby toward the library, hiding Nancy's ten-dollar bill in the folds of her garment.

Nancy arched an eyebrow and stared pointedly at Nuri's departing back, but she didn't make an issue. Nuri needed the money.

Outside the hotel, lightning flashed, thunder boomed, and the rain lashed at the windows. All they needed now, Nancy thought, was for the lights to go out and a mysterious stranger to appear. She spotted Fitz talking to Will at the bar and walked toward him.

"We should get to the séance room early," Nancy said. "According to the notice, it's in the library. We need to claim our seats and check for any gimmicks under the table or attached to the chairs. I'd like to be seated close to the medium."

"Who is this supposed medium?" asked Louise, who'd tugged George to the bar with her.

"Madam Nuri, of course. She left to prepare for it."

"She does get around, doesn't she?" George observed.

At the library, they found Marilyn, Kaye, and Lew already waiting at the closed door. Daquon stood sentry, apologetically keeping everyone outside the room.

"We want the good seats," Marilyn said to Nancy, laughing. "We're waiting for them to open the door and let us in." Her pale blue pants suit went well with her eye color and skin tones. Kaye wore a long, slinky dress, black with silver sequins sprinkled around the low neckline. Gary wore a tux, but the other men were in casual clothes as if to show their skepticism about the proceedings.

They all turned to the door when clunks and shuffling indicated furniture being pushed around in the room on the other side. Other guests joined the group. Nancy sensed an air of anticipation and excitement. Outside, the rain hammered on the roof of the verandah and thunder crashed. Julie was right. What could be more perfect weather for a séance?

Then at nine o'clock, Julie opened the door, and Daquon ushered them in. At the center of the room stood a large circular table with chairs around it. Julie stood next to one chair that was larger than the others. It was upholstered and had arms. "This is for our medium," she explained, waving people to the other chairs, which were simple wood chairs taken from the dining room.

Aside from Cole, Aysha and the kids, all the guests were present and after Julie's comment, scrambled to claim a seat for the best view.

Nancy took a chair between Fitz and Louise, and George sat on Louise's other side. As the others took their places, Nancy was amused to see Lew push himself into a chair beside Kaye and then watched Marilyn deliberately take a seat next to Sarah and Gary, on the far side from Lew. Harvey and Malcolm followed Kaye, but Malcolm weaseled himself ahead of Harvey to sit next to Marilyn. Then Evan came in and sat on the other side of Harvey with Ann and Lula completing the circle.

Everyone had taken their places and waited as a hush fell over the room. Julie dimmed the lights and opened the door. "We at Lilac Inn are pleased to introduce you to Madam Nuri, Queen of the Gypsies," she intoned in a deep and theatrical voice, bringing the palms of her hands together and bowing as the medium entered the room. "Welcome," she said to Nuri and then faded back against the wall.

Nuri had plastered her face with make-up, outlining her eyes in black, layering on the mascara, and painting her lips a dark red. Her hair was pinned up in an old-fashioned chignon with tortoiseshell combs. She had exchanged the multi-colored woolen shawl of the fortuneteller for a red-fringed shawl sprinkled with silver sequins, but her black gown remained the same. She now wore a gold necklace with cameo pendant, gold hoop earrings and gold bracelet. The effect was dramatic. Nancy would not have recognized this medium as the fortuneteller in the lobby. Awed silence filled the room as Julie lit a candle and placed it in front of Nuri, then slowly dimmed the lights and turned them off, leaving only the flame of the candle.

"Thank you," Madame Nuri said in a low, soft voice "You will all join hands." She waited. Her imperious voice and demeanor discouraged banter. "Some of you are doubters, disbelievers, I know." Her sharp glance pierced Lew's latent buffoonery. Her presence became command-ing, powerful, and there was menace in it. Nancy shivered. She didn't think any of them would dare go up against this woman right now. Lightning flashed across the windows, then the rumble of thunder. The storm must be overhead.

Nancy watched the woman in the dim candlelight, wondering how she would manage any of a medium's usual tricks. For a few seconds, Nancy could see an aura around Madam Nuri's head and shoulders. The last time she'd seen an aura was when it surrounded a woman re-counting her horror at visiting Auschwitz. That experience stifled Nancy's skepticism about auras. Was Madam Nuri so emotionally invested in the séance that she, too, gener-ated an aura?

"I must have complete silence," said Madam Nuri. "You must hold hands tightly and concentrate your energy on calling the spirits." Nancy watched Nuri's eyes dart around the table until she seemed satisfied. "Now I will extinguish the candle, and we will all close our eyes to concentrate on calling the spirits."

Nancy closed her eyes but listened intently. Julie did not move from her place against the wall. Madam Nuri spoke quietly. "I must withdraw my hand for a moment," she intoned. A few seconds passed.

Nancy had been waiting for this typical but clumsy séance trick that allowed for a variety of shenanigans while the hand was free, but the savvy mediums managed without obviously freeing their hand. Madame Nuri was only an amateur, hired to entertain.

"Thank you," Nuri said. "Our hands and our spirits now flow together as one power. We wait for the spirits of this house to come to us. They cannot speak, so they will signal their presence by other means." The quiet intensified even though rain drummed on the roof. The atmosphere felt dense, too warm, and soporific. Nancy could feel herself falling asleep.

"Now," Madam Nuri intoned. "We call on the spirits to join us." She paused and then spoke in a low commanding voice. "Oh spirits, we are gathered here tonight and eagerly seek your guidance. We beg to hear from you." She paused. "Is there a message for anyone here tonight?"

Nancy heard only the sound of breathing, intensified in the silence. Madam Nuri asked again, "Is there a message for any of us gathered here tonight? We wait for your response. You may communicate with us. Please knock on the table. One knock means yes. Two knocks mean no. We wait on you, kind spirits."

A loud knock shocked Nancy awake. She heard gasps around the table.

"We seek help and counsel, kind spirit." Madam Nuri continued. "To those of you around the table, you must keep your eyes closed to concentrate your energy."

"Do you have a message for someone here?" she asked.

Another loud knock.

"Is it for a woman gathered here tonight?"

Knock.

"Please enter my soul so I may speak your message."

Nancy had been wondering how this particular medium would translate the "Yes" or "No" knocks into a meaningful message. Kudos to Madam Nuri for overcoming that little problem.

Madam Nuri began moaning. Louder and louder. The moans stopped and in a deep voice totally unlike her own, she spoke. "Beware. Beware." She stopped and took a deep breath. "All that is real is not real. All that seems true is not true. Fakery. Fakery. Fakery. Everywhere. Everywhere."

Nancy thought she sounded uncannily like the drowning Wicked Witch in *The Wizard of Oz*.

"I cannot go on. Please, bring the lights up slowly."

Julie must have been waiting by the door because the room became lighter.

"You may open your eyes, but stay quietly in your seats," said Madam Nuri. "Do not break the circle." She continued to keep her eyes closed and to hold hands with those on either side. She took deep breaths. Slowly, she opened her eyes and released the hands she was holding. She pointed towards Sarah, or maybe Gary, or could it be Marilyn? Then she turned to face Harvey or Malcolm. Nancy couldn't tell and suppressed a nervous giggle. As usual, spirits never could get anything right. She noticed the others had opened their eyes and glanced from one person to another, probably wondering who was a fake, who was in danger.

"I'm sorry." Madam Nuri called their attention back to herself. "I am exhausted. I can endure no more tonight. I do private readings. You may make appointments with me through Miss Julie. I will come to your room." She stood. Julie came forward and helped her out the door.

Nancy peered at the medium's dress as she walked, hoping to see if a contraption for making knocks was hidden there. She saw nothing unusual, so she turned to watch the reactions. Kaye seemed the most shaky as she smiled uncertainly around the room. "That was certainly . . . something, wasn't it?" she said.

Sarah stood, a grim frown on her face. Gary was ready to laugh it off with Lew who pushed back his chair and stood, announcing loudly that it was "all a bunch of crap. Good thing I didn't spend money for this bilge."

Marilyn whispered to Louise that "if it helps her keep the roof on that shack she lives in, then, I'm all for a little show like this. Don't believe a word of it."

Louise nodded. "How do you suppose she made that knocking sound?"

Sarah came over to Nancy. "That was certainly ridiculous, wasn't it?" Sarah said. "She actually got us to sit around a table holding hands and waiting for ghosts!" Then she mimicked Madam Nuri's dramatic voice. "Fakery, fakery, fakery."

"Oh well," Nancy said. "It was all in fun on a rainy night."

"Julie ought to talk to that fortuneteller-madam whoever she is." Sarah leaned over to Nancy. "We knew about the flaw in the emerald, of course, but it didn't affect the beauty of the stone or the necklace, and it certainly didn't make the stone a fake." She whispered, "Rude of that tea leaf reader to mention it, though. I mean really."

"Forget about it," said Gary. "The woman's jealous—you can bet she doesn't have anything close to that necklace of yours."

Evan glanced at his watch and left with no comment to anyone.

Nancy saw Malcolm nudge Harvey and whisper, "Do you suppose that medium really knows a fake when she sees one?"

Harvey grunted. "She ought to. She is one."

Ann and Lula were laughing with George as they walked down the hall. None of them seemed affected. They were treating the performance as a big joke.

Nancy walked out of the room with Fitz. Julie stood at the door saying good-bye and good night to them. "How did you like it?" she asked Nancy.

"Great show," said Nancy. She'd seen better with her late husband Bill, who liked to attend séances with a critical eye, especially the flamboyant ones with spirits supposedly playing trumpets or tambourines and ghosts speaking from the grave.

"Enjoyed it," added Fitz.

"I wonder how she managed those knocks," Nancy said. Sometimes mediums hid contraptions that made knocks under their clothes or attached under the tables. In one case, knocks in a room mystified police and magicians alike. Later, they found out that the teenager who was always present when the knocks happened made the sound by cracking her ankle bones.

Julie winked and whispered. "I'll never tell."

Later that evening, Nancy set up her laptop and e-mailed Julie. She needed social security numbers for the employees and home addresses for staff and guests. Then she could run a check on each person through the various databases she subscribed to. She did have an address for Patty, that is, Patricia, Hovermale aka Madam Nuri, as well as her deceased husband, Robert Hovermale. Nancy ran a Google search and checked her databases on their names. She turned up an obituary for Robert Hovermale, deceased at age 53. He had been a writer for the Department of Justice but was on a leave of absence to "pursue other interests." Nancy guessed he was hoping to write the great American novel.

Patty Hovermale's name came up with several theatrical notices for Nuri Lovelle and a glamorous photo that was unmistakably Patty Hovermale. Why had Patty not gone back to the theater when her husband died? Nothing showed up in the criminal databases for either Patty or her husband.

Nancy searched Google on the other names. She found Chef Tom Boysie's website as a chef and a number of articles about awards he'd received and comments he'd contributed on various cooking websites. Names of the other staff brought up so many listings for different people of the same name on the Net they were useless.

Evan's name appeared in a photo caption for a USDA Forest Service publication. He was identified as an entomologist specializing in forest insect pests. Did that explain his long hikes into the Wildlife Management Area? Probably, but he was a loner, for sure.

Ann Bashaw's name was listed as an executive director of a professional association in Washington, D.C. Nancy found no listing for Lula but the next time she met Lula she'd ask her what she did.

Malcolm Smithson owned a jewelry store in Alexandria, Virginia. His website offered appraisal services and custom jewelry design. The website listed Harvey Smithson as a consultant, and he had his own website as well.

Gary Lochowsky's name, his professional credentials, and a beaming photo appeared on a website for his insurance company. There was no listing for Sarah. Nancy wondered what her previous or maiden name was.

Marilyn's name drew up hundreds of listings, most for other Marilyn Goldfarbs, but browsing through the entries, Nancy found at least ten references to articles related to assisted living and rehab services that carried Marilyn's photo as staff. The agencies were hundreds of miles apart. Marilyn couldn't possibly work at all of them, but some places didn't update their websites for months, even years. Even so, Marilyn changed jobs frequently. Was it a restless urge on her part or layoffs initiated by her employer? Maybe she didn't work well with others.

A search on Kaye Anderson also netted hundreds of listings, none of which could definitely be linked to the Kaye Anderson staying at Lilac Inn.

Searching the names of Cole and Aysha Robinson turned up a lot of similar names, but again, nothing that could be definitely linked to the couple staying at the inn.

Then on a whim, she Googled William Harris, but pages of listings came up for such a common name. Going to the Lilac Inn website, Nancy found a link from his name as owner to his LinkedIn page. His profile there showed a steady progression from research engineer to development director and then to Lilac Inn. Julie Harris's profile on LinkedIn showed a similar progression to upper management, but she worked in a large chain hotel in Pittsburgh. Unlike Will, she was well-trained to run Lilac Inn.

Nancy logged out. She felt on firmer ground, knowing a little more about the background of the guests at the inn, but she'd found nothing helpful and nothing that pointed to a thief.

*** 

### Note to Guests

We hope you enjoyed our impromptu entertainment last night. The storm overhead lent the right atmosphere for our gypsy fortuneteller and the séance. As we're sure you understand, these events are purely for entertainment and not to be taken seriously. Because of the scary nature of the séance, children were not permitted. We hope parents with children can find many other entertaining activities to do with their children here at Lilac Inn.

*Julie and Will Harris, Owner/Managers*
*Lilac Inn Resort and Restaurant*

# 13. Early Tuesday Morning
# FIVE DAYS TO GO

Nancy woke suddenly. What was that noise? She listened, scarcely daring to breathe. A soft swishing sound as if someone were walking in his socks seemed to cross outside her door and move down the hall. Her clock said two a.m. Who would be sneaking down the hall at this hour? Was he coming back from a party run late? It wasn't here at the inn where the séance was the last event of the day. Someone on staff making the rounds to check on everything? One of the security guards?

She quietly slipped out of bed, put on her robe and slippers, and tiptoed to the door. She listened again and hearing nothing, silently twisted the knob and opened the door.

The hall was lit by two lamps attached high on the wall and turned low. No one was in the hall. Who else slept on this floor? She and Louise had the middle two bedrooms, across the hall from each other. Lew was also on this floor. The stairs and the elevator were halfway down the hall from the center in one direction. Another set of stairs went down the opposite end of the building. Whoever it was had headed toward those stairs. Nancy ran to the elevator in her slippered feet. She wasn't as concerned about the noise as the other person. She might be able to beat him to the first floor.

Where else would he go?

When she stepped out of the elevator on the first floor, she stood in the dark recess near the hallway to the offices and from that position watched both sets of stairs. The door to the stairs on her right opened and out walked Lew Cookson. She saw him glance around the lobby as if to reassure himself that he was alone. He stopped to slip on his loafers.

Questions raced through Nancy's mind. She quickly dismissed the idea that he was the supplies thief since he had arrived on Saturday for a week's vacation as had the other guests. So what was he doing? He turned to look in her direction as if he knew she lurked there. Nancy shrank back against the wall, but there was no place to hide. If he came into the hall, she would be discovered.

He did not. Instead, he strolled toward the front door, unlocked it, and slowly opened it wide enough so he could squeeze through. Nancy rushed forward to watch him walk down the verandah steps onto the path. The rain had stopped, but the trail was wet and glistened in the low lights on the verandah.

Nancy gave him a good head start, then she, too, squeezed through the door and followed him, keeping to the dark shadows along the laurels lining the path, hoping she wouldn't be seen if he looked back.

He walked toward the barn. Nancy followed at a distance. Did he know what Will was inventing in the barn or was he curious? Lew stopped, lit a cigarette, and stood in place. The red tip of his cigarette glowed in the darkness. He seemed to be contemplating the existence of such a structure and what it might hold. Had Will hinted to him and perhaps others at something going on in the barn besides the usual maintenance tasks and tools? He had done that to Nancy and Fitz, but they had cornered him there, and he knew they were to be trusted.

On the other hand, Nancy had never seen Lew light a cigarette before. Perhaps he was a smoker and kept it to himself except for excursions like this one late at night. She sank back into the shadows and waited to see what he'd do next. He seemed to be staring into the night as he smoked. Then he heaved a long sigh. As Nancy listened, she felt the heavy weight, the unbearable sorrow in that sigh. Following Lew no longer seemed like the normal activity of a detective but more like an unspeakable intrusion into someone's soul.

He was on the move again. Nancy watched as he ambled to the side door of the barn and tried to open it. Unsuccessful, he strolled around the building. Nancy had done that once and knew there were no windows. Lew came back to the front, threw his cigarette on the path, and ground it with his foot. Then he picked up the butt and put it in his pocket.

Amazing, thought Nancy. He actually picked up the butt. After hearing the well of sadness in his sigh and now watching him pick up the dirty remains of a cigarette, she decided maybe Lew had some good points after all. Perhaps he had unseen depths. Then she realized that he probably didn't want Will or Daquon to know they had a spy interested in the barn, so he picked up the butt. Will certainly tried to keep his activities there a secret. What was he building inside that space?

She hid behind a tree to let Lew pass by, then followed him back to the hotel and waited for him to return upstairs to his room before she mounted the veranda steps.

The coast was clear. Nancy stepped up to the door and

twisted the knob, but Lew had locked the door. Now what? She shivered as she debated what to do. She glanced around the yard for the security guard but saw no one. The Harrises lived in a separate building a long walk in the darkness from the hotel. She didn't want to walk there, wake up someone, and have to invent some story. She shivered again in the cold night air. Then she turned in sharp attention as the door lock clicked. Someone was opening the door. Lew? She took a deep breath, ready to scream as she watched the door open.

Louise poked her head out. "Come on in out of the cold," she said.

"How did you know?" Nancy asked in relief.

"You think you're the only one who can hear mysterious footsteps in the night?" Louise whispered. "I cracked my door open, saw you follow Lew, and I followed you, only I was smart enough to stay inside." She grinned. "Good thing, too."

Nancy nodded. "Good thing."

"So where did he go?"

Nancy shrugged. "The barn to look around. And smoke. I don't know which was his real goal."

***

**Lilac Inn's No Smoking Policy**

For your health and the protection of our environment, smoking is only permitted in the parking area which has receptacles placed there for the butts.

*Will and Julie Harris, Owner/Managers*
*Lilac Inn Resort and Restaurant*

# 14. Tuesday Breakfast

Nancy groaned, turned off the ringing alarm clock, and rolled over. Six a.m. Way too early, especially since she'd been up half the night. She groaned again. Fitz was probably already dressed and waiting for her in the lobby. What possessed her to agree to join him on the bird walk before breakfast this morning? She slid out of bed, sleepwalked into the bathroom, showered, brushed her teeth, and dressed. More awake now, she checked her watch. Six twenty-five. Plenty of time to meet Fitz at six-thirty.

Once they were out in the cool, fresh, morning air, Nancy's mood improved, and she walked beside Fitz with enthusiasm, listening to the group leader and trying to see the birds he pointed out. She found birding frustrating, squinting into the shrubs and up into the trees to spot a brown bit of fluff, but Fitz knew them all. At least, he said he did. Nancy smiled at the heretical thought.

Evan Lester and Kaye Anderson also came along on the walk. Evan added bits of information to the leader's descriptions and sightings and pointed out various insects. Occasionally, he took out a small notebook and wrote in it. Knowing that Evan was an entomologist, Nancy looked at his actions as confirmation of his profession.

Kaye Anderson seemed distracted and bored. Why had

she come on this birding walk if she wasn't interested? She might find Evan attractive, since he was single, but he certainly wasn't holding her interest. Hard to tell what he thought. Kaye seemed to be spending more and more time with Lew, and birding wasn't Lew's sort of activity at all. She thought of Lew's nighttime walk. What exactly was Lew's sort of activity?

As they returned to the hotel for breakfast, Fitz held Nancy back to let the rest of the group move on ahead. "Did you hear the bit of dust-up last night?" he asked.

"What dust-up?" Had Fitz seen Lew go out, too?

"Your friend Harvey from Whisperwood and his brother were going at it with their fists hard and heavy. Must have been right after the séance. In the hall outside my door. Couldn't help hearing it." Fitz glanced inquiringly at Nancy.

Nancy shook her head as she kept her eyes on the ground. She didn't need to twist an ankle by tripping on a vine. "I'm up on the fourth floor. You're on the second. What was it about?"

"Quite a silly patch." Fitz took her elbow as they negotiated a clump of tree roots. "Seems Harvey beat out Malcolm in some game. Competitive, those two, what?"

"They're both odd ducks," said Nancy as they climbed the steps to the verandah. She saw Lew exit the elevator, and then Kaye rushed forward after him, her face flushed and eager. "Lew! You missed the bird walk!"

Lew slapped his forehead and groaned. "Sorry, honey. Plum forgot about it."

Nancy watched them walk toward the dining room together. Had Kaye tapped into a side of Lew beneath his brash rudeness or was she simply needy for any kind of male attention?

Gary and Sarah waited at the dining room door. "Opens for breakfast at seven-thirty," Gary said, holding up his watch. "In one minute."

Nancy glanced at Fitz and inclined her head toward the couple. He nodded. Nancy walked over to them. "May we join you?" she asked. She needed every opportunity to talk with the guests and here was a good one. What had the fortuneteller said to Sarah?

Sarah glanced nervously at Gary. "I suppose so. Honey?"

"Sure, sure." Gary studied Nancy. "I hear you're a great detective, Nancy."

"Detective?" echoed Sarah.

"Not any more. Retired," Nancy murmured as she always did to the question. "I'm here to enjoy a week with my friends. I suppose you've been talking to George or Louise?"

Gary cleared his throat. "Met George on the golf course. Said you almost got killed in the last three. . .cases, he called them."

"You almost got killed?" added Sarah. "That must have been thrilling. You caught the criminals and everything?" There was something off about her tone that Nancy didn't like. Patronizing. Perhaps it was jealousy. Sarah probably heard awe in Gary's voice and didn't like it. Or could it have been fear?

Fitz took Nancy's hand. "Wrong place, wrong time, that's all," said Fitz. He squeezed her hand.

Nancy felt uncomfortable. Gary was too interested;

Sarah was on guard, and now everyone would know she'd been a detective. The other guests would be watching her, wondering. She'd have to talk to George and Louise, tell them to cool it on the detective bit. "I am retired," she repeated, "but we got in a bit over our heads trying to help some friends out. We don't do that kind of thing anymore."

"No mysteries here," said Sarah firmly. "We're plain ordinary people. That's all."

"That's Nancy and me, too," confirmed Fitz, again squeezing her hand in a reassuring gesture. Nancy understood what he meant. He wasn't patronizing her. He was playing along.

"I guess you got a good fortune last night from the gypsy," Nancy said, watching Sarah's response.

Sarah's eyes narrowed. "What would you know about that?"

"Nothing." Nancy laughed to disarm her. "You looked pleased when she finished, that's all. Most fortunetellers wouldn't want to upset their clients."

"Pleased?" Sarah shrilled. Then she caught herself, and a phony smile slid across her face. "Yes, of course. How was your fortune?"

"Fine. Nothing special," Nancy said. "She saw a long journey by sea ahead, usual hackneyed stuff."

"Yeah," said Sarah. "All baloney. I tried to get my ten dollars back, but she refused. She's a scam artist, is what she is. I should complain to the manager."

They turned to watch the morning's host unlatch the dining room door. "Good morning," she said, inviting them in. Nancy recognized Bridie Callahan, the intern from Ireland. "Sit yourselves down wherever you like," she added.

"And you can be helping yourselves to the coffee on the sideboard." Her lilting accent and friendliness lent sunshine to the room.

Nancy followed the other three to a back table outside on the verandah. With a swift move, she beat Gary to the seat against the rail, so she could view the entire dining room. She could see Gary wasn't pleased and wondered. He was supposed to be an insurance salesman. Why would he follow a policeman's habit? Nancy answered her own question. He probably enjoyed watching the people come in as she did.

"We're pleased to be here," said Nancy. "This is a beautiful resort. Everything you could ask for. My friend Louise's great-niece and her husband own it, and they offered us a free stay since the season hasn't started yet." She glanced at the door to see Evan Lester wander in, followed by Marilyn Goldfarb. Evan took a table by himself. Marilyn walked in the opposite direction, waved to Nancy, and also took a table alone. Then George and Louise walked by, waved to Nancy, and took the adjacent table next to the rail. They invited Lew and Kaye to join them. Louise glanced at Nancy and winked. They were all being detectives this morning.

The server immediately appeared, filled their cups, and also invited them to the breakfast buffet. Nancy recognized the young woman and a look at her name badge placed her as "Missy." Missy Crain, sous chef and the housekeeper's daughter. Nancy smiled a thanks to Missy, then turned to Sarah. "I love the quiet, peaceful atmosphere here. It feels so safe."

"I have to wonder about that," said Gary. "A valuable

ring was stolen yesterday."

"Whose ring?" asked Fitz, as he poured sugar and cream into his coffee.

"Cole's," said Sarah. "Out of their cabin. They never lock that place up because the kids run in and out."

"The hotel has a safe," said Nancy. "Might want to put your necklace in it."

"We'll do that after breakfast," said Gary. "A lot of foreigners here."

"Only two, actually," Nancy said. "Those two delightful girls. One from Ireland and one from Norway."

"They may seem all right," Sarah sniffed, "but you never can tell."

"Did you hear the row last night?" asked Fitz to defuse the situation. "That pair of brothers, you know?"

Sarah laughed. "We did. They're always fighting, and it's usually over something trivial, like who won a game. They bet on everything. I even heard them bet on who would be first to arrive for dinner. They're like a pair of two-year-olds."

"I thought this was some kind of bonding vacation for them," threw in Nancy.

"Not much bonding there," Sarah said. "Accusing each other of cheating and what not." She signaled the server as she raised her coffee cup.

Nancy glanced over to see how Louise and George were faring. Lew seemed to be doing all the talking across the table, and it sounded like he and George planned a round of golf after breakfast. Kaye seemed distinctly unhappy, and Marilyn watched them with a faint smile. Evan was sitting alone, as usual, but Nancy noticed his eyes follow Missy and Bridie as they moved from table to table. Neither Lew nor Evan wore wedding rings, and both were here by themselves. She hoped Louise was pumping Lew. He had mentioned a wife but what about Evan? Was he married? Divorced? Widowed? Gay? Why were they here?

This led her to think about Kaye Anderson and Marilyn Goldfarb. Both were single, and both had chosen Lilac Inn to get away from their usual routines and maybe to forget, but what did they want? What were they hoping for? They both seemed transparent enough, but were they really? Kaye seemed to be carrying a heavy burden, but was that because she was dumped or hiding something? Louise hadn't mentioned anything off about Marilyn, and they'd spent most of the day together yesterday. Still, why was she here? A New Yorker. How did she find out about Lilac Inn? Why did she really choose to come here? Nancy found it hard to like Marilyn after the bird incident.

Her attention was drawn to the door where Ann Bashaw and Lula Beall had appeared. Nancy saw their eyes rove across the room, hesitate briefly, and then smile at Nancy and her table and then Louise, before they entered and selected a table near the center of the room. Both of them were golfers, and Nancy had seen them play a mean set of tennis. They might be what they seemed—a couple out for rest and recreation, but did they have another, more sinister, agenda?

Neither Harvey nor Malcolm Smithson showed up for breakfast. There seemed to be no love or respect between the brothers, so why were they here? They certainly weren't bonding.

Nancy lingered through the meal, listening for any clues that might lead her to the thief and hoping Louise, Fitz, and George were doing the same. She planned to make notes when she got back to her room.

After breakfast, the diners dispersed. Fitz left for his room, and Nancy passed the Robinson family in the lobby waiting for the van to take them to a coal mine exhibit near Charleston.

"Too nice a day to go down a coal mine," said Aysha to Nancy as she passed, "but the kids are excited about it, so here we are." She added glumly, "The sacrifices we parents make."

Nancy laughed and wished them well. She returned to her room and spent an hour noting what she had learned so far about the staff and guests. Then the phone rang. It was Julie.

"Nancy, can you come down to my office?" she asked. "As soon as possible?"

She sounded upset. Worried. "Of course," Nancy said, putting down the phone, picking up a notepad, and heading for the elevator. Louise waited for her in the lobby, and together they walked to the manager's office and knocked on the door.

Julie unlocked it. "Good. Come in. More problems," she said through clenched teeth, and she brushed one hand across her forehead.

"What's up?" asked Nancy as Julie checked the hall, closed the door, and motioned to them to sit.

"Gary and Sarah Lochowsky were in here a few minutes ago, reporting that her necklace was stolen, either last night or this morning," Julie said. "This thievery has got to stop, or it will ruin us." She stared at them with hollow eyes, clenching and unclenching her jaw.

"She's sure it wasn't misplaced?" asked Nancy. "We talked about it this morning. They were going to put it in the hotel safe."

"Should have done it in the first place," grumbled Louise. "Didn't need to be wearing it here."

Julie paced back and forth, rubbing her arms. "That's how they know it's gone. They looked for it, planning to bring it down to the safe. It wasn't in its box or the suitcase or with the dress she wore last night. They couldn't find it anywhere."

"What floor are they on," asked Nancy.

"Second," Julie said, despondently.

"Second floor." She and Lew were on the fourth floor. Had Lew come back from stealing the necklace? It didn't make sense that he would turn around and go downstairs and out to the barn if he were stealing necklaces. *Unless he knew I was watching him.* He might have led her on a wild goose chase to divert suspicion. If he had stolen the necklace and if he was afraid someone had seen him up and about. All that sounded far-fetched to Nancy.

"I saw Lew Cookson leave the inn late last night," she said and recounted the story. "Lew didn't stop at the second floor, and he wasn't holding or hiding a necklace when I saw him."

"That's odd." Julie sat behind her desk, picked up a paper clip chain, and shuffled it from hand to hand. "It's probably our no smoking policy that got him up." She frowned. I'll have to check Lew's room when Carola cleans it today."

Nancy cupped her chin in her hand and quickly reviewed in her mind the other guests she'd met. "What about Madam Nuri? Has she been around this morning? When does she leave at night?"

"Yeah. I thought of her, too," said Louise. "Obvious suspect, and she knew about those emeralds."

Julie put down the paper clips. "Of course. Will and I are both suspicious of her. We keep an eye on where she goes, what she does. She didn't go upstairs last night, and I haven't seen her around this morning." She dropped into her chair. "Obvious suspect, I suppose, but I don't think she had the opportunity."

"She keeps mumbling about fakery and frauds," Nancy said. "Upset a couple of guests. Someone said Patty and her husband were interested in cold case files."

Julie nodded. "That's right. She used to bring those magazines about crime and criminals over here while we were working on the place. I wasn't interested and didn't think they were appropriate for guests, so I told her to keep them home."

Nancy sat quietly, staring at the floor. She'd watched Julie distracted by one guest, then another, directing the interns, answering the phone, fielding the complaints, and dealing with the thefts. She had a lot on her plate. "What about the stolen ring?" Nancy asked.

"Cole Robinson's diamond pinkie ring. They're in the first cabin, so access would have been easy." Her fingers fiddled with the paper clip chain. "Those cabins aren't secure, and since we're out here in the woods and we have a security guard on the premises, most people leave their doors open. Especially if they have kids. Anyone could have gone in and stolen the ring."

"We should talk to the security guards first," said Nancy.

Louise agreed. "Good idea."

Julie reached for the phone. "I'll bring him in." She tapped in the numbers and sent out a message for the guard on duty to come to her office. "They usually don't patrol the upper floors where the guests stay unless there's a problem."

She turned to Nancy, her hand still resting on the phone. "We contract with a security company for the guards, and we have a turn-down service here."

"I noticed," Nancy said. "Thanks for the chocolates on the pillow."

Julie managed a small smile. "Guests like it, and it gives us a chance to check the rooms." Her eyes rolled. "You'd be surprised how many people want to light candles in their rooms and then forget to snuff them."

"I can't believe it," groaned Louise. "This place is wood. A tinderbox."

Julie shook her head. "Not that bad. We've made every effort to fireproof this place. Smoke alarms, sprinklers, and fire extinguishers are all over the building." She leaned back in her chair. "We do have to be careful, and we absolutely do not allow candles in the guest rooms or smoking anywhere on the grounds except the parking area." She sighed. "Still, we need to check and keep our eyes open, knowing how some people are."

A sharp rap sounded on the door. "Come in," Julie called.

An average-sized man with a slight paunch stepped in. He was wearing a navy-blue uniform with the logo of Apex Supreme Security Company on his sleeve and shirt pocket.

A badge over the pocket gave his name as Brewer. "Yes, ma'am," he said. He took off his cap and shuffled it around in his hands.

"When you came on at eight this morning" asked Julie. "Did you notice anything different or odd on your rounds?"

"No, ma'am," he said. "Nothing out of the usual. I met with Tom Simmons, who's on during the night, and he didn't report anything unusual."

"We had a theft during the night or early this morning." Julie watched the man intently. "A diamond and emerald necklace out of Room 203."

"We patrol the entire hotel and grounds, ma'am," he said. "We have cameras set up around the property, too, but we haven't spotted any unusual activity. Has the sheriff been notified?"

"They were called, and a report was filed. They'll be checking the pawn shops. This is the second jewelry theft with these guests." Julie frowned at him. The guard studied the floor. "Yes, ma'am," he said. "We've got our eye out for anything unusual."

"The pinkie ring was stolen from one of the cabins."

"Easy to get into and out of those cabins, ma'am," said the guard, still shuffling his cap." Those people in the cabins need to lock their doors. One man can't properly do the job here . . ."

"Yes, yes. I want you to keep your eyes open. You know we've got a thief here, and we need to get that ring and the necklace back. Our own supplies, too. If you see anyone carting around our housekeeping and office inventory, get the name and notify me." She nodded at him.

"Yes, ma'am." He turned and put his cap back on as he

walked out the door.

Julie sighed again. "I called the night security guard, who also saw nothing unusual. What with our supplies going missing, I feel I can't trust the staff or the guests and have to watch everyone. Do you suppose it's the same thief?"

"Did you get my e-mail?" asked Nancy.

Julie picked up several sheets of paper from her desk. "Here's the list with the information you requested. Good luck with it. Our staff are carefully vetted through the security company we use and that goes for the interns, too. I have names and addresses for the guests, but we only take their address, phone number or e-mail, and credit card info on them. Good luck."

A diamond pinkie ring for a man and a diamond and emerald necklace for a woman. Pricey things, unlike hotel supplies, but who would steal those items? Nancy thought of Malcolm and Harvey Smithson. They would know how to dismantle the jewelry and redesign it into new pieces, and they'd have the contacts to sell it. They would take a huge risk to do such a thing, and she didn't get the impression that either one was so hard up as to risk such thefts. Of course, handling stolen jewelry might be one way they could maintain an expensive lifestyle—as long as they didn't get caught.

Sarah wouldn't steal her own necklace although Nancy had read mysteries where the owner stole a valuable necklace to cash in on the insurance money. Or to add another wrinkle, if one spouse needed a lot of money for a reason they didn't want the other spouse to know, like to pay a blackmailer. They might fake a jewelry theft and claim it was stolen. Did such a scenario fit Sarah and Gary?

Possibly. There was something distinctly odd about the way Patty, aka Madam Nuri, interacted with Sarah. It was as if Patty knew all about Sarah and what she knew wasn't savory. Julie said she and Will watched Patty when she was at the inn, but how could they? Julie spent most of her time in the office, and Will was busy in the barn or fixing problems in the building much of the time

Anyone at the inn, guest or staff, could have a kleptomania problem. It might show up as she ran the names and personal information on them through the databases she subscribed to. She might pick up something the security company missed.

She didn't think the same person stole the supplies and the jewelry. The theft of supplies had been going on for weeks, but the jewelry thefts only occurred in the last several days. An employee would be the obvious suspect for the supplies, but the nature and timing of the jewelry thefts pointed to a guest. Which one?

This was Tuesday. All the guests, including Louise and herself, would leave on Saturday. There wasn't much time to find out.

***

**Notice to Guests: Protect Your Valuables**

Lilac Inn is an informal resort where you can relax and enjoy the ambiance and the activities of a rural setting. If you have expensive items such as jewelry with you, please bring them to the reception desk in the lobby and check them into the hotel safe until you leave. This service is free.

Lilac Inn cannot be responsible for lost or stolen personal property. Thank you.

*Will and Julie Harris, Owner/Managers*
*Lilac Inn Resort and Restaurant*

# 15. Tuesday Morning

Nancy and Louise left Julie's office and walked out to the verandah. "Wait a minute," Louise said. "I promised George I'd meet him on the course." She shrugged, "I don't play golf, but anything to keep him happy." She reached for the banister with one hand and held her trekking pole in the other. "See you later."

Nancy watched her head down the path, then noticed Will walking toward the barn. He waved at Nancy as he crossed the yard. Tilly followed behind, gently wagging her tail.

Will seemed to spend a lot of time in the barn, Nancy thought, with and without Daquon, who was busy pulling out the honeysuckle vines creeping in under the lilacs. Curious as always, Nancy followed Will and hid behind a tree as he opened the sliding barn door. Before he stepped inside, Tilly ran off into the meadow, distracting Will and giving Nancy time to run to the door before he could close it. Acting as if she were on a casual walk about the grounds, she stepped inside before he could slide the door closed.

"What?" Will cried, whirling around to face her. "You're not allowed in here," he said. He reached for her arm. "Out! And I mean now!".

She dodged his hand and stepped farther into the barn

away from his reach. He flipped the switch and a bank of fluorescent lights lit up the room, momentarily blinding her.

As her vision cleared, she could see tools mounted on pegboard panels that stretched the length of the barn on both side walls. The floor was laid in heavy wood planks, stained dark by oil spills and scattered sawdust. Overhead was a giant pulley on gearwheels. Nancy remembered seeing something similar in a museum replica of Thomas Edison's workshop. In the middle of the room sat a large contraption that resembled the skeleton of a giant dragonfly.

"Hi, Will," she said brightly. "How great you have such a huge workplace. Did it come with the property?"

Will stood gaping at her. After a moment as he seemed to gather his wits, he said, "This is private property, you know. You have no business coming in here."

Nancy saw she needed to pull her dumb and doddering act. "I'm so sorry," she said. "Isn't this part of the hotel property? I didn't think anything was a secret." She walked to the huge metal beast in the middle of the room. "This is fantastic. What is it?"

"Don't touch it." Will regarded the contraption with a slight smile, and Nancy saw fondness and pride in his eyes.

"It's scary. I've never seen anything like it," gushed Nancy. "You must have spent hours building it."

He nodded. "I have." He ran his hand along one of the steel rods. "It still has a long way to go, though."

She walked closer. She still couldn't imagine what it might be. "What does it do?"

He put his hands on his hips, his eyes glittered in the harsh light, turning his expression sinister. "This is an improved ultralight plane."

"An ultralight?" Nancy said, stepping back from him with a blank expression on her face.

"I suppose you don't know what an ultralight is." He regarded her with distaste. "You should have paid some attention in all your ninety-plus years." He banged his fist on a wooden post. "You should know what an ultralight is."

Nancy gaped at him, stunned and speechless at such single-minded absorption in his project.

"Just a minute," he said as he slid shut the barn door and turned to look at her. "It's a small plane." Will was impatient now. "Only I've made it quieter and more comfortable than most ultralight planes you might have seen." He glared at Nancy. "I guess you haven't seen any."

Nancy shook her head. The man must be deranged. Poor Julie.

Arms akimbo, he regarded his invention as he spoke. "You're Julie's friend, and you're supposed to be investigating here, so I'll fill you in on this." He brought his eyes back to glare at Nancy. "You keep this to yourself, you hear? I don't want any nosy parkers coming over from town to find out what I'm doing."

Nancy nodded, backing away from his pointing finger. "Of course." She felt like running away from this lunatic, but he'd shut the barn door. He'd catch her and then what? Was he violent? Would he attack her?

He stared at her for a moment before adding in a calmer voice, "Okay, then. There's a meadow behind the barn that makes a good runway. Short, but I don't need a lot of length. Only a clear space. I've been testing it out in the early evenings when most of you guests are in for supper." He stepped forward and slid between the rods and wires to a seat Nancy hadn't noticed before. He flicked a switch and the propeller in front of the structure began turning. Nancy could hear the motor gain power. It sounded like a gasoline engine. She could smell the fumes, but the garage door was closed. A vision of her body, overcome by carbon monoxide gas, crossed her mind.

Will flipped another switch and red lights came on in front. "I'm only using the red lights right now," he said. "Haven't rigged the running lights yet."

"The garage doors are closed," she said.

He glanced at her. "Don't worry. Good ventilation in here."

Good ventilation? Nancy didn't trust that statement, not from the maniac in front of her. She glanced casually toward the door. Could she slide it open and run out before he could catch her?

"Come on over here. Take a closer look." He motioned to her. Love for his machine shone in his face. "Pretty interesting, don't you think?" His anger had dissipated as pride took over.

When Nancy recovered from her astonishment at Will's swift transformation, she asked, "Do you try it out much in the open?"

"I'm improving it all the time and take it out to test it." Will turned off the lights and the motor. The propeller slowed and then stopped. He climbed out of the contraption.

"But what do you plan to do with it?" Nancy asked, feeling his enthusiasm.

"A lot of people would want a small, easy-to-fly plane that didn't need a long runway for short hops," Will said.

"Like an air car. Could have entertainment value, too, for our guests."

Nancy nodded. "I guess so."

"Look at this." Will walked to the back of the garage. "See what I'm making here?"

She saw a metal frame that looked like it might one day be a boat. "Julie loves to canoe and kayak, but she gets frustrated with trying to haul a heavy 10-footer or 12-footer on top of her car, secure it on top, and then take it down and carry it to the water. She's always wanted a maneuverable, good-tracking canoe or kayak that was light enough for her to carry, small enough to put in her car, and affordable."

Nancy saw the value of that design. She loved to canoe and kayak, too, and finally decided to resort to outfitters who provided the watercraft and the transportation. "This is excellent," she said. "Good luck on that. I'll be one of your first buyers."

"Deal," he said, hands on hip. "But don't tell anyone. Deal's off if you do." He steered her toward the side door. "I've got work to do."

Will no longer seemed menacing. She hovered at the entrance. "Thank you for showing me your inventions," she said. "I'm captivated."

Will frowned. "Keep it quiet for now. I don't want any hassles about this. Or sightseers either."

"Of course not," said Nancy, "but I'll bet your guests would find your work here fascinating . You might even develop a pool of potential investors or buyers when you're ready to manufacture these for sale.

He shrugged. "You could be right, but I'm not ready for anything like that yet."

Nancy stepped out and heard him lock the door. As she walked toward the hotel, she wondered how much all those tools and equipment cost. Where did he get the extra money? He seemed more invested in his inventions than in the hotel. She'd understood Julie and Will had put all their savings into the resort. Was Will only paying lip service to running the hotel? Is this really why Julie was so worried?

***

**NOTE TO GUESTS**
**What to See and Do in Our Area**

This part of West Virginia is close to the state capitol of Charleston, coal mine museums, llama farms, scenic beauty, waterfalls, antique and art shops, and gardens. Each month features a festival celebrating an aspect of living here. Ask your hosts for the latest calendar of events.

*Julie and Will Harris, Owner/Managers*
*Lilac Inn Resort and Restaurant*

# 16. Tuesday Noon

Nancy left the barn and set out in search of Malcolm and Harvey Smithson. She found them on the verandah, stretched out in two cushioned wicker chairs with a coffee pot and two mugs on the wicker table between them.

"Good morning, Nancy," said Harvey, glancing up from a jewelry trade magazine. Malcolm had been dozing but opened an eye in her direction.

"I need to talk to you two," said Nancy, pulling another wicker chair toward them to sit.

"Anything you want," said Malcolm drowsily.

"Two jewelry thefts have occurred here in the past couple of days," began Nancy.

"Really," said Harvey, looking at her with interest.

"You don't say," said Malcolm, opening both eyes and suddenly awake.

"The thief has to be one of the guests here," Nancy said.

"No kidding. But what about the staff?" asked Harvey.

"Could be a staff person, I guess, but nothing belonging to a guest has gone missing before this week."

Harvey laid aside the magazine and sat up. "Police been notified?"

"Of course. They'll check all the pawn shops around

here and the neighboring areas, but the jewelry may never turn up there. Meanwhile, we only have about four days to find and return the items stolen before we all go home." She took a deep breath. "You could help me catch the thief."

Malcolm now sat up. "Really? How?"

"Do you have an expensive piece of jewelry I could borrow?" She saw the doubt on Malcolm's face. "Not for long. You'd get it back tomorrow morning."

Malcolm nodded approvingly. "I see. You'll use it as bait. Maybe catch the thief. Sure. I got a diamond and ruby brooch I picked up from a consignment shop a few days ago." He looked her up and down. "Brooches are out of fashion, mostly, but someone of your age . . . you could carry it off."

Nancy's eyes narrowed. Had she been insulted? He was implying that she was "out of it," unaware of trends, old-fashioned. She longed to kick him in a sensitive spot. She smiled with her teeth. "Yes, I guess I have a twinset in my wardrobe." She didn't, but she could still wear a brooch. "That will do nicely, thank you. May I wear it this evening?"

"Sure," said Malcolm. "I'll run up and get it now. You can wear it all day." He pulled himself out of the chair and headed for the elevator.

"It might work," said Harvey, opening his magazine, "but I wouldn't count on it."

Nancy glanced at him. "If you have a better idea . . ."

"No, no," murmured Harvey, his eyes on the open magazine.

Nancy waited until Malcolm returned with a blue leather box. "I'm going to reset these stones into something different," he said, "but it'll do for now." He gave her the box. "Don't lose it," he added, "and don't forget it someplace where you can't find it."

Nancy didn't respond to the jibe. She opened the box and caught her breath. The brooch was lovely, designed with alternating round rubies and baguette diamonds in a circle. She tore her eyes away from the piece and closed the box. "Thank you," she said. "I'll watch over it carefully." She would. The piece must be worth hundreds.

She'd worn a white T-shirt under a navy sweatshirt and khaki slacks for the birding walk and breakfast. She took the elevator up to the fourth floor to find something more appropriate to wear, something that would fit a diamond and ruby brooch. She hadn't brought many clothes, but the black, short-sleeved turtleneck would serve with the brooch at the neck. Black jeans would work, too.

Feeling slightly uncomfortable, she wore this dramatic outfit to lunch, taking a table and waving at Fitz when he came in to join her.

"That's a nice outfit," he observed. "Beautiful pin. Are those real diamonds?"

"You'll be surprised to learn you gave it to me," Nancy said. "And I'm so thrilled by it I'm wearing it all day."

"What?" Fitz sat back with a confused expression.

"Yes," she nodded. "However, you should know. . ." She filled him in on the jewelry thefts. "I'm hoping the thief will go after this brooch, and we can catch him."

"Nancy," said Fitz, putting his hand on hers and gazing at her, a faint smile on his lips. "I would love to give you a brooch like that."

For a moment, Nancy felt stunned. She was afraid to

lift her eyes to his. She suddenly realized that he was quite serious. Her heart stirred, but she found she couldn't speak. What would have happened next was interrupted.

"How'd the morning go?" said a boisterous voice. Louise glanced from Nancy to Fitz. If she noticed anything unusual, she didn't let on. She took a seat, collapsed the trekking pole, and laid it on the floor beside her.

"I was out chatting up Marilyn and Kaye, but they don't seem to have any clue about the jewelry thefts." She glanced at Nancy. "No, I didn't say anything about the thefts. I was very circumspect but tried to find out more about them through chatter. I'm a world-class chatterer when I want to be." She picked up the menu and perused it.

"Did you learn anything useful?" asked Nancy.

Louise shrugged, keeping her eyes on the menu. "Kaye was dumped and came here to console herself. We already knew Marilyn had been laid off as a nurse and needed to decide what to do next. She's considering a career change."

"I imagine any kind of medical job could get intense, and you'd want a break." Nancy thought of the kind and expert care the hospice nurses had provided during the last days of both her husbands. How would she ever have gotten through that terrible time without those nurses?

"She worked in nursing homes, rehab places," said Louise. "Tough job."

"I thought nurses of any sort were in short supply," said Nancy. "Why would they lay her off?"

Louise shrugged, then George wandered in and took the fourth chair. Nancy told him about the thefts and her plan to catch the thief.

George shook his head. "I don't know about you, but I

can hardly keep my eyes open at night. All that golfing and fresh air, you know."

"Not to worry," said Nancy. "I'm also not eager to stay up all night. Need my beauty rest like all of you."

"What's your plan?" asked Fitz.

"Tonight Madam Nuri will be reading palms and tarot cards again. Everyone will be milling about. I'll hang around, parading my brooch to make sure everyone notices it. Then I'll go up and change clothes to something warmer because, I'll tell everyone, Fitz and I are going for a moonlit walk."

"New moon," grumbled George as if its darkness was on purpose to thwart their plan.

Nancy waved that objection aside. "No matter. We are going out, everyone will know about it, everyone will see I'm not wearing the pin, easy to guess it's on my bureau in my room."

She looked at Louise and George. "You two will sneak away and watch for anyone entering my room and catch them."

Louise rested her chin on her hand thoughtfully. George pushed his lips in and out. Finally, he said, "Ought to work." He nodded. "Yep, ought to work. I'm game."

"Me, too," said Louise. "My room is across from yours, Nancy. We can watch from there."

"Okay then, we have a plan." Nancy picked up her menu.

***

After lunch, Nancy sat at her laptop, checking the names and social security numbers of staff against the criminal databases to which she subscribed. No one came up with any kind of criminal record. She also checked the guests again, using the addresses they'd given Julie when they made their reservations. Lew showed up with a long backlog of driving infractions, parking violations, and unpaid fines.

Nancy searched Gary Lochowsky again. His name appeared in several other mentions on other sites, such as the local Rotary Club meetings. She was hoping for a wedding photo and article, but none appeared. She supposed it had been a small, private wedding, since it probably wasn't the first for either of them.

Sarah Lochowsky's name also didn't show up in any criminal records. Nancy checked the marriage records for Ohio and Pennsylvania, likely states for the Lochowsky wedding. Bingo. Gary Lochowsky married Sarah Marie Milford of Canton, Ohio, a little over a year ago. They'd said they were celebrating their first anniversary, so that part was true. She ran Sarah Marie Milford's name through her criminal database for a match but found none. Then Nancy tried for a match on LinkedIn and Facebook, but dozens of women with the same name showed up, some with photos and some without. Nancy narrowed the possibilities down to five, three of which had photos attached that could be of Sarah with a different hair style or color, but the likelihood of that was probably nil.

***

**Special Event: Tonight Only**
**Informal Jewelry Appraisals**
Two professional jewelers, brothers Malcolm and Harvey Smithson, will remain in the lobby from seven-

thirty to eight-thirty this evening to appraise your jewelry. These will be simple off-the-cuff appraisals for your amusement only. For a formal written appraisal, please use a professional appraiser's services in your home town. The reception desk will be open until ten p.m. tonight so guests may return their jewelry to the office safe. The management cannot be responsible for thefts or loss of personal property.

*Julie and Will Harris, Owner/Managers*
*Lilac Inn Resort and Restaurant*

# 17. Tuesday Evening

That evening after dinner, the guests casually drifted to the library for cards or the verandah for after-dinner drinks and conversation. Julie walked among them reminding guests of the informal jewelry appraisals and announcing Madam Nuri was available to read palms and tarot cards for guests again that evening. The usual table was set up in the lobby for Nuri's use.

Another table was set up on the verandah for the jewelry appraisals. A lamp sat on the table along with two loupes. Harvey and Malcolm insisted on sitting outside in their usual chairs. "These are simply informal but informed appraisals. Nothing legal. Only for fun," said Malcolm, "but we are professional jewelers, and we know our business.".

As she passed through the lobby, Nancy saw Madam Nuri in full gypsy costume—large golden hoop earrings, strands of beads around her neck, frilly blouse with a shawl across her shoulders, and a long and full black skirt. She was laying out cards for Kaye Anderson, who leaned back in her chair, a dubious expression on her face and narrowed eyes. The black carry-on was set again behind the fortune-teller's chair. Nancy paused to watch Nuri cast shrewd, intelligent glances upon Kaye. Knowing Madam Nuri was an actress and highly intuitive, Nancy thought she would have no trouble undermining Kaye's obvious skepticism and telling her what she wanted to hear. Nancy casually stood by, seemingly engrossed in reading Julie's daily newsletter of events and places to visit in the area.

Nuri put aside the cards and took Kaye's hand, turning it over to search the palm. "I see you have endured a great disappointment," purred Nuri, "recently. This is true, is it not?"

"Oh yes," said Kaye hesitatingly. "How did you know?"

"You are heartbroken, yes?" Nuri kept her eyes on Kaye's palm.

"Yes, yes, you see. . ."

Nancy listened. Was Kaye eating it up?

"But now you have met someone . . . ." Nuri softened her words and peered into Kaye's face.

"I have. How could you know? He is so nice . . ."

"He is nice, you say, but he is not nice." Nuri ran a finger across Kaye's palm. "This man, he is not for you."

Kaye's lips trembled. "But he is nice. I like him, I truly do."

"Of course you do," said Nuri. "But he will betray you." She put down Kaye's hand and perused the cards she had laid out. "I see here that you will take a long voyage."

Kaye's eyes roamed over the cards. "A voyage?"

"Yes. And it may be on that voyage, you will meet the man of your dreams, the right man." Nuri looked at Kaye, shook her head slightly, and continued. "I am not sure. The cards can not tell me . . . it may be you will meet the man on the voyage or perhaps after, maybe before, I do not know. The cards. . ." She lifted her hands as if she were helpless to further explain the cards. "That is all I have for you now."

She gestured to a small wooden box, open on the table. "Please put ten dollars in the box. Thank you."

Kaye put a ten-dollar bill in the box and pushed back her chair. "Thank you, Madam Nuri. You give me hope." Madam Nuri bowed her head, and Nancy watched Kaye leave with an odd expression on her face.

Still seemingly engrossed in the newsletter, Nancy felt appalled at what she'd heard. She agreed that Lew Cookson was not the man for Kaye, but to suggest that she'd meet someone on a voyage who would be the man of her dreams! That was irresponsible. Thank goodness Nuri softened that bold statement with maybes.

Nancy changed her position but still stood by as Sarah came over to Nuri. Gary followed and pulled the chair out for Sarah before passing on to the bar.

Nancy wondered why Sarah would come back to Nuri. Trying for a better reading? She was curious about Sarah. What would Nuri say this time?

Again, Nuri began by laying out cards, but then she took Sarah's hand and lightly ran the fingers from her other hand over Sarah's palm. She shook her head. "We have met before, have we not?" she asked.

"Of course," Sarah said with disdain. "Yesterday."

Nuri raised her eyes to stare into Sarah's. "Before that, surely?"

Sarah bristled. "No, no, of course not."

"But yes, I do know you," insisted Nuri. "I know you from many places. Cincinnati, Pittsburgh, Baltimore. Many places. I see bad things there. Evil things."

Sarah snatched her hand back. "I'm sorry, but I've never seen you before in my life."

"Perhaps, then, in another place, another life," purred Nuri. "I will read you the cards."

"Only good things," said Sarah. "I'm on my second honeymoon."

"But of course." Nuri cast her eyes across the cards. "But I am afraid the cards tell me nothing. The future is cloudy. We must meet again later. Perhaps in your room. Perhaps you visit me in my home, yes? I think we have much to talk about, and then we will try again."

"Oh. Okay. Sometimes it doesn't work, I guess." Sarah bounced out of the chair. She reached for her purse, but Nuri placed her hand on Sarah's arm. "Later. You will pay me later."

Nancy stood by, astounded at the menace in Nuri's voice—and her refusal to take the money.

"Next time." Sarah said and walked away with a puckered brow and a frown.

The next person was Marilyn who took a seat but stared at Nuri with a quizzical expression.

Nancy saw Nuri turn away from Marilyn to glare at Nancy, ready to chastise her if she remained standing so close. *She knows I've been listening.* Nancy looked away. She shouldn't be lingering here, anyway. She needed to flaunt her brooch. Nuri laid a hand on Nancy's arm and beckoned her closer.

"You wear a beautiful piece of jewelry," said Nuri. "I have not seen that before."

"My friend Fitz gave it to me," Nancy said, glad Nuri had noticed it. Nuri was a suspicious character to say the least.

"Ah, a special friend. I understand." Nuri nodded and

began to lay out the cards as she greeted Marilyn.

Nuri was right. Fitz was a special friend. *How special?* Nancy wandered into the card room where Louise and George played bridge with Ann Bashaw and Lula Beall.

Louise primed the pump. Looking up from her cards, she said, "Nancy, that's a beautiful brooch you're wearing. Where did you get it?"

"Fitz gave it to me today," Nancy said on cue. "It's all diamonds and rubies."

"Wow. Must be worth a pretty penny," George exclaimed.

"Pipe down, George," said Louise, winking at Nancy.

What a comedy. Nancy waved and moved on to the puzzle table where Gary Lochowsky and Cole Robinson were hovering over the pieces. Gary looked up and smiled a greeting. "That's a pretty piece of jewelry you're wearing," he said.

Cole glanced up and nodded. "Watch out for it," Cole said. "Remember, my ring was stolen."

"And my wife's necklace," added Gary.

"I will," said Nancy. "I know it's valuable, and I certainly wouldn't want it stolen."

She wandered out to the verandah. Malcolm Smithson did the honors this time. 'Good job," he said softly for Nancy's ears alone, then louder, "Beautiful brooch you're wearing."

Lew Cookson glanced at the brooch and nodded. "Sure is. Quite a bunch of diamonds," he commented. "Big money for that, I'd say."

Evan Lester, sitting nearby with a book, also looked up. Nancy saw him notice the brooch, nod, and return, seemingly uninterested, to his book.

Fitz came out to the verandah. "What do you say we go for a walk, Nancy?" he asked.

"Sure. It's kind of chilly, though. Let me change to something warmer." Nancy replied.

"Wait a minute," said Malcolm in a loud voice. "Do you want me to give you a quick appraisal on that brooch?"

Nancy glanced at Fitz. "Sure," he said. "Give it a go."

Nancy took off the brooch and passed it over to Malcolm. He picked up a loupe from the table and examined the brooch, taking an inordinately long time, Nancy thought.

"I can give you a rough estimate, but I don't have the facilities here to weigh the stones." He continued to act as if he were studying the brooch. Then he sat back and handed it to her. "I'd insure this lovely piece of jewelry for five thousand dollars," He said at last and winked at her.

"That much?" Nancy said, stunned. Could this brooch be worth that much really or was he pulling her leg?

"Quite an expensive piece," He looked pointedly at Fitz. "He must like you very much, eh? The man who gave this to you." He laughed at his little joke, knowing it put Fitz on the spot.

"Yes, he does," said Fitz.

Nancy blushed. She pinned it back onto her turtleneck. "Thank you for the appraisal."

"Not a problem. Glad to do it." Malcolm looked beyond Nancy to Marilyn who held a necklace in her hands.

She stepped forward. "I'd like an appraisal of this necklace. Maybe you can tell me what the stones are."

Nancy and Fitz walked back into the lobby, then into the card room, with Fitz following.

"How's the game going?" she asked Louise.

"Only a game," grumbled Louise.

Fitz took his cue. "What do you say we go for a walk, Nancy?" he said, repeating the intention for the game players in the room.

"Sure. It's kind of chilly, though. Let me change to something warmer." Nancy also repeated for this audience. She made a show of unpinning the brooch. "I'll be right down," she said.

"Okay. I'll wait for you down here," said Fitz.

Nancy left to go up to her room and change, placing the brooch squarely on top of the bureau. Too obvious, she said to herself. She wrapped it in a scarf and put it in the top drawer. The thief would expect to hunt for it.

She rejoined Fitz in the game room. "Care to walk with us?" Fitz asked Louise and George.

"Nah," said George. "I'm bushed. I'm going up to bed soon as I finish this game."

"Me, too," said Louise. "It's tough hanging around here on vacation." She grinned at the absurdity.

Nancy laughed. "Okay, you guys. We'll see you tomorrow." She and Fitz walked out to the verandah and down the steps to the path in full view of anyone outside. Then they disappeared into the darkness of a moonless night.

They were alone, strolling along the wooded path that led to the bird blind. Lights from the hotel penetrated through the trees so they could still see their way. Nancy waited for Fitz to say something as she remembered his words at lunch. What did he mean? She thought of when they first met, many years ago, at a troubled time in both their lives. Of the terrible loss he suffered when his son was killed while riding his bicycle. Of the support he'd offered her when her first husband died. They had lost track of each other for years after that except for the ritual exchange of holiday cards. Then he showed up at Whisperwood.

Fitz cleared his throat. "Beautiful evening," he said.

Nancy nodded. "Yes, it is."

They walked along in silence.

Nancy didn't often feel tongue-tied, but her feelings were so confused she couldn't get a word out. She glanced up at Fitz. He stared straight ahead, his dark face in shadow.

Finally, Nancy ventured a few words. "I was so glad when you turned up at Whisperwood last year. I. . ." she took a deep breath. "It made me realize how much I missed you."

His hand reached for hers and squeezed. "Me, too," he said. "You were the reason I moved there."

"I'm glad." She looked up at him, and he gazed down at her and slowly, tentatively, his face lowered to hers and their lips met. Then their arms wound around each other.

"I love you," said Fitz against her face.

"Yes," said Nancy. "I love you, too. From the moment I saw you in the elevator at Whisperwood." She felt something inside her heart flutter, break free, and fly.

Some time later, their arms around each other, they continued their walk. Nancy thought back to all the times they'd lived through yet, until a few months ago, they had only been friends. Then he shared his personal tragedy with her, a story she had never known, and she saw his vulnerability. Something changed at that moment. He touched her heart. When had it changed for him? What was he thinking about now? She looked up at him, and he turned his face to her. "I love you," he said again, his voice trembling.

"I love you, too," Nancy replied, feeling herself folded into his arms and realizing it felt good to be there.

Eventually, they turned their feet back toward the verandah and stepped away from each other as they returned to the lobby, hand in hand.

***

### Notice to Guests: Evening Activities

Games, puzzles, movies, books, and good conversation are all available to you in the evenings. Madam Nuri, our local palm and tarot card reader, medium, and fortuneteller, often visits and can be coaxed to read your fortune if you cross her palm with silver. All in good fun, of course. Enjoy yourself.

Don't forget: Tomorrow's movie in the library at 7 p.m. is *E.T.*, a suitable movie for the entire family.

*Will and Julie Harris, Owner/Managers,*
*Lilac Inn Resort and Restaurant*

# 18. Wednesday Morning
# FOUR DAYS TO GO

Nancy lay in bed, reflecting on the night before and Fitz. Dear, wonderful Fitz. How did he feel this morning? Their long-time friendship had ramped up to a new level. She would need time to adjust. Fitz probably would, too. Maybe they'd gotten carried away last night. She'd have to take it slow. He might already be regretting what happened. She didn't, though, but she wasn't going to presume anything yet. *It's my age and my profession. Can't fully trust anyone or anything.*

That settled, her thoughts took another turn. She considered their lack of progress so far in finding out who was stealing the hotel supplies and the jewelry.

Last night, when she and Fitz came back from their walk, Louise burst out of her room across the hall. "You're back. Good."

George waved at Nancy from a chair. "Been up and down a dozen times," he said. "Taking turns peeking through the door. Most boring job I've ever done."

"More than boring. Absolutely no action, Nancy," added Louise. "No one tried your door. No one stopped and knocked to see if you were in. I'll bet the brooch is still where you left it."

"Let's see." The foursome trooped into Nancy's room. Nancy opened the drawer and unwrapped the scarf. They stared glumly at the brooch.

"It was a good idea, Nancy," said Louise. "But it didn't work."

Nancy grimaced. "I don't think anyone was onto us, and we'd pointed the brooch out to all the guests. I'd hate to think it was someone on staff."

"Back to the drawing board," grumbled George.

Nancy put the brooch into her pocket, and they returned to the hall. The stair door opened and Evan Lester walked out. He stopped, appearing startled, when he saw Nancy, Louise, George, and Fitz staring at him. No one spoke, then Evan cleared his throat. "Sorry. Thought this was the third floor." He turned and disappeared down the stairway.

Nancy glanced at the others. "That was odd."

"If he's the thief," grumbled Louise, "he's too late."

George nodded. "Or you came up here too early."

Fitz laughed. "I think we're all too suspicious. He made a simple mistake."

Nancy shook her head dubiously. "It's possible, I suppose." How could you miss walking an extra flight of stairs or mistake the third for the fourth floor? Evan is a bright man. Is he also the thief? "Where is his room?"

"Third floor," said George. "Right above mine."

Nancy was sure the thieves must be two different people. Stealing hotel supplies had been going on for several months. It indicated a thief who was on staff. Someone with access to the storerooms who knew how to sell the stolen merchandise and who would buy it. She hated to think that of one of the staff people here, but they were the most logical thieves. She had visited the kitchens and met Missy and Chef Pierre. They both lived nearby, had excellent resumes, and no criminal record. The housekeeping staff outdid themselves making sure guests had everything they needed, nobody had a criminal record, and the rooms were clean and comfortable. The interns seemed like earnest, honest young people. They shared a room in Julie's house, so they had no place to hide stolen goods and no way to dispose of them. Julie showed Nancy their resumes, references, and applications. Nothing suspicious there. Everyone she met had been pleasant to her. All open books. No one seemed to have a hidden agenda.

But someone was stealing the supplies.

The same went for the stolen pinky ring and the necklace. Those items might be more tempting to a wider variety of people—the guests, for instance, but no one she'd met here seemed to be anything more than they appeared. She'd searched the criminal databases she subscribed to and didn't find any staff member or guest listed there except for Lew and his parking tickets.

Her thoughts turned to Patty, or Madam Nuri as she preferred to be called. She was the most likely suspect for the jewelry thefts. Financially, she was on shaky ground, dependent on fortunetelling and an occasional séance. Hard to pay the bills with an income like that. Where did she live? Did she have any family? How long had she been in the area?

Nancy glanced at the bedside clock. Seven-thirty. She was to meet Louise and Fitz for breakfast at eight. They'd signed up for the canoe trip this morning on the New River. The guide was picking them up at ten and would return them to the hotel by three p.m. after a picnic lunch. She wondered who else had signed up for the trip as she dragged herself out of bed and into the shower.

Louise sat at their usual table when Nancy arrived. Fitz caught up with Nancy as she walked in, taking her hand and squeezing it while giving her a special wink. She smiled at him. She was too shy to do more in a public situation with Louise's eagle eyes picking up on any nuance. Half an hour later, George showed up, already complaining.

"I never get up this early at home," he said. "What's so darn important that we're all here at the crack of dawn?"

Louise laughed. "Crack of dawn." She looked pointedly at the shafts of sunlight turning the gray decking to silver. "Hardly."

George tucked a napkin into the bright yellow collar of his polo shirt. "It is to me," he said.

Nancy saw Julie poke her head into the dining room and nod at Nancy before withdrawing. Nancy laid aside the menu and stood as the server came by to fill their coffee cups. "Excuse me," she said. "I'm going to see if Julie's in her office. I'll be back in a few minutes."

She tapped softly on the office door, heard Julie say "Come in," and slipped into the room, closing the door behind her.

Julie looked up from a spreadsheet and forced a smile, but Nancy could see the troubled lines on Julie's face. "What happened last night? Did you see anything suspicious? Nail the culprits?"

"We did a good job with the bait," said Nancy. "But nobody took it. I'll return the brooch to Malcolm today."

Julie shook her head and sighed. "It's not your fault,

Nancy. You're doing the best you can."

"I've run all the guests and staff through my criminal databases. Nothing suspicious on any of them. Except one odd item. Marilyn had gone through four jobs in short order, moving from state to state. Nothing negative was said in any comments from her employers. She wasn't an exemplary employee but apparently not a bad one either." Nancy paused and shrugged. "Maybe she just liked to move from place to place. Odd but not criminal."

"Moving from job to job is a red flag," said Julie "Some people get away with it because most employers and human resources people won't say anything negative about an employee no matter what they do. Afraid of being sued. However many jobs she had, it's no concern of mine. She's a guest, not an employee. Her money is as good as anyone's."

"That's true, I guess," said Nancy.

"I'm glad everyone checked out okay," Julie said. "The security company looked into the backgrounds of all the staff before we hired them. I'm confident none of them would steal from us." She fingered the spreadsheets she'd been poring over. "Good to know your search validated the security company's findings."

"What can you tell me about Patty?" Nancy asked. "Where did she come from? How long has she been here? What do you know about her?"

Julie leaned back in her chair. "We thought of her as our poor orphan child, you know, Nancy. Pathetic, really. She and her husband bought a few acres with an abandoned apple orchard and a log house, a shack, really, down the road. They had plans to build a new house. Then her husband died, so she lives in that awful rustic wreck, hidden down a dirt road full of ruts and weeds."

"What about money?" asked Nancy. "How does she survive?"

Julie shook her head. "She ran out of money a year ago. Now she scrapes along with the fortunetelling. She gardens, too, and sells whatever she grows. We buy her herbs. She has a wood stove for heat, an outside well, and an outhouse. At least she has a cell phone, charges it here. But she's a sad case. We try to help her out however we can."

"Where did Patty come from?"

"Outside of Washington, D.C. someplace. I know she wasn't brought up that way. Her clothes are quite beautiful, some of them. That's about all she has of her former life, whatever it was." Julie picked up a cup of coffee and sipped it.

"She must have had a good job in D.C.," Nancy said, wishing she'd brought a cup of tea with her.

Julie nodded. "I suspect that's the case. A lot of people from the D.C.-Baltimore area try to leave the rat race by moving back to the land for a simpler lifestyle. They can buy thirty acres here for a fraction of the cost elsewhere. Some succeed and manage to build a different kind of life. A lot of them are happy with their decision."

"What about Patty? Do you think she's happy?" asked Nancy, sitting back.

Julie sighed. "I don't see how she could be, but she doesn't have the money to do anything else." Julie took another sip. "If she could sell that property. . ."

"Has she tried?" Nancy wondered who might buy such a place.

Julie shook her head. "People have suggested selling, but she won't." Julie grimaced. "Thinks it would be disrespectful of her husband." Julie leaned back in her chair. "She's still mourning him, I guess, but it's been five years now."

Nancy understood. Memories of her own losses sometimes weighed down her spirits no matter how many years had passed. She shook herself to banish the memories. "Does she have a car?" Nancy asked, answering her own question in her mind. How could Patty afford a car?

Julie shrugged. "She catches a ride with one of us when we're going into town."

"Tough life." Nancy rose to leave.

Julie stood, too. "Yeah. Tough life."

Nancy glanced at her watch, "Not quite eight. How do you get to Patty's place?"

"Turn right onto the road, go about a quarter mile and you'll see an overgrown dirt road on the right, making a path through the roadside honeysuckle. Walk down that, past the gnarled old apple trees. You'll see the cabin on the left. I've been down the road out of curiosity but never imposed on her and never went inside." She smiled. "Afraid of what I'd find, you know."

Nancy turned to leave as Will poked his head in, then he saw Nancy. "How's it going?" he asked, his heavy-lidded eyes making his face appear reptilian.

Nancy glanced at Julie who was gazing at him fondly. Looks meant nothing as Nancy well knew, having exploited stereotypes and assumptions in her business as a detective. Who would believe he was a talented inventor? Who would believe he had a plane in his barn? There was no sign of any such thing outside the barn. He was very secretive. In fact, she reflected, the secretiveness made him look sneaky, even untrustworthy. That's the feeling she got when she talked with him, but now she knew about his inventions, so perhaps she could think of him in a more kindly way. She managed a reply to Will's question, although she had to admit to herself they had gotten nowhere so far. "We're working on it," she said. "No new thefts?"

Will leaned against the door frame, hands in his pockets, and looked her straight in the eye. "The staff are keeping a close inventory and watch on the storerooms, and the security guards are on the alert." He smiled at Julie.

Nancy watched him closely, trying to get a fix on the guy. She was reassured by the tenderness in his face when he looked at his wife, but he resembled a movie con artist. All he needed was a thin mustache. Could he be the thief? Maybe he stole the housekeeping items and sold them to support his inventions. Julie said they sank all their money into this place. Could he have stolen the jewelry, too? Where did he get the money to build a plane?

***

### NOTICE TO GUESTS

The County Extension Office offers workshops on Saturdays related to income-producing endeavors for local residents, many of whom live at poverty level. This Saturday, workshops will be on managing a woodlot and growing emus for meat and other products. This might be an educational stop on your way home. Information available at the reception desk.

*Will and Julie Harris, Owner/Managers*
*Lilac Inn Resort and Restaurant*

# Chapter 19. Wednesday Morning

Nancy checked the time. Nine a.m. She had an hour before the canoe trip to talk to Carola, who headed the housekeeping staff. Nancy took the elevator to the top floor where she found Carola with the cleaning and supply cart. "Can I speak with you a few minutes?" asked Nancy.

Carola stopped chewing gum and looked dubiously at the clipboard in her hand. "I guess so," she said. "I don't know anything, though." She spoke with a slight lisp, and one of her front teeth was missing. Her hair was tightly curled in a neat close cut, and her blue maid's uniform was spotless.

"Sometimes people notice things they don't know they noticed," Nancy said. She felt it was a redundant exercise since Julie had already questioned the staff, but something new might pop up. "I'm talking with everyone who works here. Do you have any thoughts on how the thefts of hotel supplies occurred?"

Carola shook her head as she ran her hand along the top of the cart. "I account for the supplies I use every day," she said, "and I lock up the supply closet every night. Since the thefts, I always keep it locked when I'm out on the floor, but other people have keys, you know, and Julie keeps a spare set on the wall in her office. She doesn't always lock her office when she leaves." She spoke breathlessly as she chewed the gum, and her hands gripped the cart handle. "Does now, though."

"I see," said Nancy, noting Carola's defensiveness.

"I didn't steal the supplies," Carola added. "Sometimes I take the used soap bits or the end of a toilet paper roll, but what use does the hotel have for those?"

Nancy smiled benignly to help Carola feel more at ease. "Of course. I often wondered what you did with those tiny bars of soap when they'd been used. You couldn't give them to the next guest."

Carola laughed. "That's for sure."

"You have access to the entire hotel. Have you noticed anything unusual going on here? Maybe something odd you couldn't explain. It doesn't necessarily have to connect with the missing supplies."

"I don't have access to the barn, you know. Something for sure is odd there," Carola said, "but that's Mr. Harris' place, and he doesn't allow any of us in there. Except Daquon, of course."

"No one wandering the halls who shouldn't be here?"

Carola sighed. "Ma'am, how would I know? We get new people every week. I don't know any of them. I'm here to clean the place. I don't socialize. Now is that all? I got to get back to work."

"One more thing," Nancy said. "Is there any particular time or day the supplies go missing?"

"Not that I know," said Carola. "I show up and sometimes the supplies are missing but most of the time not. I leave the housekeeping cart in the hall while I'm cleaning the rooms. Don't count the supplies every time I go in and out, you know. Sometimes I grab something and notice there aren't as many of whatever it is as I thought. Never see anyone in the hall what could have taken it. Most of the time, I think they take the stuff after hours or before. Probably pick the door of the supplies closet, my guess." She turned to her cart, ready to roll. "That all?"

"Thank you for your time." Nancy said. "I really appreciate it and so do Julie and Will. If you do see anything unusual, though, please let them know as soon as possible."

Carola began moving her cart, her feet in time with her gum chewing. "I will, ma'am. I most certainly will."

***

The canoe trip scheduled for that morning drew most of the guests to the verandah to wait for the guide. An alternative shopping excursion to Charleston had drawn no takers. George smirked at Louise as he passed on his way to the Pro Shop. "I'll take civilized sports like golf any day," he muttered. "Not going to catch me out in the middle of nowhere in an open, tippable scow. Probably alligators and moccasins in that river. Maybe the Mothman, too."

Louise laughed. "We're in West Virginia, George. Not Florida," she called after him. "And it's a canoe, not a flat-bottomed barge."

Malcolm and Harvey did not join their excursion. Nancy couldn't imagine either of those hothouse plants in a canoe, so she wasn't surprised. Nancy had asked them about it, though, out of curiosity, but they claimed business in town. Jewelry business? Had they stolen the jewelry and were finding a fence? They would know valuable jewelry when they saw it, and Sarah had certainly flaunted her necklace Monday evening. On the other hand, they were jewelers.

Business men. Reputable business men. Why would they risk their reputations and their businesses on thievery? They also knew that the brooch Nancy wore was a trap. If they were the thieves, it was no wonder no one sprung the trap.

Evan Lester was also missing, but Nancy heard him tell Julie that he was going for an early morning hike and then driving over to find where the original Mothman was seen. Aysha carried a huge backpack from which bottles of water and trail mix spilled out. Kaye wore a black fanny pack and carried a small paperback in a large pocket of her khaki pants. Sarah's purse hung on her arm. The others all carried small backpacks.

"What's the river like, anyone know?" asked Nancy.

Lew turned around and surveyed her with distaste, head to foot. "We had rain a couple of nights ago, but not much. The river's pretty fast most of the time." He paused, hands on hips and squinted insultingly at her. "You sure you're up to it?"

Nancy turned away, not bothering to respond. She'd won plenty of canoe races in her time, the last one only a couple of years ago. She saw the angry glint in Louise's eye. She looked ready to raise her cane to strike him, but Nancy shook her head. *Keep things pleasant for Julie's sake.*

Nancy noticed Marilyn standing silently by, brooding. Was she worried about not having a job? This resort wasn't cheap. "How are you doing?" Nancy asked, using an innocuous question to start a conversation. There was something odd about Marilyn. Maybe she didn't get along with her coworkers and that's why she moved from job to job.

Marilyn looked up, startled. "I'm fine. No problems." She recovered herself. "I love canoeing, don't you?"

Nancy nodded, then she heard the rumble and rattle of a

vehicle coming down the drive.

The guide pulled up in an old school bus painted white with "River & Trail Outfitters" and a website painted in large green letters on the side. A young man in jeans and T-shirt hopped out of the bus, clipboard in hand. "Everyone here going on the canoe trip today?" he called out.

"Yes sir," Cole boomed. Kai and Kimberly clapped their hands and yelled, "Hooray!" The others nodded and smiled their assent.

"Good. I'm your trip leader and guide, Drew MacDill. Yell out when I call your names, okay?" He began reading names from the clipboard. He glanced up and smiled as each person responded. "Okay," he said as he lowered the clipboard. "We've got fourteen. That's seven canoes. Everybody got a partner?"

Fitz smiled at Nancy and whispered, "We're partners, right?"

Nancy returned the smile, considered the subtext, and nodded. "You bet." She noticed that Louise and Marilyn were standing together. Lew walked over to Kaye's side.

"All aboard, then."

Nancy saw Lew leave Kaye to take Drew aside for a private word. She dawdled along to hear because she'd seen him nod her way as he talked.

"We can go at our own pace, right?" Lew asked.

"Sure," answered Drew, "but I'll be bringing up the rear in case there's any trouble."

"Good. Some people don't know when to stop." Lew nodded her way again. "Know what I mean?"

Drew frowned at him. "Sir, you may be surprised. I've seen twenty-year-olds who couldn't paddle a raft in a puddle. That woman there, she looks like she can handle a canoe all right. Excuse me." He left Lew to help the Robinsons negotiate the huge backpack and the two kids.

Nancy's heart warmed toward Drew. *A very nice young man.* She stepped up into the bus behind Gary who helped Sarah with the steps and then let her take a window seat.

Once onboard the bus, the group settled down for a long ride to the put-in place. Nancy and Fitz sat in front of Kai and Kimberly who bounced in their seats.

Kai leaned forward and whispered in Nancy's ear, "Want to know what we saw?"

"Sure. What?" said Nancy. Louise turned her head and leaned back to listen.

"The Mothman!" Kai and Kimberly said together.

"The Mothman?" Nancy glanced at Fitz.

Kimberly pushed herself forward. "Yeah! He was big, and he had long wings like a giant dragonfly and big red eyes!"

"Really," said Nancy. "And where did you see this creature?"

"In the sky over the woods. Coming out of the trees! It was huge." Kai spread out his hands to show how big.

"Bigger than that!" said Kimberly. "And it chased us!" Her eyes grew large and round. "We were scared."

"We ran fast back to the hotel." Kai shook his head. "It didn't follow us. We were scared. Really scared."

"Good thing you escaped this monster," said Nancy, glancing at Aysha.

Aysha shrugged. "Kids have such colorful imaginations, don't they?"

Nancy didn't think the kids had made up the story.

Someone else was spreading stories about the monsters, too. Investigations of the earlier Mothman sightings determined it was a large sandhill crane seen at dusk or evening. Of course, the children embroidered the story so the details might be made up. She noticed Louise, sitting behind Aysha, roll her eyes. Louise also thought the kids' colorful imaginations were at work. Nancy resolved to ask them exactly where they saw the Mothman. Pretend or not, it was still worth investigating, and Nancy had her own suspicions.

The bus turned down a dirt road and bumped along for half a mile to a cleared and sandy area by the river. Canoes were lined up along the edge, and a teenager in torn cut-offs and T-shirt stood by a pile of life jackets and paddles. At this point, the river was as narrow as Nancy's living room and overhung with trees and vines that trailed into the water. Peering downstream, she was reassured by the prospect. Flatwater. No rapids that she could see. She liked to observe the birds, wildlife, and plants along the river; she didn't want a ride that was fast and harrowing. As each person got off the bus, the teenager handed out a paddle and PFD to each of them.

The boaters followed Drew to the water's edge to claim a canoe.

Drew halted them before they stepped into the watercraft and confirmed Nancy's impression. "This is mostly flat water with a bit of a current, faster than usual because of the snowmelt and recent rain. There's one stretch of Class I rapids. Shouldn't cause trouble for any of you experienced paddlers." He winked at the group, gave them a few safety instructions, and concluded with, "I'll stay in the rear to pick up the stragglers, but remember," he paused for his big line, "you all have to paddle your own canoe." He waited for the laugh, then held up his hand. "When you get to the bridge, pull out on the right. There's a beach there, and it's where we'll have lunch."

Nancy preferred to take the stern seat and steer, but Fitz weighed significantly more than she did, so he took the stern. That put her in the power seat, but she didn't think she'd have any problems. She settled back to enjoy the wild scenery on both banks as the river wound through the valley. She could hear the Robinson kids squealing and laughing as they sorted themselves out in two canoes, one parent in each trying to instruct Kai and Kimberly on the art of paddling. Nancy was glad to leave them and their yelling far behind. Gary Lochowsky sat in the back of his canoe with Sarah in front. Her paddle rested across her lap. She clearly had no intention of contributing to the effort. Gary's face had a strained look on it, but he seemed experienced and frequently let the boat drift with the current.

Lew was paired with Kaye Anderson who chattered as she dipped her paddle. Still, happiness did not light up her face. She looked more as if she were living under a black cloud. Nancy hoped Kaye was not too taken with Lew. The man was married, and from what she'd seen of him, Nancy would have placed him as bigoted and not too bright. What stopped her from a total dislike was that long heartfelt sigh when he thought he was alone. Another deeply troubled person—like Kaye. Was that the attraction between the two?

Ann and Lula argued about who would steer and finally agreed on a compromise with one steering before lunch and the other after lunch. Nancy paddled faster to get beyond earshot of their bickering.

Thinking of Sarah's necklace caused Nancy to watch for Sarah and Gary on the river. How were they doing? Was their paddling arrangement a metaphor for their marriage? Was Gary spending his marriage years paddling for both of them? She considered the idea as she spied them ahead near the bank on the left. They seemed to be arguing. Nancy glanced back at Fitz who had been watching them, too. He steered closer to the bank so they could listen without being obvious.

"I think we should leave," Sarah was saying, "before something else gets stolen."

"We paid for a week," said Gary. "People would wonder if we left early."

"So what? Anyway, it's no one else's business." Sarah replied. "We were victims of a jewel thief. Victims. Nobody would blame us for leaving after being robbed."

Gary glanced up from the water and noticed Nancy close by. He waved and called out, "How ya doing?" Sarah smiled and waved, too.

"Fine," said Nancy.

"Current makes this easy," added Fitz. "Beautiful day out here." He added power to his stroke, and Nancy and Fitz left the other couple behind, soon losing them out of sight around a bend.

"What did you think of that?" asked Fitz softly.

"Sarah's ready to leave," Nancy said. "I'd hate to see them do that. You know Sarah will tell everyone she knows back home about the theft. Bad publicity for Will and Julie."

"Whether they leave now or at the end of the week, they're still going to tell tales," said Fitz.

"If they stay, we might find the necklace. There might even be some reasonable explanation for its disappearance. Maybe she misplaced it or dropped it behind sofa cushions or something. I can't imagine anyone at the hotel, guest or staff, being such a brazen thief." Nancy shook her head. "Someone's a thief, though," she amended.

"Do you have any ideas about the thefts?" asked Fitz. "I don't."

"I don't either. Only a few vague suspicions. I wonder why Evan Lester showed up on the fourth floor last night?"

"An absentminded mistake," said Fitz.

They paddled on in silence. Nancy noticed Louise steer her canoe toward a bank to point out the blooming redbud trees to Marilyn, who nodded but responded half-heartedly, her thoughts elsewhere.

Sarah and Gary floated along in a grim silence. Gary kept his eye on the river ahead while Sarah studied her fingernails. Somewhere way behind them, the Robinsons were stalled against a sunken tree trunk. Nancy could hear their shouts, muted in the distance. Lew and Kaye had passed them some time ago and were far ahead. Nancy smiled grimly. Lew was proving his superiority, no doubt. Pathetic.

She tried to ignore the constant bickering from Ann and Lula. Lula sitting at the stern and steering couldn't run the straight course in the middle that Ann insisted upon. The two sniped at each other from the moment they stepped into the canoe.

Nancy grimaced. She'd seen canoe trips break up relationships. It wasn't the first time she'd thought couples should canoe together before they got married. Afterward, they might not want to. Get married, that is. She glanced back at Fitz. They were so in tune with each other in their paddling, they must be a perfect couple. She grinned at the thought.

"I think we're a perfect couple," said Fitz.

Nancy laughed. "I was thinking the same thing." She wanted to say more, the words trembled on her lips. She turned around to gaze at him. "Last night was wonderful. I'm so glad."

"Me, too," said Fitz.

They continued to paddle contentedly downstream. Enveloped in a warm glow, Nancy sensed Fitz's regard behind her. He felt the same way she did. Love. And at her advanced age. His background, beginning in Jamaica but growing up in New York and then traveling and living around the world, was much broader than her own. Yet, they connected on many levels.

The time passed. Nancy began feeling hungry for lunch when, at last, the bridge loomed ahead. She saw Lew and Kaye's canoe pulled up on the beach. Fitz steered their canoe toward shore and with a powerful sweep of the paddle, pushed it up on the beach alongside the other canoe.

Soon, the entire party sat on the bank, eating sandwiches, apples, and potato chips. Water and soft drinks were hauled out of Drew's canoe and passed around as well.

The Robinson family were in dripping clothes after numerous capsizes, but the day was warm, and the kids finished their sandwiches quickly to play tag in the clear, cold water.

Nancy listened to the conversations around her, seeking clues to the personalities and backgrounds of the guests. She watched Lew try to impress Kaye, who was willing to be impressed, telling her he was an assistant branch chief for some federal government agency in D.C. He didn't specify which agency, but assistant branch chief was specific enough and mid-level enough to be real.

Kaye worked as an administrative assistant in the Treasury Department. Neither she nor Lew seemed likely to skulk corridors as a jewel or supplies thief.

Nursing was fraught with emotional crises, and Marilyn must have seen her share. That probably accounted for the brooding. A heavy frown rested on her face, and Louise sat uncharacteristically silent next to her.

Were Sarah and Gary Lochowsky what they seemed? She had found nothing suspicious about the couple on the database, except for the void on Sarah. That was easily explained by their marriage since Sarah had changed her name to Lochowsky. Sarah's demeanor was often guarded. Gary's stolid face revealed little about what he thought or felt.

And that brought Ann Bashaw and Lula Beall to mind. Ann seemed competent and stable. Lula was a comfortable and amiable kitty cat. They were a pleasant couple with a few hard edges, but no wonder considering the abuse and misunderstandings they must have encountered trying to be true to themselves. They bickered incessantly on the river, but otherwise seemed like ordinary, law-abiding citizens. Nancy couldn't see either of them stealing jewelry, but she'd been wrong before.

That left Evan Lester. He seemed to be a loner and given to long hikes with his bird guide and his binoculars. It all fit since he was an entomologist. Judging from the articles and information on the web, he must be well-respected in his field.

"Mulling over the suspects?" whispered Fitz, sitting next to her.

Nancy ran her eyes across the group assembled on the bank. "Do you have any thoughts?"

Fitz shook his head. "Not one. All look innocent to me. I'm relying on your expertise."

"Retired," said Nancy automatically. "Long time ago." The phrase was becoming a habit. "I do try to keep up with my profession, and I'm interested." She saw Drew packing up the picnic debris. She stood, brushing off her shorts, to help.

He blew a whistle. She heard Kai and Kimberly squeal, then saw Gary sit up, blinking his eyes, as Sarah emerged from the woods. Ann and Lula weren't speaking and glared at each other. One by one, everyone walked down to the canoes, and Nancy, who had a long-time experience with boats, helped them get seated and then pushed them off.

"One stretch of easy rapids up about a quarter mile," Drew called out as they left, "then it's a smooth paddle the rest of the way as the river gets wider. We'll be pulling out at the River & Trail Building. You can't miss it. There's a sign over the dock." He shoved his canoe into the water and leaped in, then back-paddled to stay in place so he could watch the others launch the canoes and head down the river.

Nancy observed the way the others interacted, watching for any signs of a tendency toward thieving although she wasn't sure what those signs might be and nothing struck her as significant. She found Sarah irritating for continuing to let Gary be the sole paddler of their canoe. His face was red, and he was perspiring from the effort and the heat, but he didn't complain. Kaye finally shut up, having received no interest or reinforcement from Lew since before lunch.

Louise and Marilyn seemed to be congenial, cooperative partners who easily forged ahead of the others. Louise usually led and Marilyn followed. Nancy and Fitz also found the trip easy and relaxing, enjoying each other's company.

Ann and Lula didn't speak to each other, paddling their canoe as drudgery rather than joy. As they pulled it onto the shore, Ann turned her back on Lula and muttered, "I'll never paddle with you again. Next time, separate canoes."

One by one, the boaters arrived at the pull-out place and dragged their crafts up on the beach. They dropped their paddles and life preservers at the door of the office and waited.

The Robinsons were the last to arrive. Kai and Kimberly scrambled out of the canoes and into the water to push their parents and the canoes onto the beach. Cole and Aysha apologized for being the last as they struggled to heave themselves out and onto land, but only Lew Cookson seemed annoyed.

The bus took them back to Lilac Inn to be greeted by Julie offering soft drinks, bottled water, and cookies in the lobby. "Come to my office," she whispered to Nancy. "I need to talk to you. Something terrible has happened."

***

**Notice to Guests: Kayaks Available**
Lilac Inn has two kayaks for use on the pond. Adults only, please. Sign up to borrow a kayak at the Pro

Shop. Pick up paddles and a personal flotation device (PFD) there, too. All boaters must wear a PFD.
*Will and Julie Harris, Owner/Managers*
*Lilac Inn Resort and Restaurant*

# 20. Wednesday Afternoon

Nancy saw the worry, fear, and tragedy on Julie's face. What horrible thing could have happened?

"Is George all right?" Louise asked, a tremor in her voice. "He wasn't on the canoe trip, and all of us came back okay."

"He's fine," Julie said, "but I need to see you both right away. In my office."

"Okay. We'll follow you," Nancy said, wondering what had happened while they were gone.

"Me, too," said Louise, walking behind Nancy. "As long as George is okay . . ."

"Close the door behind you," Julie said, taking her place behind the desk. She wiped a hand across her brow. "Please. Sit." She motioned to the chairs in front of the desk and leaned forward as Nancy and Louise sat.

"What's happened?" asked Nancy. Had Will been hurt?

"Patty has been found dead," Julie said. "Will is over at her place now, talking to the police."

Nancy gasped. "Dead? How? Was it an accident?"

"It was not an accident," Julie said, staring ahead at the wall. "She was shot in the head during the night or early this morning. No signs of vandalism. That's all I know. She would have lain there for days if she hadn't asked Will to pick her up to go into town this morning. She wasn't waiting in her drive as she usually does for a pickup, so Will walked down to her cabin to fetch her."

Julie reached for a tissue and blew her nose, then swept the tissue across her eyes. "We worried about her, all alone down that dirt road—especially with the thefts going on here. This county has a low crime rate, but still. . . "

Nancy sat back and drummed her fingers on the chair arm. "Was she well-liked among the staff here?" she asked.

"Oh, well, she was a curiosity, you see." Julie sighed. "Not a question of liking or disliking. She did add interest and color when she came around. Guests loved the séances—who does that anymore?—and the fortunetelling."

"I could see where the fortunetelling might have struck a nerve," added Louise, "in somebody with a guilty conscience."

Julie nodded. "Her comments could be entirely innocent and innocuous, but the client might interpret them differently."

"She sometimes probably hit the mark too closely," commented Nancy.

Julie looked at them with a rueful smile. "She wasn't known for tact and sensitivity."

"Sarah Lochowsky wasn't pleased with her readings," Nancy said. She heard the clomping of boots in the hall.

"Here comes Will," Julie looked toward the door. "He can fill us in on what happened."

Will threw the door open, walked in, nodded to Nancy and Louise, and reached back to shut it behind him before dropping into the other chair.

"What happened?" asked Julie.

"They think she was shot early this morning," Will said. "But wait till you hear this." He pulled a rag out of his pocket and wiped his brow.

"What?" said Julie, Nancy, and Louise simultaneously.

"I found out where all our supplies have been going."

Julie gaped at Will. "Patty? Patty was stealing from us?"

"Sure looks like it." He stretched his legs out in front of him, stowing the rag back in a pocket. "Her place was packed with our stuff. Hardly room to turn around. Stacks of canned goods. Piles of flour sacks, sugar sacks. Cleaning supplies. I couldn't believe it." He whipped his hat across his legs. "I'll bet it's all there. Even the missing towels and sheets."

"Unbelievable," said Julie, sitting back, shock on her face.

"Are you sure they're from your resort?" asked Nancy. "Could it be stuff she bought herself?"

"Special brands made for hotel use. Stuff missing from our pantries and storerooms. Our wholesaler. Can't draw any other conclusion," Will said. "Also, there's so much. Piles of it. I don't think she was selling it. More like she hoarded it."

"Are they going to return our stuff?" asked Julie. "We've got receipts for all those supplies."

"I talked to the sheriff, told him we could prove it was ours," Will said. "We did file a report of the thefts with him. Might take a while."

Julie put her head in her hands. "I can't believe it."

Will clenched his teeth. "Neither can I. Shows you what a good deed will do. We tried to help that woman, give her an income. . ."

"But why was she killed?" asked Nancy. "It wasn't because of the stuff she stole."

"Yeah," said Louise. "The murderer didn't take any of that. It was still there for you to see."

Neither Julie nor Will had an answer.

"Did you see any signs of an intruder?" asked Nancy. "How was she lying?"

Will took a deep breath, shaking his head. "I was too shaken to notice much. She was lying on the floor . . . on her stomach as if she'd tried to run." He thought a moment. "The killer must have come in through the front door. I guess she let him in. No broken windows." His eyes roamed the walls. "That I saw, I mean. I didn't notice the details. Just went outside and called the police."

"Do you think she stole the jewelry, too?" asked Nancy.

"Don't know," he replied.

As they sat there, mulling over the news, Nancy heard a soft, timid knock on the door. Julie called out, "Come in," as Will opened it. Kimberly stood outside holding onto Tilly, the golden retriever, with her mother behind her.

"Go ahead," prodded Aysha to her daughter. "Tell them."

Her eyes big and round, Kimberly held up a glittering diamond and emerald necklace. "The doggie f-found this, ma'am." The girl gulped. "He had it in his mouth."

"I'm right, aren't I?" said Aysha. "This is the missing necklace?"

Nancy stepped forward. "It certainly is. Thank you for coming forward with it, Kimberly."

Kimberly stroked the dog. "It wasn't me. It was the doggie. He's a retriever, isn't he?"

"Quite a good one," said Julie with a smile. "And thank you, too." Julie glanced at the mother. "I'll call Sarah right away."

"Good. We're pleased to help, aren't we, Kimberly?" said Aysha.

"Yes, ma'am," Kimberly said dutifully. "Can I go now?"

Aysha nodded and Kimberly ran out of the office toward the verandah. Julie watched her until she disappeared around a corner. "Extra ice cream, for sure," she said.

Aysha frowned at Julie. "Please keep us out of this. We simply found the dog with the necklace in his mouth and returned it to you so you could give it back to Sarah. Nobody needs to know we had anything to do with it."

Julie nodded. "We're all glad it's found," she said, "and I'll certainly say nothing of your involvement. I'm sure Sarah would want to thank you, though."

"Not necessary. We're glad to help." Aysha stepped away from the door and turned toward the elevator.

Julie held the necklace up for Nancy, Louise, and Will to see. Nancy took it and examined it closely. "This looks like the necklace Sarah was wearing," she said, handing it back to Julie. "I wonder where the dog found it."

"Thank goodness, the girl saw it hanging from his mouth," Julie said. "He could have dropped it back in the woods somewhere." She reached down to pet the dog. "Good Tilly."

"So Patty didn't steal the jewelry," said Nancy. "Do you suppose Sarah dropped it somewhere the dog could pick it up?"

Julie shook her head. "Sarah specifically said she put

it away in her jewelry box when she and Gary returned to their room after the séance. Gary confirms it. Someone had to enter their room and take it."

"But why steal it and then leave it where the dog could find it?" asked Will. "I don't get it."

"It's like a-a prank." Julie shivered. "I don't see why someone would do this to us. They could ruin our business and for what? Nobody else has an inn like ours nearby."

"I took a good look at the necklace when she wore it," said Nancy. "I love to see fine craftsmanship, and I noticed the settings had delicate prongs for holding expensive stones, not mirror-backed pieces of glass. The stones could be synthetics, I suppose, but the clasp is quality, too."

"I noticed that," said Julie.

"Patty may have stolen our supplies and hoarded them," added Will, "but she didn't steal that necklace only to return it." He paused. "Unless she did steal the necklace, and the murderer found it. It would be very suspicious if he were found with it, so he threw it where the dog would find it."

Nancy remembered Patty's comment about the necklace on Monday night. "She did know about jewelry, though. She could have stolen it."

***

**NOTICE TO GUESTS AND STAFF**

We regret to inform you of the passing of Patty Hovermale, who as Madam Nuri, gave us many hours of entertainment as a medium and fortuneteller. We will miss her. If anyone has any information regarding her untimely death, contact Corporal Yost of the local Sheriff's Department at 304-555-7300. If you have any questions, please see Julie or Will Harris. A memorial service will be arranged for her at a date to be announced. If you would like to attend, please let the front desk know and you will be notified of the arrangements.

*Will and Julie Harris, Owner/Managers*
*Lilac Inn Resort and Restaurant*

# 21. Wednesday Evening

Patty's death cast a pall over the afternoon cocktail hour. Conversation was hushed out of respect for her, but speculation hung in the air.

"It couldn't have been one of us," Sarah said, speaking softly to Nancy and Louise. "We barely knew the woman." She sipped from her glass of wine while casting an eye over each person in the room. "Most of us were out on the canoe trip, anyway."

Nancy didn't tell her the murder happened late the night before or in the early morning, long before the trip departure. If Sarah was guilty, she was doing a good job of pretending innocence. Any of them could have done it, but who here would have a motive? It must have been someone Patty knew from town. She was vulnerable to thieves and vandals, too, living alone and isolated in that cabin although apparently nothing was stolen from her house. Quite the contrary.

Evan stood nearby and heard Sarah's last words. "I wasn't on the canoe trip," he said, "and I didn't kill her, either." He held a cocktail in one hand, the other nervously hovered around his mouth as if he wanted to bite his nails. "Nancy, can I speak to you a minute?" He took Nancy's elbow and steered her toward a vacant corner of the room.

"You used to be a private eye, right?"

Nancy sighed. Once again, she repeated, "Retired a long time now." Then she saw Evan's troubled face and shaking hands. "I do try to help when I can," she added.

"I'm sure, but you must still remember the ropes." He glanced at the others. "What to look for. Who's lying. That kind of thing, I mean." He stared at her a moment. He seemed to be assessing her, making up his mind. Finally, he said, "I'm worried."

He certainly seemed worried. Had he some connection with Patty he was afraid the police would find out about? And why was he on the fourth floor last night? Had he really mistaken the floor or did he want to see someone there? Or had he planned to steal the brooch?

"Worried about what?" Nancy asked.

He grabbed her arm. "I didn't kill her," he said, staring into Nancy's eyes as if willing her belief. "I wandered by her cabin yesterday morning, only I didn't know it was hers." He shook Nancy's arm. "My field is entomology, but I'm a lifelong birder, too. I walk all over the place, searching for birds in different habitats. Insects, too." He stopped to take a breath, suddenly noticed he still gripped Nancy's arm and let go with an apologetic shake of the head. "Sorry," he said.

"You found her cabin?" asked Nancy, seeing where this was going.

He nodded as if relieved. "Her orchard. Overgrown. A mess. Trees past their prime, all twisted and gnarled. Infested. No one has paid attention to that orchard for years."

"Dozens of people must wander by her place, even through her orchard, every month," said Nancy. "Hikers and birders like yourself. Hunters, even, in season."

"Sure." He bit his lip. "I didn't see her cabin at first, you know, but when I went farther down that road, I found it. I didn't see anyone around, so out of curiosity I walked up and knocked on the door. Thought I'd suggest ways to fix up that orchard." He'd been speaking fast and stopped to take a breath. "Nobody answered."

"Then what did you do?"

"I tried the door knob, but it was locked, then I called out. No one answered and I thought the place was vacant, so I. . ." He hesitated and darted a look at Nancy. She waited.

"I peeped in all the windows." He shot another glance at her as if seeking her reaction. "I was curious," he repeated, as if to defend himself. "All right, I was plain nosy. Anyway, someone could have been hurt inside or something."

"Of course." Nancy waited, keeping her expression blank, carefully nonjudgmental.

Evan swallowed and went on. "She had piles of junk in that place. Couldn't see across the room for all the stuff."

"But you didn't go in?"

"No, I didn't go in." He sounded relieved. "But the police could find my prints on the doorknob and window sills, couldn't they?"

"I suppose the ones on the doorknob would be obliterated by those who came in afterwards, but the window sills . . ." She glanced at Evan's ashen face and changed the subject. "Did you see her body?" she asked. "Patty was probably dead by the time you arrived."

"No, oh no." He looked at her in horror. "If I'd seen her

lying on the floor, hurt or . . . but I didn't. I didn't see anything but piles of junk. " He shook his head. "What should I do?" He seemed so worried Nancy took pity on him.

"Tell the police your story before they track down your fingerprints and have to drag you in."

Evan bit his lip as he stared at the floor. Nancy saw Louise give her a quizzical raised eyebrow. Nancy shook her head, then turned back to the poor man and watched him deliberate.

"What am I going to do?" he moaned softly to himself. "They'll think I did it for sure."

"If you're that worried, maybe you should get a lawyer," Nancy said. "I think it will look better for you if you simply tell them you passed by yesterday and peered in the windows because no one was there, and you thought the cabin was abandoned, along with the orchard."

He nodded. "Yeah, that's right. Anyone would do what I did." He looked at her. "That's what you'd advise?"

"Friend to friend, yes," she said, suddenly wary of the tone in his voice. "I'm certainly not a lawyer, and I'm not a detective anymore, and I'm not billing you. It's a friend to friend suggestion."

He laughed. "Okay. I get it. Not going to sue you no matter how it turns out. I'm innocent of any crime but nosiness, and that's not a crime."

"That's right. You're an entomologist, aren't you? You could say you were interested because of the infestation in the orchard."

He took a sip of his cocktail. "Yeah. That's an idea. And it is true. There is one other thing, though."

Nancy looked at him. "What's that?"

"Her kitty cat," he said. "That was one sweet kitty. I'm worried about her, too."

"I suppose the police will call animal control."

Evan nodded, staring at his feet as he muttered, "I'll ask about her when I see them. I'd sure like to adopt her." He laughed. "Unless they arrest me."

Nancy smiled, appreciating the unseen depths in Evan. He was quite a nice person. Just introverted. "I hope it works out."

"Thanks, Nancy. I'll talk to the police in the morning."

Fitz walked in. Nancy left Evan to greet him. "Everyone's talking about Patty," she said.

"Yeah. Hard to believe," Fitz replied. "Even harder to think she's the supply thief and a hoarder. Especially in the shack she lived in. A fire trap. She must have really been messed up. Husband dying so suddenly and living alone there. Understandable, really."

Nancy remembered her own days as a widow. How difficult it was to get through the nights. The days were hard, too, but she'd had friends around her, interests to pursue, and a comfortable income. She felt a profound pity for Patty, left alone in a new town with no friends, no income, and no support system. If hoarding was a symptom of trauma, Patty had reason enough, but why would someone murder her?

"Any thoughts on the killer?" Nancy asked.

"A few, yes," said Fitz. "Seems like the guests here made up her social life and much of her income—other than what she made selling the produce she grew and the supplies she stole."

"She didn't sell the hotel's supplies." Nancy walked

with him as he headed for the bar. "Will said they were stacked all over the cabin. She didn't try to sell them or even use them."

Fitz ordered a Heineken. "She definitely had a screw loose." He glanced around the room. "She didn't own a car. Do you suppose she knew any neighbors besides the people here at Lilac Inn? I didn't see any houses as I drove here."

Nancy nodded. "I wouldn't think she'd have anyone visit her," she said, "but a hotel guest could have gone there to talk with her. Someone with a problem they wanted to keep private."

Fitz signed the bar bill and picked up the beer. "I'd look for the killer here at Lilac Inn."

Nancy sipped her wine and surveyed the other guests over the wine glass. "I think you're right, but who would kill her and why?"

Fitz took Nancy's hand and led her to a quiet corner away from the others. "That's what I've been trying to figure out. All the guests here came for the week. The interns are from overseas and wouldn't have a history with her. She was pretty much a loner and seemed to antagonize most of the staff, so none of them had much interaction with her, either."

Fitz nodded. "Not a winning personality."

"She was an odd character," said Nancy. "She told fortunes to the guests and seemed to take more risks at what she told them than most so-called fortunetellers would. They rely on making intuitive lucky guesses and being vague. She told me my past would catch up to me. If I were a different sort of person, like maybe a jewel thief, I might worry she knew too much about me. If she saw she'd worried me enough, would she pursue that line, embellish it?

Try blackmail?" She bit her lip thoughtfully. "Julie thought she was helping Patty out and providing a little entertainment for the guests."

"The police will check her bank account looking for clues, like big deposits. I hope they search her mattress, freezer, and sugar jar," said Fitz. "If she was working blackmail, she'd have to hide the money somewhere. She sure didn't spend it."

Nancy glanced at her watch. "Let's see if Julie is in her office. Maybe she can tell us a little more about Patty." Nancy set her wine glass on a serving table, and Fitz followed her down the hall. Nancy rapped softly on the office door and walked in when she heard Julie's pleasant "Come in."

She smiled as she saw Nancy and Fitz. "Thank goodness. I don't need any more aggravations today, and I hope you didn't bring me one."

Nancy shook her head and sat in one of the chairs. Fitz took the other. "We need to know more about Patty." she said.

"Patty." Julie sat back and crossed her legs. "I don't know much. She asked if she could come by in the evenings and tell people's fortunes, promising not to make a nuisance of herself. She did have manners, you know, and usually knew when to back off. The guests enjoyed the entertainment. I never heard any complaints."

Nancy disagreed with Julie's impression. "You think she knew when to back off? You didn't notice her antagonizing or distressing anyone?" Nancy had sensed a malicious cast to Patty and watched her deliberately give unkind and disturbing fortunes to the guests rather than innocuous or optimistic ones that most so-called fortunetellers would offer. Patty loved true crime stories and collected "Wanted" flyers. What if she recognized a wanted felon?

Julie leaned back, tapped her pencil on the desk, and regarded Nancy. "What do you think?"

"Something odd had been going on between Patty and Sarah," said Nancy. "Twice when she looked at Sarah, she started talking about frauds and fakes. If I'd been a different kind of person, she could have pressed one of my buttons. I wouldn't kill her, but someone else with a dangerous secret might."

"Did she have any relatives nearby?" asked Fitz. "Family? Friends?"

Julie shook her head. "As I told you, she and her husband moved here from D.C. to get away from the rat race. After a couple of years he died, and she was left alone in the cabin. By that time, they'd probably used up whatever resources they had." Julie thought a moment, then added, "But wait a minute. Hovermale is a common West Virginia name. Her husband might have had relations near here. That might be why they chose this particular part of West Virginia, but I never heard her speak of them."

"Do you suppose the property could be worth anything?" asked Fitz.

"Property values around here are depressed. That's why we could buy this place. I can't imagine her property is worth killing someone for. The orchard is in terrible shape."

Fitz nodded. "No mineral rights? No diamonds? Gold?"

Julie smiled. "You've got to be joking, If you find some, though, we could sure use the income."

He laughed. "Okay, okay. So who inherits the property?"

"That's a good question." Julie shrugged. "I don't have the faintest idea."

Nancy rose. "I hope her death won't affect your business," she said.

"I'm very sorry she passed," said Julie. "I liked her, and I liked her spirit."

"Yes," Nancy said. "She was quite a character."

"Of course, that was before I found out she stole our supplies." Julie shook her head with a rueful smile.

"I suppose losing her husband and worrying about money unhinged her," Nancy said, getting up and heading for the door with Fitz following.

Julie snapped her fingers. "Wait a minute. I forgot to tell you."

"What?" said Nancy, turning at the door.

"I am so relieved," Julie said. "We returned Sarah's necklace, and now we've found Cole's diamond pinky ring."

"That's great news," Nancy said. "Where was the ring?"

"On the floor in the dining room. In plain sight." Julie grinned at them. "One of the interns spotted it and brought it to me. Thank goodness." She paused, then added, "Cole was glad to get it back. Sentimental value. Belonged to his grandfather and then his father."

"I have a ring like that," said Fitz. "Belonged to my dad, but I never wear it." He stepped forward and opened the door for Nancy.

Both the missing pieces of jewelry returned, Nancy thought, and the culprit for the missing hotel supplies identified. All very neat. Patty couldn't have stolen the jewelry as well as the supplies. She was dead before the necklace and ring were returned. Why steal the jewelry and then return it?

*I need to take a close look at the ring.* Nancy had some experience with jewelry. She might be able to spot some fakes substituted for the genuine article. She'd have to ask Cole and Sarah about that. Not that they would know. We're all amateurs, she thought, but either of the Smithson brothers could check the jewelry and make sure substitutions hadn't been made.

Could the murder have frightened the jewel thieves so much they returned the jewelry?

Could it have been the kids playing a game? No. Kai and Kimberly were neither stupid nor disrespectful. They were good kids. Other kids who lived in the area? She hadn't seen any. This hotel was too remote, away from family homes.

Nancy walked out with Fitz, her mind back on Patty's murder. "I'm going to contact the Hovermales around here. Patty's husband might have had relatives nearby."

Later that evening, Nancy found an old telephone directory in the library and searched for Hovermales. There were other spellings of Hovermale, like Hawvermale and Havermale, but she ignored those. She made a list of six families with their addresses and then retrieved the county map she'd picked up at the Chamber of Commerce in town. Louise loved exploring country roads and so did she. As long as they didn't get shot for trespassing, they should have an interesting day tomorrow.

***

## NOTICE TO GUESTS
### Tomorrow: The Great Bug Search and Honey Tasting!

Guest Evan Lester is a well-known entomologist and has offered to take anyone interested on a hike tomorrow to find, identify, and learn more about the bugs and beetles around us. He promises to talk about butterflies, moths, and bees as well. Join him on the verandah at 10 a.m. Thursday morning. Thank you, Evan!

**Honey Tasting**: Thursday at 4 p.m. Guest Louise Owens is bringing her collection of honeys from around the world for a tasting. What honey will become your favorite?

*Will and Julie Harris, Owner/Managers,*
*Lilac Inn Resort and Restaurant*

# 22. Thursday Morning
# THREE DAYS TO GO

On the way to breakfast the next morning, Nancy read the notice on the lobby bulletin board. Evan was leading a bug hunt this morning. He'd probably add a lot of interesting bits of information, too. She shook her head with regret. She would love to join the hunt. So would Louise, but they had other plans for today, and no time to waste. She walked into the dining room and spotted Fitz and Louise seated outside on the verandah. George rushed into the dining room behind Nancy. The morning already felt warm, and the dew was heavy on the grass, but the sky was clear.

She filled a plate from the breakfast buffet, then joined the others. George took a seat next to Louise and smiled approvingly at his plate as he laid it on the table.

Louise stared at his fuchsia polo shirt and pale pink slacks. "I see you dialed down the brightness today," she said.

George ignored the sarcasm. "I'm glad you like it."

"Fuchsia is my favorite color," Nancy said, but then she turned serious. "We found out who stole the hotel items," she said, "but now we have a murder and two jewelry thefts to solve and only three days left to do it."

As if on cue, Louise chimed in. "Someone killed Patty,

and people here at the hotel aren't the only possible suspects."

Nancy nodded. "She must have known people in the community, and they would have known her. What about relatives?"

"You're right, luv," said Fitz, sipping his coffee.

"I propose to drive around today to explore the countryside and, incidentally, to drop in on the local Hovermales. Some of them might be related to her deceased husband and give us some clues. Who wants to go with me?"

"I'm in," said Louise without hesitation. "Country drive it is."

George sniffed as he speared a piece of sausage. "If you need muscle to whip the varmints into shape, call on me. I'm the guy with the clubs, but I'm planning to use them today on the course."

"Let me see," said Fitz with a smile. "I could sit in the bird blind and find new species for my life list or I could sit by the pool and read or maybe find someone to play tennis with. Or I could drive into the countryside with Nancy. The drive, hands down." His smile widened to a grin as he winked at Nancy.

Nancy beamed at them. "Good, because I don't know what I'm going to get into. This is Hatfield and McCoy country, you know. Bootleggers, stills, bad dogs, and I don't know what else."

"All stereotypes," put in Louise, "and you know how I feel about stereotypes. Lot of nice people, intelligent people in West Virginia, too. What I tell people," she waved her fork to make the point, "is that the crusty old codger in bib overalls sitting in a rocking chair on his front porch in the West Virginia hills could easily be a retired physicist from NASA."

"Ain't that the truth," said George. "Ain't that the truth."

"I have a list of Hovermales in the county," said Nancy, "with addresses."

"Let's check the list with Julie—she might have a local map," said Fitz. "We don't want loose directions that say to turn where the church used to be."

"Good idea," said Louise. "Some of these roads don't even have names."

"Not to worry." Nancy buttered her toast. "I have a map, but it's an old one, printed before the county brought in the 911 system. With the new system, the county had to standardize and eliminate duplications of the road names." Picking up the raspberry jam, she added, "Trouble is I used an ancient phone book to get the names and addresses, and it listed the old road names. If Julie can't translate the old names into the new ones, we'll go into town to the Chamber of Commerce. They should be able to set us straight."

Louise looked up from her oatmeal. "I need to get back by three this afternoon."

"Of course. We'll be more than ready to come back by then," Nancy said, adding a squirt of honey to her tea. "Your honey tasting is at four."

"Yep," Louise said with pride. "Julie's putting up more announcements now. Seems like today will be insect day here at Lilac Inn."

"I'll be done by four," said George. "I'm looking forward to the tasting."

"Wouldn't miss it," added Fitz.

After breakfast, Nancy took the list to Julie's office.

"I'm going to visit the people on this list and see if anyone is related to Patty," Nancy said. "Do you know how to get to these places?" She unfolded her map and spread it out on Julie's desk.

Julie skimmed the list, then she studied the map. "This is an old map. Chamber of Commerce printed up new ones with the new road names. We were all confused there for a while, and some businesses out of town lost customers. Here's our inn." Julie picked up a pen and wrote an "X" on the map. She referred to Nancy's list and one by one, added an "X" on the map for each name on the list. She folded it and handed it back to Nancy. "Most of the people around here are nice people, but you never know. Some are suspicious of strangers, and some plain don't like them. And most of them have guns. Be careful."

"Louise and Fitz are going with me," Nancy said. "We'll try to keep out of trouble."

"You could call the people on your list and ask." Julie handed her the phone.

"I'd rather catch them by surprise." Nancy headed out the door. "Thanks," she called back, reflecting that person-to-person chats had always given her more information than a phone call.

As Nancy drove to town, Louise took over the map and drew a line for their routes from stop to stop. They easily found their first stop, a tiny frame house on a side street with an even smaller yard of hard clay sparsely covered in weeds. A sign in front said, "Tina's Beauty Salon. Walk In."

Fitz took one look and said, "I'll stay in the car. This is your territory."

"Wait a minute," said Nancy. "Probably no one has heard the news yet that Patty's dead. Let's use present tense in speaking of her to avoid muddying the waters."

Fitz and Louise nodded. "Good idea," said Louise.

Nancy and Louise followed the broken sidewalk to the door and entered. A plain-looking woman with dark brown, wavy hair nodded at them as she swiftly wrapped strands of a scrawny woman's gray hair in papers around narrow rods and wound them tightly to her scalp. The woman in the chair wore a faded housedress and observed them with eager bird-like eyes.

"We're looking for Tina Hovermale," said Nancy. Country music turned down low fought with the noise of hair dryers and a dripping window air conditioner.

"I'm Tina. Take a seat, please." As Tina worked, she glanced at Nancy. "What can I do for you?"

"I'm new in town, but a friend told me there's an excellent fortuneteller here named. . ." Nancy pulled a paper out of her purse and pretended to refer to it. "Patty Hovermale. I saw your name in the phone book, and it's Hovermale, too. Do you know her and where I can find her?"

"I've heard of her." The hairdresser continued to work, keeping her eyes on her customer's hair as she talked. "Not related. Lots of Hovermales around here, you know."

"Do you think she's any good?" asked Nancy while Louise hovered behind her. "As a palm reader, I mean. You probably hear something about her from your customers."

"Have no idea. You're a fool if you believe in that stuff." She kept working while she talked. Her customer looked on with interest. "Anyway, she's a newcomer and sticks to herself. Don't see her in town."

"All right," said Nancy. "Thank you for your help."

"Wait a minute." Tina put down a curler and faced them, arms akimbo. "Did you find out what you came to hear?"

Nancy gaped at her. What did she mean?

"You newcomers act like we're all a bunch of hillbillies, like we don't know nothing. But I know Patty's dead. I hear everything in this beauty parlor." Tina's eyes sparked. "We don't know why she was killed or who did it. Is that why you came sniffing around here?"

"We knew her, too," Nancy stammered as she backed toward the door. "We wanted to help."

"Then you can go now." Tina turned to her customer. "And stop treating us like idiots."

Properly chastened, Nancy followed Louise to the car. Once safely behind locked doors, they looked at each other and laughed.

"What happened?" asked Fitz from the back seat.

"Should have known," said Louise, "They hear everything at the beauty salons."

Nancy nodded. "I guess so." She told Fitz about the encounter, then started the car.

"Next," said Louise. "Go through town and turn right on Cotter's Mill Road."

"Okay." Nancy followed directions as Louise navigated her down the road to a rusted mailbox with number 525 on the side in black paint. A white picket fence surrounded the house and enclosed a swing set and a colorful array of plastic toys. "Day care," Louise said.

"I'll stay in the car again," said Fitz. "Too intimidating with three of us. I'm here if you need me."

Nancy and Louise walked to the door and knocked. After the third knock, an anorexic woman in an apron came to the door and stepped out. Rummaging in an apron pocket, she found a packet of cigarettes and a Bic lighter. "Nap time," she said as she lit up. "You don't have any kids, do you?"

Nancy shook her head. "Are you Ms. Hovermale?"

She blew out a flume of smoke. "Why?"

Louise stepped forward. "We're looking for relatives of Patty Hovermale. She's a widow who lives next to Lilac Inn."

"Yeah. I know about her. Related somehow long time ago. Distant, you know? What happened to her?"

"Why should something have happened?" asked Nancy. Do day care operators hear everything, too?

The woman drew on her cigarette, blew out the smoke, and then replied. "You wouldn't ask otherwise."

"Can you tell us anything about her?"

"Nope." The woman leaned back against the house and peered at them through suspicious eyes. "She's new here. Don't know her and don't want to know her. Stuck up like all them come-heres." She frowned. "Why are you looking for her? She done something?"

"No, no. I've heard so much about her," Nancy said. "She's an excellent fortuneteller, my friends tell me. I want to hire her for a party I'm giving, but she doesn't have a phone, and I don't know where she lives."

The woman took another drag. "Sorry. Can't help you. I could use some fortunetelling myself." She laughed. "Only the good kind. Don't need no bad news."

Nancy pulled a card out of her purse. "Can I give you my name and phone number in case you hear anything?"

"No point to it. Unless she needs child care, she won't be talking to me."

A child cried out inside the house. The woman dropped her cigarette, ground it with her foot, and went back inside. "Good luck finding whatever you're after," she said over her shoulder.

As they trudged back to the car, Louise muttered, "Seems like that old saw about small towns is right. You gotta be born here to get accepted."

Nancy pulled out her cell phone and tapped in a number. "We need Patty's husband's first name."

Julie answered the call. "Randall," she said. "Randy."

At the third place on their list, down a long, rutted dirt drive, a chained Rottweiler growled at them, then exploded into barking as a middle-aged man in undershirt, ripped and dirty jeans, and greasy beard came from behind the house and stared at them. He hushed the dog and walked toward their car.

This time, Fitz got out of the car and met the man. They shook hands.

"Y'all lost?" The man asked.

"Are you Sam Hovermale?" asked Fitz.

"I am. Who are you?"

Fitz introduced himself, and Nancy stepped out of the car. "We're looking for relatives of Randall and Patty Hovermale," she said.

Sam turned friendly. "He's my cousin. That is, he was, but he up and died awhile back. His widow's doing the best she can to keep body and soul together. Why do you want to know?"

Nancy chewed her lip, trying to decide which tack to

take. She made up her mind and lied. "We're thinking of hiring her for a party at the inn and wanted to know more about her. Do you think she can handle a large group?"

"Oh, sure." Sam gazed across the meadow. "Randall was handy at a lot of things. He had a good job in Washington, D.C. Yessir, he sure did. I always heard she did, too. Both of them."

"Why did they move out here?" asked Louise.

"Can't imagine. There ain't nothing out here. That's why his widow's having such a hard time. We offered to help, but she won't have none of it. She ought to go back where she came from."

"What's she like?"

He leaned back and squinted his eyes at them. "I'd think she'd do a good job for you at fortunetelling. If you want to know whether I liked her, then no, I didn't. Most people wouldn't like her. She was stand-offish. Too good for the likes of us. Turned her nose up at my place, and she was sarcastic. She has no right to judge me. Look at what she's got? My place is a darn sight better'n hers, right now."

"I guess," Louise drawled, "you didn't like her very much."

He laughed. "Can't say I did 'cause I didn't. Not at all. When she did come here, she was always snooping. I stopped inviting her to come over after Randy died. Didn't need that kind of person around here. Anyways, she never invited us to her place, even when Randy was alive."

"Does she have any other relatives close by?" asked Nancy. "There seem to be a lot of Hovermales."

"Sure there are. Maybe we're related way back, but most of us keep ourselves to ourselves, if you know what

I mean. I'm the only one who made an effort to welcome Randall to these parts. Not that she was interested." He stepped back from the car. "She'll do a good job for you, though." He laughed at them with folded arms. "She needs the money."

Nancy waved as they turned around to head back down the rutted dirt road.

"Not sure how much we got out of that," said Louise. "What are we trying to find out exactly?"

Nancy nodded. "We should have planned our questions better. I was mainly on a fishing expedition."

"At least we found one relative," said Louise. "But next time we see him, he'll know we lied, and he'll know she's been murdered."

"Sounds like nobody visited her much," added Fitz.

Nancy turned onto the road. "He sidestepped the question about other relatives."

Louise referred to the list. "There are four more names on the list. We could try one more, but it seems like we could find out more about Patty from Julie than any of these people. That is, until we come up with more specifics on what we need to know." She glanced at her watch. "Anyway, I'd like to get back early to get ready for the honey tasting."

Louise was right. They weren't getting anywhere tracking down the Hovermales. Any relation would be on Randall's side, not Patty's. Her property wasn't worth much, and if she had anything else to leave, which seemed unlikely, she wouldn't will it to any of his people who seemed so uninterested in her. Who would she leave it to?

This was Thursday morning. Time was getting short.

Julie had given her and Louise a week's stay to solve the problem of the supply thefts. That problem had been solved, but not through her efforts and a murder was the result. On Saturday, they would leave Lilac Inn. They had two more days to find the murderer and the jewelry thief, not that she and Louise were expected to solve those crimes, but she hated to leave them unsolved. She didn't like to leave anything unfinished.

"Okay. One more Hovermale, then," she said. "Who's next?"

Fitz referred to the list. "Horace Hovermale on New River Road, other side of town. It's on our way back to the inn."

"Good," said Louise. She navigated, and fifteen minutes later, they found themselves in front of a cottage with a row of large windows across the north-facing front. A blue ceramic bird bath stood in the front yard and out near the mail box was a modest wooden sign which said "Horace Hovermale, Potter and Artist." Nancy drove onto an overgrown patch in front and parked.

This time, all three went to the door. Nancy pulled the rope of a brass bell hanging to the left of the door and loud, clear tones rang out.

Inside, a man's voice yelled, "Wait a minute. Wait a minute." Then the door opened and a tall, skinny man stood there in jeans and white T-shirt. Both were splattered with paint and mud-colored stains.

Clay, Nancy thought. The sign said he was a potter.

"Come on in," the man said. He held out his hand to Fitz. "I'm Horace Hovermale. You folks here to see my studio?"

Nancy stepped forward. "We'd love to see your artwork, too, but we're actually here to ask if you know Patty Hovermale."

"Patty? Sure, I know her." He turned and gestured for them to follow. "She and her husband, now what was his name?"

"Randall," said Louise.

Horace glanced at her. "Yes, that's right. Randall. Writer. Died too soon." He shook his head as he led them up a step into what must once have been a family room. Now it was crowded with tables, an easel, a small printing press, and paintings stacked against one wall. Shelves against another wall held mugs, vases, bowls, and other pottery.

Nancy took a closer look. "These are beautiful," she said. "I want to buy one of your bowls and a mug. I love the blues."

Fitz had also picked up a large bowl and was studying it. "I used to do pottery," he said. "A hobby for a while."

"I'd love to see something you made," said Nancy. Fitz was full of surprises.

Fitz laughed. "I never made anything as good as this."

Horace nodded with satisfaction. "Some of my best work over there." Then he eyed Nancy speculatively. "Say, aren't you all staying at that new inn down the road?"

She glanced at him, still engrossed in the pottery. "Yes, that's right. Lilac Inn. Patty lived next to it."

"You could do me a favor," said Horace. "Talk to the owners over there about displaying my pottery and art. They'd get a commission on what sells." He scratched his head. "I've talked to them, but they were too busy trying to get open to pay attention. It'll help both of us if you mention it to them."

"I'd be happy to do that. I'll show her the pieces I buy." Nancy held up a small bowl. "You do fine work."

He brushed the compliment aside. "Appreciate it. I'll give you my card." He ambled to a desk crowded into a corner of the room and covered with papers. He handed Nancy a card, then leaned against the desk with folded arms. "What d'you want to know about Patty? She's okay, isn't she?"

"Are you related to her?" asked Nancy.

"Not to her. To her late husband," Horace said. "Only met her once, but I think I'm the closest relative she has around these parts even if it's on Randall's side." He hesitated, then added, "Whatever you want to know, why don't you ask her?"

"We met her at the inn," Nancy began cautiously. "She told fortunes there."

"Oh, brother," Horace said. "I need to go talk to her. She could work with me. Darn sight better than tarot cards."

"We didn't get to know her very well, and then. . ." she glanced at Horace, "and then she was found murdered yesterday morning."

"What? Are you kidding me?" His mouth dropped open.

"I'm very sorry, but it's true." Nancy saw Fitz and Louise hanging back but watching.

Horace scratched his chin, eyes on the floor. "I wonder who gets her property now?" he muttered.

Nancy didn't think he meant anyone to hear those words. She pretended to browse a little longer, but Louise broke into her thoughts. "It's almost lunchtime. I want to get back to the inn."

Nancy and Fitz paid for their purchases and joined Louise waiting impatiently at the door to walk back to the car.

"He's a possible heir," said Nancy. "Do you think he really didn't know about the murder?"

"Sounded too glib to me," said Louise.

"But he does good work," added Fitz.

They returned to the inn. As they walked up the verandah steps, Kai and Kimberly ran down. They stopped, waving their hands excitedly.

"You know what we saw this morning?" said Kai.

"It was real early," added Kimberly. "Mom and Dad weren't even up, but we wanted to pick blackberries before breakfast and. . ."

Kai interrupted. "You know what we saw?"

Nancy smiled at him. "No, what?"

"Let me tell her," Kimberly broke in, clapping her hands. "We saw the Mothman again!"

"Yeah!" Kai's eyes grew large. "The Mothman. Or maybe it was the Green Monster!"

"We saw it! It had big red eyes and it was flying. Like we said. It looked like a giant bug!"

"You really saw it?"

"We did! We did! The two kids jumped up and down and then ran down the steps toward their cabin.

Something that looked like a flying bug with red eyes. Kids had big imaginations. Maybe Evan pointed out a critter to the kids, and it grew in their minds. If they could turn a bug into a space monster, what would they do with Louise's lecture on bees and honey?

***

## LOCAL NOTES
### Antiques and Art

This area is known for its art studios and antique shops as well as its quaint boutiques. Tomorrow morning at ten. the van will take guests on a tour of the local studios and shows. This early spring show has been arranged especially for our guests. Sign up now at the reception desk to reserve your place. Space is limited to the seats on the shuttle.

In the future, the works of these local artists will be shown at Lilac Inn and will be on sale here.

*Will and Julie Harris, Owner/Managers,*
*Lilac Inn Resort and Restaurant*

# 23. Thursday Noon

"What do you suppose those kids saw?" Fitz said, thoughtfully watching the kids disappear into the cabin.

"Early this morning, they said," added Louise.

"Another mystery." Nancy crossed the lobby, but stopped as she saw a man in the uniform of a West Virginia sheriff's officer—black shirt and hat with a gray tie and slacks, a star on his shirt pocket and a sheriff's office patch on his sleeve. His belt with its holster and other paraphernalia creaked with each step as he climbed the stairs to the verandah. He looked limp from the heat and his face was grim, but he had the command bearing of a cop. She would have known he was a law officer even without the uniform and was glad to see him. About time the sheriff got around to questioning the people at the inn.

"Excuse me," she told Fitz and Louise. She greeted the officer as he arrived at the desk. "Can I help you?"

"Corporal Dwayne Yost, ma'am. I'm looking for the person in charge here," the man said, doffing his hat. He was gray-haired and slim and kept his face blank.

"You're investigating Patty Hovermale's murder." Nancy said. It wasn't a question.

He frowned. "The manager's office, please, ma'am."

Nancy walked him to Julie's office and rapped on the

door before she ushered in Corporal Yost. Julie paled and stood. "I'm the manager," she said. "You're here about Patty."

He pulled a small notebook out of his back pocket and referred to it. "Yes, ma'am. I'm looking for anyone who might have seen anything or anyone unusual that might have a bearing on the murder of Ms. Patricia Hovermale."

"Patty was a frequent visitor here, Officer," said Julie, "But she lived in a remote shack by herself down the road, as you know. You saw what it's like. She didn't entertain visitors at her place, and I'm sure none of our guests would wander that way. Anyway, she had nothing to do with our staff, so why would they go there? Guests wouldn't go there, either. If they wanted their fortune read in private, she met them in their room here at the inn."

Nancy and Fitz stood back against the wall. She wanted to support Julie and hear the conversation.

He glanced around the office and penciled something in his notebook. "I'd like to speak to the staff here, and I want to look at the path from your property to hers. There is clear and direct access from here to there?"

"It's a rough trail, not really a path," Julie said, "but why would anyone at the hotel want to kill Patty? It doesn't make sense."

Nancy felt sorry for Julie.

"Yes, ma'am," said Officer Yost, not arguing the point. "Any other access points?"

"The road," Julie answered reluctantly.

He flipped his notebook shut and tucked it into his pocket. "Yes, ma'am. Now I need to talk with your husband. He does the maintenance, correct?"

Julie nodded. "Along with his assistant, Daquon."

"All right, I will talk with them and check out the property. You may tell your guests and staff if they saw or heard anything suspicious, to talk to me while I'm here or to call the number on my card." He pulled a card out of his shirt pocket and handed it to Julie.

"Okay," Julie said. "That's fine. I'll talk to the guests. I'm sure they'll want to help, but you can start with me. I know nothing about what happened to Patty. She often came here in the evenings to entertain the guests. The last time I saw her was Tuesday evening when she did a little palm reading for them. She was pleasant enough. People enjoyed her readings, but I'm sure nobody took them seriously. Then she went home. We were shocked to hear about the murder and even more shocked to learn she had stolen our supplies."

"Yes, ma'am," he said, as deadpan as ever as he jotted a few notes. He turned to Nancy. "What about you, ma'am?"

Nancy started in surprise when he addressed her. She remembered Patty's odd reaction to Sarah. Should she mention it? "I don't know anything," she said, hedging. "Patty did say something to Sarah Lochowsky as if she knew her from someplace else, but. . ." She shrugged and then asked, "Do you know when she was killed?"

"I'm asking the questions, ma'am," he said. His face remained impassive.

"I wondered if she'd been killed soon after the readings she gave here, That's all," said Nancy. "Maybe she came too close to someone's secret."

"You're a guest here, ma'am?"

"Yes, I am." Nancy introduced herself. Really, if he

said "ma'am" one more time, she was going to hit him on the head. Did they think that impassive expression helped them do their job? He'd get a lot more out of people if he acted more human and friendlier.

"Is that all?" Julie asked. "You're free to go anywhere on the property and ask your questions. I'll make an announcement at lunch. Also," she paused and looked Officer Yost directly in the eye. "We miss Patty here. We want to help you capture the killer as soon as possible. I don't believe anyone here is responsible. We'll do anything we can to help."

"Yes, ma'am," he said. He nodded at Nancy as he swiveled and stalked out.

Julie glanced at Nancy and laughed. "If he'd said "ma'am" one more time. . ."

"I know what you mean." Nancy turned to leave but stopped at the door. "What are you going to tell the guests?"

"The truth, I guess," Julie said. "There probably are a lot of rumors flying around here. Our guests need to know what's going on."

"Good idea." They walked out together toward the dining room.

As they approached the hostess, Nancy saw George, Louise, and Fitz perusing menus at a table for four. She glanced questioningly at Julie who shook her head. "I won't be joining you. Too much to do."

Nancy nodded toward her friends. "I'll sit with them," she said to Ingunn, the Norwegian intern, acting as hostess.

George looked up as Nancy took her seat. "I hope you all did better than I did on the golf course," he grumbled, setting down the menu and shaking his head. "Those two women beat the heck out of me."

"We had a nice drive, did some detecting, but I don't think we learned anything, did we?" Louise looked at Nancy.

"I bought a beautiful bowl, luv," said Fitz.

"Me, too, and a mug, and we can cross some of those people off our list." Nancy thought about Horace. Who inherited Patty's estate? Was he an interested party? It was a lead, but they certainly hadn't distinguished themselves so far. The hotel supplies thief was exposed but not through their efforts. Now the supplies thefts were eclipsed by a much bigger crime. Two crimes if you included the jewelry thefts, even though the jewelry was returned.

Julie remained at the hostess desk. Behind her stood Officer Yost. She tapped a spoon on a glass for attention. "I apologize for interrupting your lunch," she began, looking as if she had approached a guillotine. Nancy smiled at her for encouragement, and Julie glanced Nancy's way but didn't acknowledge her.

"As you know," Julie began, then cleared her throat. "A terrible tragedy has occurred. The fortuneteller, whom many of you have met, was killed early yesterday morning at her home down the road. This tragedy has nothing to do with Lilac Inn, but," she nodded at Yost, "this is Officer Yost. If you have any information to contribute about this tragedy, please talk to him or call him at his office. His phone number will be at the registration desk."

She stepped aside to let Officer Yost come forward. "Thank you, ma'am, and thank you to all of you guests at Lilac Inn. I'll be on the grounds this afternoon, and Miss Julie here will know where I am, so if you have any information that might help us solve this crime, please pull me aside and talk to me." He paused and scanned the room. "Or, if you'd prefer, you can call my office, 304-555-7300, and leave a message there. Any questions?" Yost waited, but no one raised a hand. As he turned to leave, Julie led him to a table and gave him a menu. "On the house," she said.

***

## NOTICE TO GUESTS AND STAFF

The Sheriff's Department is investigating the untimely death of our neighbor, Patricia Hovermale. If you have any information that might help the investigation, please call Officer Yost at 304-555-7300. We assure our guests that Lilac Inn maintains a Security Patrol 24 hours a day everyday. All staff are required to report unusual incidents or strangers on the grounds. If you have any concerns, please let us know, but also be assured you are safe here.

*Will and Julie Harris, Owner/Managers,*
*Lilac Inn Resort and Restaurant*

# 24. Thursday Afternoon

Nancy excused herself after lunch and walked to the Pro Shop. She hadn't yet talked to the golfing pro, Sam Johnston, who ran the shop. She found him poring over a spreadsheet behind the front counter at a scarred wooden desk he used for an office.

"Excuse me," Nancy said, tapping on the counter.

Sam looked up. He laid the spreadsheet aside and walked to the counter. "How can I help you?" He wore a white polo shirt, white shorts, and an orange ball cap that shaded his eyes.

"I'm Nancy Dickenson, a guest here," Nancy began.

"Oh, yeah. You're here to find out who stole our supplies." He grinned. "Guess you're out of work now, what with the thief being murdered."

Nancy kept her face blank at his rude tone and held back a response.

He pointed his finger at her. "I never did like that woman. She'd poke her head in here, see me, and move on. You ask me, she was looking to steal from me, too."

Nancy nodded. "Did you think she was a thief?"

"Not then, but I didn't like her." Sam picked up a golf ball from a bucket on the counter and threw it from hand to hand. "Thinking back on it, though, it makes sense. Why else would she come snooping around here? That fortune-telling stuff was a way to worm herself into the place. You ask me, she stole the jewelry, too."

"You know about the missing jewelry?" Nancy asked.

"Everybody knows everything around here. We all like our jobs and don't want to lose 'em. The way things were going with all the thefts, we weren't sure Julie and Will could stay in business." He stopped and watched one of the landscaping men walk in, put a dollar bill into the Coke machine, and walk out again with the soft drink.

"We're glad someone was looking into it, and we're glad the thief's been found. Deserved what happened to her, I think." He leaned toward her. "It seems to me, your job is done, isn't it?"

"Pretty much," Nancy admitted. "I'm trying to tie up some loose ends. Did you notice anything odd going on around here the past couple of weeks?"

"Other than the customers?" He chortled. "Some of them are strange enough, but they're all here on vacation. The honeymooners, the singles, people like yourself, out for rest and relaxation. The Pro Shop closes at six p.m. I'm busy all day, then I go home. I haven't seen anything odd going on around here."

Nancy thanked him and left. She wasn't going to get anything useful out of him. Fitz might have better luck in a man-to-man way of loosening him up. She walked back to the inn and on up to her room.

***

Louise knocked on Nancy's door at three-thirty, waking her from a nap. "Show time!" she said. She beamed as she handed. Nancy a bag containing the plastic sampling spoons and napkins. She lugged a cart behind her loaded with a box of honey jars, her beekeeping outfit, and hive materials. Together they made their way to the meeting room off the lobby. Julie stood at the door, smiling as she greeted them. "The room is ready for you. Tell me if you need anything." She stepped aside into the hall to let them enter and then greeted the guests, arriving early for the honey tasting.

Cole, Aysha and the kids bounced in first, full of questions and enthusiasm.

"Do you really have a bee hive?" asked Kimberly. "Do you get stung a lot?"

"I've been stung twice," added Kai. "You didn't bring any bees in, did you?"

Louise smiled at them. "I brought my beekeeping suit so you could look at it and maybe try it on. Bees won't sting you unless you interfere with them or mess with their hive. I mess with their hive, so I wear the suit with gloves and the hat with netting, but I haven't been stung once."

She picked up the bee hat and placed it over Kimberly's head. "A bit big for you, but with that on, they can't sting your face." She turned to Kai. "People are always saying they were stung by a bee when they were actually stung by a yellow jacket or wasp."

"They let you have a bee hive at Whisperwood?" asked Aysha. "Aren't they afraid the other residents will get stung?"

"Nah. The hive is out of the way behind the garden, and the gardeners love those bees." Louise left the kids trying on the beekeeping suit and went back to arranging the jars of honey on the table. "Anyway," she said over her shoulder to Aysha, "I only buy gentle bees."

Standing by, Nancy wondered when any of them mentioned Whisperwood to Aysha. How did she know where they lived?

Lew Cookson swaggered in, a beer in hand, wearing tight jeans, a black T-shirt, and a belt to contain his girth. "My Dad kept bees. They didn't bother me none. I wouldn't let 'em." He saw Kaye exit the elevator and edged in her direction. "Come over here next to me," he said to her. "I won't let those bees get near you."

"Oh." Kaye stopped walking toward them. "Are there bees here?"

"Of course not," Louise glanced at Nancy and rolled her eyes. "Come on over here. This is a honey tasting."

Kaye let Lew put his arm around her and draw her in close. "I hate bees," she said. "And wasps." She paused, then added, "And especially yellow jackets."

Marilyn ran up the verandah steps and arrived, holding her tennis racket. "I'm not too late, am I?"

"Haven't started yet," said Louise.

Evan followed Marilyn and stood outside the group clustering around Louise. He nodded approvingly at Louise. "I had a hive when I was a kid. Made extra money selling honey and beeswax candles."

"People die from insect stings," said Marilyn. "I've seen them."

Malcolm and Harvey walked down the stairs, squabbling between themselves. Malcolm's jaw was set, and Harvey seemed disgruntled.

"I kept bees once," said Malcolm. "Had twelve hives."

"Twelve hives!" Louise looked at him. "That must have

been a lot of work."

"Nothing to it," he said. "Let them do their thing and collect the honey when it's ready."

"Really." Louise looked him up and down. "Nothing to it, huh? How'd you learn that?"

He winked at her. "I was a natural-born beekeeper, that's all."

Nancy knew the hours Louise spent trying to protect her hive against moths, mites, diseases, and wildlife. She waited for Louise's cutting remark, but Harvey interrupted.

Yeah," Harvey said, "like I'm a natural-born airline pilot." He glared at Malcolm. "Which I'm not. And you had two hives, not twelve. They didn't make it through one winter."

"No, you're not an airline pilot." Malcolm glared back. "In fact, you're nothing but a pissant."

"Oh, yeah?" said Harvey. "And you're a liar."

"Boys, boys." Louse looked at Nancy with an air of disbelief.

Nancy agreed. These two brothers never grew up. Still carrying on a ridiculous sibling rivalry. She stepped between them. She was not going to let their bickering ruin Louise's presentation. Louise had worked hard on this, and she had an interesting lesson to share.

Ann and Lula poked their heads in the door, then walked in. "Came right from the course," said Lula.

"Thought we'd see what's happening," added Ann. "But I'll tell you, I kill wasps and hornets and anything else that gets in my way."

The comment drew Nancy's interest. Her glance at Ann took in Lula's expression. Lula stared at Ann, and there was no mistaking the look of fear on her face. "You don't mean that," Lula said tentatively.

Ann glanced at the startled faces staring at her and flicked a finger. "Of course I do. I don't let anything bother me." Then she laughed and added, "I mean bugs, of course."

There was a moment of silence, then Julie pulled over a couple of chairs and continued to greet guests as she arranged seating. The group was now assembled around an oval table. Julie stood at one end.

"I think everyone is here," Julie said. She surveyed the group and nodded at Officer Yost, standing at the door and watching. "Thank you for coming to the unique program we've lined up for you this afternoon. Also, special thanks to our beekeeper, Louise Owens, who is my great-aunt and one of our guests this week, and she's a West Virginia beekeeper."

Julie cleared her throat and began her pitch. "We at Lilac Inn are proud to be an ecotourism site in West Virginia. We plan our resort and our activities to be environmentally conscious and protective."

"Hear, hear," said Louise, applauding.

Julie smiled at her and continued. "As we all know, honeybees are threatened worldwide. We at Lilac Inn want to do our part to protect them, so we don't use pesticides anywhere outside, and we plant native species in our landscaping. Native species provide the habitat and food that our native animals and birds—and bees—need."

Louise broke in again with loud clapping. George, Fitz, and Nancy grinned. They all knew about Louise's successful campaign at Whisperwood to plant native species and avoid pesticide use in the landscaping there.

Julie smiled at Louise. "Now I'll step aside to let my Aunt Louise tell you about beekeeping and honey."

Louise nodded at Julie and stepped forward to the demonstration table. Guests crowded around. Kai and Kimberly leaned on the table in front of their parents.

"Honey isn't the only product we get from bees," Louise began. "There's also royal jelly, propolis, beeswax. . ."

"What's that?" asked Kimberly, pointing to a square wooden box about the size of a kitchen drawer but open on the top and bottom. Lined up inside the box were ten removable frames side by side.

"This is a super," Louise said. "To make a beehive, we stack these boxes over a deeper box that's the same length and width. The queen bee is kept in the deeper box to lay her eggs there. The worker bees make the honey and do all the work required in the hive, like cleaning it, feeding the queen and baby bees, guarding the hive, and so on." She pulled out one of the frames spanned by a plastic sheet imprinted with honeycomb cells in wax. "The imprinted cells help the bees make cells that are uniform and easy for honey extraction." Louise gave the frame to Kimberly. "Pass it around when you're through looking at it."

"I'm not touching that," said Kaye.

Lew took the frame instead and pushed a finger through the wax impression. "Oops, sorry. Don't know my own strength."

While Louise glared at Lew, Nancy took the frame and passed it to Kimberly. Lew had poked his finger through it deliberately. Louise continued her lecture. "A beehive has a queen whose job is to lay eggs. The male bees are called drones, and their job is to fertilize the queen so she can lay those eggs. Most of the bees are worker bees, who are females and," she said with a wink, "they are busy little bees."

"When do we get to taste the honey?" asked Kimberly, passing the frame to her mother.

"In a minute," Louise replied. "You have to know how it's made first." She put the frame into the super and laid it aside.

"How do you get the honey out of the frame?" asked Kai.

"You ever hear of centrifugal force?" asked Louise. "We cut the caps off the cells, then put the frames into a barrel-like machine called a honey extractor, spin it around and the centrifugal force propels the honey out of the cells, then it drips down to the bottom where we can drain it into jars."

"Sounds like a lot of hard work to me," said Kaye. "And dirty work, too."

"Yep. That's what agriculture is," said Louise.

"How much honey do you get from a super?" asked Marilyn. Louise smiled at her. Marilyn seemed the most interested of them all, and she said she was a city girl.

"This is my first season managing a bee hive," Louise said, "so I'm not sure, but a beekeeping friend said I'd need a lot of clean quart jars."

"Wow," said Kimberly.

Louise smiled at her. "You're right. I'll bet everyone's had clover honey and maybe orange blossom honey or wildflower honey, right?"

"I've tasted about every kind of honey there is anywhere," said Malcolm.

Harvey snorted. "You wish."

Louise ignored them. "I've had friends sending me honey from around the world, and I've got them here. How about we try some lemon blossom honey from Israel?"

"Israel?" said Lula. "I've spent time in Israel. Never tasted their honey."

Louise opened a bag of small plastic sampling spoons and allowed each person to dip a spoon into the jar for a taste. "That's really delicate," said Aysha. "I love it."

"Now for something completely different. "She opened a jar of heather honey from Scotland. "Take a new spoon, please."

Again, each person picked up an unused spoon, dipped it into the jar, and took a taste.

"Gross," said Kimberly.

"Really strong flavor," added Marilyn.

"Strong flavor, yes," said Lew. "My kind of honey. You got any for sale?"

"I've heard of tupelo honey from Mississippi," said Evan. "I'd like to try that." He took a new spoon and dipped it into the jar, tasted it, and nodded. "I know people who think this is the best-tasting honey." He smacked his lips. "They're right."

"Now try this honey from Ethiopia." Louise held up an open jar and turned it upside down."

"Wait a minute," said Ann. "It'll drip all over the table-cloth."

But nothing poured out. Louise dug a spoon into the jar and brought out a mound of honey that was white, waxy and solid.

Everyone around the table clamored to try it.

"It tastes like. . .honey," said Kai in a disappointed tone.

"That's what it is, dummy," said Kimberly.

"Delicious," said Lula. "They're all delicious."

"I could see using a honey flavor to enhance some reci-pes," added Ann. "Orange blossom honey as a sweetener for an orange cake, maybe."

"You make any money selling your honey?" asked Gary as he dipped a clean spoon into a jar and offered it to Sarah.

"It's only my first year," Louise answered, glancing at him, "and it's a hobby with me."

"I'm glad you work in a good office job, sweetie," said Sarah to Gary. "I never want to keep bees for a living."

The tasting took about an hour until only Evan, who wanted to learn more about Louise's experience with the current problems in beekeeping, remained and continued to ask questions.

***

### The Lilac Inn Daily Notes
### Much Ado About Honey

Many thanks to guest Louise Owens for her informa-tive talk about beekeeping and the wonderful honey tasting. Our own Chef Pierre will honor Louise by us-ing honey in all the desserts served this evening. We will also offer the honey wine called mead at today's cocktail hour.

*Will and Julie Harris, Owner/Managers*
*Lilac Inn Resort and Restaurant*

# 25. Thursday Evening

The guests drifted away from Louise and on to the late afternoon happy hour. Louise packed the jars into the box they came in, and Evan hung around helping Louise load the cart. He then pulled it, still asking questions, all the way to her room.

Despite Julie's fears, none of the guests, even Sarah, expressed anxiety at the happy hour over Patty's death. In fact, by some tacit agreement, Patty's name was never brought up in conversation. The intern Bridie mingled with the group offering tiny quiches and stuffed mushrooms while Missy stood behind the bar. "We have mead tonight," she announced. "On the house."

Louise joined Nancy, George, and Fitz a short time later and accepted the thanks and congratulations of the others for her demonstration as her due. "I thought Evan would never stop asking questions," she said, wiping a hand across her brow in jest.

"He was interested." said Nancy. "The kids liked it, too."

"Everyone did," said George. "Julie might make you a regular part of the entertainment here."

"Good audience. Didn't know how much they'd stand for a description of the hive, so I kept it simple." Louise plucked a stuffed mushroom from a passing tray.

"You've learned a lot about beekeeping in a short time," Nancy said.

Fitz brought two glasses of wine from the bar, handing one to Louise and one to Nancy. "Did you notice how competitive Malcolm was?"

"Yeah," added George, beer in hand. "To hear him talk, he's done everything bigger and better than anyone else."

Nancy shook her head. "Poor Harvey. He's been putting up with that all his life."

"Sarah seemed tense, too," said Fitz. "Gary's always hovering over her."

George pursed his lips. "He may be overprotective, but if you ask me, she's too clingy, like she doesn't want Gary to get away."

Louise tossed her braid. "He does everything for her."

"Kaye acts clingy, too," said Nancy. "Lew's lapping it up."

"Why would she get involved with that man?" asked Louise. "He said he's married."

Nancy shrugged. "I have no idea."

As the guests gradually drifted away toward dinner, Nancy noticed Officer Yost, still on the job, sitting near the entrance and scribbling into a notebook. He'd taken off his hat, and it dangled on the chair arm. Nancy casually walked to him. "Did you get any useful information today?" she asked. She didn't expect much by way of an answer. She didn't get any.

He nodded at her. "Ma'am."

She tried again. "I hope we could help you."

"Thank you, ma'am. Do you have any information

about the crime? See anything suspicious?" He folded his arms, his expression noncommittal, and his tone patronizing. He didn't expect anything from her.

Nancy shook her head. "Nothing," she said, pleased to fulfill his expectations. With his ominous watchful presence, she noticed the conversation at happy hour was a bit more subdued than on previous nights. Everyone kept it light. Nancy listened for hints of dissatisfaction or fear or plans to leave early, but heard only pleasant chatter about their day's activities.

Later that evening, Nancy sat out on the verandah with Sarah, Gary, Lula, Ann, and Marilyn. Ann and Lula were smiling at each other, the trials of paddling the river forgotten. What was that little episode at the honey tasting about? Ann had looked fierce then, and Lula had seemed scared. Lula mentioned she'd been in Israel, but Nancy couldn't see any way that snippet of information could cause trouble between them or be helpful to her.

Aysha and Cole had retired with the kids to their cabin. Kaye and Lew had gone for a walk. Evan was in the bird blind with Fitz, both of them intent on listening and looking for night birds and bats. Louise had already gone to bed. George was in the library reading.

Ann looked at Nancy. "You're a detective, aren't you?"

Nancy smiled graciously and played it down as usual. "I retired. A long time ago." How did word get around? She hoped Julie hadn't mentioned her previous occupation to anyone else. Better not to.

"What about all the thefts around here?" asked Sarah. "Any ideas about that? Those thieves must have murdered Patty, too. Maybe they worked together."

Ann spoke up. "I've been thinking about that. I heard she stole supplies from the hotel. She could have stolen your necklace, too." Ann glanced at the silver bracelet on her own wrist.

"Gary gave me that necklace. I sure am glad to get it back,' said Sarah. "The thieves must have killed her for it."

"If they killed her," Gary said reasonably, "why'd they return it?"

Sarah lifted her chin, "They didn't return it. The dog retrieved it."

"Hard to believe thieves and a killer work around here," added Lula. "Everyone is so nice and pleasant. Whoever killed Patty must have been some roughneck she knew from town."

"Must have been," Sarah agreed.

"Could be," said Ann, sipping drowsily on a glass of wine. "But I think she stole those supplies for some reason. Supplement her income probably. Maybe she tried to short-change the fence she used. Those people are all criminals."

"That sounds logical," said Sarah. "She tried a double-cross that got her killed."

Nancy listened to the conversation, assessing the personalities and the comments. Who had killed Patty? Why? Was it the same person who had stolen the jewelry? Malcolm and Harvey were jewelers, but were they also thieves and murderers? She knew Harvey was a wealthy man as was his brother. Harvey lived at Whisperwood and contributed substantially to the benevolent fund there. His apartment reflected his eccentric—and expensive—tastes.

Malcolm seemed even more prosperous. He was over-competitive, especially with his brother, but neither of them had reason to steal. And if they had stolen the jewelry, why would they return it? Why would either of them kill Patty? They didn't seem to interact with her in any way.

She listened to Ann and Lula bat the problem back and forth. After a while, with no resolution, the topic changed to golfing and tennis schedules for the next day. Sarah and Gary listened but didn't contribute. Sarah looked exhausted. She cast frequent, worried glances at Gary. Were they having marital troubles? Or something else.

Nancy excused herself and went up to her room. She was beginning to get a glimmer of an idea. She pulled several sheets of hotel stationery out of the desk drawer and listed all the guests at the inn, but first she wrote the name Patty Hovermale. Why would anyone want to kill her?

Patty Hovermale: Lived alone in a shack nearby. Little income except what she earned telling fortunes and holding séances. Did she steal hotel supplies to resell? Her place was filled with toilet paper rolls, reams of copy paper, cleaning fluids, towels, and all manner of other supplies. She seemed to be hoarding the stuff, not selling it, and hoarding was a sign of trauma. Was she still suffering from her husband's unexpected death? Did she feel afraid to live alone on that property? Why didn't she move out?

Did she also steal the jewelry? Both missing pieces were found after she died on the grounds of the inn, nowhere near her shack. What did that mean? Did she surprise a trespasser in her cabin? A thief? Would a second thief or the murderer really want to steal hotel supplies?

Was Patty simply waiting for a way to transport all those supplies into town to sell? She would need a van to take all of it, but she relied on Julie and Will to get into town.

Was her hoard enough to kill for? She had hinted during the fortunetelling and séance that she knew secrets and that someone there was a fake. The way she ended the séance was a bit theatrical. Was she warning someone? Knowing secrets is dangerous.

Aysha and Cole Robinson: Pleasant couple with two children. Cole's ring was stolen, or had he faked the theft? Was he a victim or the thief? If a victim, was that enough for a revenge killing? Why else would either of them kill Patty? Again, they'd had little interaction with Patty that Nancy saw.

Kaye Anderson: Immersed in her own worries. Neurotic but seemed to have a good job. Would she steal the jewelry because of some compulsion and then return it? Nancy assumed she was recovering from a failed love affair, but it could have been something else. Something illegal? Something like embezzlement? Was she hiding out here? Had Patty made a comment to Kaye in reading her fortune that suggested she knew an unsavory incident from Kaye's past? Why else would Kaye kill her?

Lew Cookson: Aggressive and obnoxiously macho. Married but why is he here without his wife? He seems to be interested in Kaye. Because she's vulnerable? Why would he steal the jewelry and then return it? He was harboring some kind of secret or terrible sadness. Did Patty know his secret? Would it be bad enough for him to kill her?

Evan Lester: A respected entomologist and a loner. Likes long hikes and birding. Doesn't join in many group activities or sit with others at meals. Why would he steal jewelry and return it? Why would he kill Patty?

Ann Bashaw and Lula Beall: A pleasant couple. Get

along with everyone. Little interaction with Patty. Why would they steal jewelry or kill Patty? Ann said she would kill if something got in her way. The statement had frightened Lula. Did Patty get in her way?

Sarah and Gary Lochowsky: Sarah's necklace was stolen but returned. Why? She has seemed more and more distracted. She and Gary are older newlyweds. Could she be having second thoughts? Gary is an extrovert, seems interested in others, conventional, and over-protective of Sarah. Sometimes stares at Sarah with an odd look. Is it love? Lust? Curiosity? Patty had made several strange comments to Sarah as if they'd met before. Did Patty know a ruinous secret about Sarah that would doom her reputation and her marriage?

Marilyn Goldfarb: Seemed outgoing and friendly at first, but she is deeper than she appears. She has become quieter and more serious. She seems compassionate, and she is a nurse, but why would she kill the baby robin? Did she really think that was the right thing to do? Something is weighing her down. She is looking for a job, possibly in this area. Is there a reason she doesn't want to go home? Why would she steal jewelry or kill Patty? And why did she change jobs so often?

Julie and Will Harris: They knew Patty better than anyone else at Lilac Inn. Did Patty know something about them they'd rather keep secret? They were financially stretched too far, but would they steal jewelry only to return it later? Maybe they did steal the jewelry, but Patty's murder made them nervous so they returned it. Nancy hated to think Julie would be mixed up in criminal activities, but if Will were the culprit, Julie might know nothing about his activities. She didn't see him for much of the day. How was Will paying for his inventions? Patty also brought some entertainment to the hotel that they didn't have to pay for. For most guests, the fortunetelling act was a welcome diversion. Julie and Will lost that when Patty died.

And, of course, there were the two brothers, Harvey and Malcolm. They checked out as professional jewelers, but why would they steal jewelry? If they tried to pawn or sell it, they would risk their reputations and their livelihoods because they would most certainly be caught.

Nancy considered the hotel staff. The housekeeping and maintenance help had reason to venture into the guest rooms, but they must know they'd be the first suspects if a guest's property was stolen. They had excellent references from other hotels and inns in the state, and nothing had been stolen before. The interns were new to this country, and both had good references. They had no way to get rid of stolen property and no past history with Patty.

Actually, anyone here at the resort could have stolen the jewelry and for the simplest of reasons: To sell for the money. Patty's murder had upped the ante since the connection between stealing and murder might be an easy one for authorities to make. An excellent reason to find a way to return the jewelry.

The question of past history with Patty stuck in Nancy's mind. Patty had no money to steal, and no one took the piles of hotel stuff out of her house, so theft had not been a motive for Patty's murder. Unless a psychopathic killer had wandered through the area, the motive for killing Patty had to lie in the past. She knew something dangerous to the killer.

***

## Memo to Staff
## Safety Concerns Us All

All staff members are instructed to report any unusual, hazardous, or insecure conditions they see on the grounds. Guests are also urged to alert us to any concerns or problems you experience, so they can be corrected. We assure you that we are always looking out for your safety here at Lilac Inn. Thank you for your help.

*Will and Julie Harris, Owner/Managers*
*Lilac Inn Resort and Restaurant*

# 26. Friday Morning
# TWO DAYS TO GO

Nancy woke at seven the next morning and lay in bed thinking about how nice it was not to be poked and prodded by her cat Malone. He had a sense of entitlement that alternately annoyed and amused Nancy, but he was back home at Whisperwood, and no doubt the staff there were catering to his needs and giving him extra treats. They all knew how he'd helped Nancy and the 90s Club save their village the year before.

She gradually grew aware of low voices along with the bird songs outside her window. She'd turned off the air conditioning the night before and opened her windows to the cool outside air. The voices seemed to be arguing. They drew her curiosity. She rose and padded in bare feet to the window to look down from the fourth floor. Harvey and Malcolm stood on the path hissing at each other.

As Nancy watched, they turned and headed to the path toward the bird blind. Fitz was an early riser and probably already in the blind with his binoculars. Thinking of Fitz gave her a warm feeling and made her smile.

She longed to spend more time with Fitz, to hold his hand, to cuddle up with him. She saw the warmth in his glance when he looked at her, but neither of them wanted to draw attention to their relationship as they searched for a murderer. Nancy needed to continue to study the guests.

She glanced at her watch. Seven-fifteen. Harvey and Malcolm had never impressed her as early risers or as birders. Why were they up so early, and what were they arguing about this time?

She dressed and went down to breakfast, the first to arrive. Louise soon joined her. "Where is everybody?" she asked.

Nancy shrugged. "Difficult night, I guess. Patty's death has affected all of us."

"Even though Patty lived down the road, the murderer must be someone here," said Louise, surveying the empty dining room. A breakfast buffet was set up on the side wall with coffee, tea, and juice at one end. A server came by and filled their coffee cups.

Julie poked her head in and waved at Nancy. Then she filled a cup with coffee and joined them. "The sheriff's officer interviewed Will and me," she said, her brows drawn together in a worried frown. "I think they suspect us." She took a sip of coffee. "We had nothing to do with her murder, I swear," she said, looking earnestly from Nancy to Louise.

"Of course you didn't," Louise said.

"The guests are going to want to leave." Julie sighed. "They'll want refunds." She stared at the table, a hand across her eyes. "We can't afford that."

"They would have left Wednesday night if they were concerned," said Nancy. "Anyway, there's only one day of their week left. They'd only be entitled to a refund for one day, and you'd be right to deny it. After all, they reserved for a week, and they can have the week."

"That's right," added Louise. "The murder wasn't on the property at all, the victim was neither a guest nor paid staff, and the jewelry's been returned."

Nancy nodded. "If any guests brought valuable jewelry, they should have put it in the safe as soon as they arrived. The card in the room plainly states that. You're not responsible for the thefts or the murder."

"Anyway" said Louise. "it's a good thing we're here." She patted Julie on the arm. "Nancy will nail the culprit. She's hot on the trail now."

Nancy started to demur but stopped when she saw Louise's intense warning stare. Julie needed a bit of hope right now. "Louise and I are working on it. We don't think the staff are involved and are considering the guests carefully. It could be someone Patty knew from the past. Can you think of any guest who might have known Patty before?"

Julie gazed past the verandah into the woods. "Patty's been around since we opened, and no one has mentioned or indicated in any way—around me, that is—that they knew her from somewhere else. We don't have close neighbors, and I have no idea if Patty had interactions with someone in town. Did you track down any of her relatives?"

"We visited four Hovermales, but only two said they were related to her husband. One of them didn't show much interest in her, and the other one wondered who got her property. Of course, any Hovermales who were relatives would be from her husband's side." Louise waved at Fitz who stood at the door. He walked to their table and pulled out a chair.

Julie nodded at him and turned to leave. "Gotta get to

work," she said. " I'll talk to you later."

Fitz waved at her and grinned at Nancy. "Saw a woodcock this morning doing his mating dance," Fitz said. "Fascinating."

"A woodcock, huh?" said Louise. "I always wanted to see that. Never could get up early enough."

"Did you see Harvey and Malcolm this morning?" asked Nancy.

"I sure did," said Fitz. "They scared away a couple of mallards. Made a real nuisance of themselves. They were arguing about something Harvey wanted and Malcolm refused to consider—didn't catch what it was. They were surprised to see me and shut up."

"You didn't hear anything they were saying?" Nancy felt disappointed, but the two brothers always seemed to disagree about some trivial event, and Malcolm kept the argument going until he won. *What a pair.* "By the way, Fitz . . ."

He smiled at her. "What?"

"I couldn't get anything out of the golf pro." She grimaced. "He was too busy patronizing me, so I'm hoping you can go buddy-buddy with him and see what you can find out. Casually, I mean."

Fitz laughed. "I'm surprised. He's supposed to be irresistible to women."

Nancy shook her head. "He was cagey with me. Probably doesn't know anything, but he might divulge something interesting to you, being a man." She shrugged. "Who knows."

"Worth trying." Fitz glanced at his watch. "I'll drop by later this morning."

George arrived along with Ann and Lula, then the two women moved on and George took his place next to Louise at the table.

After breakfast, George, Lula, and Ann went off to the Pro Shop to retrieve their golf clubs and rent a cart. Fitz glanced at Nancy. "I'll drop by the shop after George and the women are out on the course, and Sam's not so busy."

Nancy nodded. "I doubt if he knows anything, but we need to try every angle. We go home tomorrow." She watched Fitz walk to the elevator.

I'll go with you to Julie's office," said Louise. They headed down the hall.

The door was open, and Julie sat behind her desk. Nancy and Louise took the chairs in front.

"Thanks for coming by. I just wondered if you can think of anything Will and I can do," Julie asked. "I feel so helpless." Nancy bit her lip. Was Julie regretting her decision to ask them to look into the odd goings-on here? Did she wish she'd hired an active, younger, still employed detective instead? Their performance so far had not been stellar.

Nancy shook her head. "I've already looked into the backgrounds of the guests and found nothing, but the answer may lie in Patty's past. The police will be checking out the strangers in the area. Have you recovered your stolen property yet?"

Julie shrugged. "Not yet, but we will. We can prove it's all our stuff. Shouldn't be a problem." She tapped a pencil on the desk. "The jewelry was returned to the owners, and I hope that will be the end of it." She sighed. "No jewelry has ever been stolen here before, so it certainly points to one of the guests this week. By Saturday, they will all be gone, and we'll have a new crop of guests—and problems."

Nancy felt Julie's distress. She hated to fail, but they only had one more day to unmask the culprit. Who would steal jewelry and then return it? What was the point? Who would do such a thing?

An idea slowly coalesced in Nancy's mind. As it sharpened, she realized she knew who the jewelry thieves were. The answer was obvious once you considered the personalities.

"Julie, will you be in the office all morning?" Nancy asked.

Julie sat up, startled. "Pretty much. Lot of accounting to do. I'll be here until eleven or so."

"Good. We didn't help you find your stolen supplies, but I'll be back in a short while with, I hope, the answer to one other puzzle here. Come on, Louise." She pulled Louise out of the chair. "We've got work to do."

Outside the office, Nancy turned to Louise. "I want you to find Will and bring him back here, then both of you stand outside Julie's office until I call you."

"What's up?" asked Louise.

"I've got an idea, and I need you and Will to back me up."

Louise saluted. 'Aye, aye, ma'am." She walked to the lobby and out to Will's workshop. Nancy watched her go, a new idea forming in her mind. She was about to solve two mysteries plaguing Lilac Inn. She was sure of it.

Nancy hurried back to the dining room. Her eyes darted from guest to guest. Most of them were heaping their plates at the breakfast bar or devouring the food with coffee at the tables. Aysha and Cole plied Kimberly and Kai with pancakes. Kaye and Lew smiled at each other over their coffee. Marian was listening to Evan, who had opened up at her interest. Sarah and Gary sat quietly, each absorbed in his or her own thoughts. Harvey and Malcolm Smithson stared glumly into their coffee cups and ignored each other. Nancy meandered through the tables toward theirs.

"Up early this morning, weren't you?" she said pleasantly.

They cast unwelcoming looks at her. "We often get up early," blustered Malcolm.

"What do you want?" asked Harvey.

Nancy sat at their table. "You two are both experts on gems and jewelry. Harvey, you helped me out with my pearls at Whisperwood, and I am truly grateful." She believed in slathering on the butter. "Because of your expertise, you two can provide important information to Julie and Will. Information they desperately need. Are you about finished with breakfast?"

Malcolm and Harvey studied each other. "I guess so," said Harvey reluctantly.

"Let's go to the office, then." Nancy stood up. "Bring along your coffee." She led them across the lobby and down the hall to Julie's office. Louise had come in from outside, and Will followed her. Nancy nodded meaningfully at Louise and then at the office. Louise nodded back.

"You two go ahead," she said to Harvey and Malcolm. "I need to mention something to Louise."

The two men walked on. Nancy whispered, "Louise, you and Will listen at the door outside while I'm in there with Julie and the Smithsons."

"What's going on?" asked Will.

"Never mind," Louise said. "Do what Nancy says."

Nancy joined the Smithson brothers outside Julie's office, tapped at the door and entered as Julie called out, "Come in." Harvey and Malcolm followed. "Sit, please," Nancy said, pointing to the two padded chairs. She pulled a third chair forward to join them.

Looking like Tweedledee and Tweedledum, they took the chairs with sideways glances at each other.

She began in a stern voice, "How about you two telling us what you've been up to."

"What's this all about?" blustered Malcolm.

"What do you mean?" stammered Harvey.

"You've been playing a game, haven't you?" Nancy persisted, keeping cold eyes on both of them. She waited.

Malcolm finally sat back and chuckled. "She's got us, Harvey. Doggone it, she's got us."

Harvey frowned at Malcolm.

"What's going on?" asked Julie, a puzzled expression on her face as she looked from one brother to the other.

"They're your jewelry thieves," said Nancy. She folded her arms and nodded at Malcolm and Harvey. "How about telling her about it."

Malcolm pushed his lips in and out, ignoring Harvey. After a moment, he laughed again. "All right," he said. "It's okay. We've been doing this for years." He grinned. "It's only a game. No big deal. We try to outdo each other as jewelry thieves."

"We always return the jewelry," put in Harvey, anxiously. "No harm done."

"No harm done!" sputtered Julie. "Our hotel's reputation was on the line. No harm done indeed. I haven't been able to sleep this week worrying about the missing jewelry and hotel supplies and now Patty's murder. It's been horrible." Her eyes welled up, and she reached for a tissue, brushing it across her eyes and blowing her nose. "You think there was no harm done. I can't believe you'd be so stupid."

"I'm sorry," stammered Harvey. "We were only playing a game."

"Don't you people have a sense of humor?" Malcolm leaned toward Julie and pointed his finger at her. "You worry too much. Worse comes to worse, you've got insurance." He leaned back comfortably, a smug grin on his face. "Once the jewelry's back where it belongs, everyone forgets about the thefts." He snapped his fingers. "Not an issue." He leaned back, still wearing the smug grin. "Pretty damn smart work, if you ask me."

Julie exploded. "Not an issue! I want you out of here today! And you are not welcome here ever again."

Malcolm studied his fingernails. "Afraid not. The police asked us to stay until they're ready to let us leave."

"Only because of the murder," put in Harvey.

Nancy folded her arms and frowned at them. "I will ask Cole and Sarah to have their jewelry checked by a reputable jeweler—that does not mean either of you—to make sure synthetic stones weren't substituted for the real ones."

"Of course not! We wouldn't do a thing like that." Harvey looked horrified. "We were only having a little harmless fun."

"And we are reputable jewelers," blustered Malcolm, his face red.

"I think not." Julie's eyes sparked. "Tell Sarah and Cole

how much harmless fun you were having."

"Now wait a minute," said Malcolm. "Their jewelry's been returned. That's all they need to know."

"You owe them an apology," said Nancy. "Of course they'll learn who stole their jewelry."

"I will be alerting my colleagues in the hotel business about this incident," said Julie.

Malcolm sat impassively, drumming his fingers on the chair arm. "We'll sue you for defamation of character. You have no proof we did this. We'll deny everything."

Nancy stood, walked to the door, and opened it. "Did you hear that?"

"We sure did. Of all the crummy tricks. . ." Louise fumed.

"You two jerks could have ruined us," added Will, his face red from outrage.

Then Julie stood, frowning with eyes narrowed in contempt, "You will be prosecuted if you do this kind of thing again anywhere. Know that. Also know that you will be suspects in any jewelry theft in any hotel."

Malcolm sputtered angrily, then he stormed out. Harvey stayed. "I'm sorry, Nancy. I had no idea. When we started this. . .game, we took inexpensive trinkets. Malcolm insisted on more and more expensive items. I should have refused, but he's so aggressive. I couldn't stand up against him. I'm so sorry." He walked out, shaking his head.

Nancy shut the door after them and turned to face Julie and Will. "Good riddance, I say."

"How did you know it was them?" asked Julie. Louise and Will looked at her expectantly.

"It's obvious, when you think about it. Malcolm is so

competitive, you see," Nancy said. "And Harvey is his brother. They've been competing and playing games and laying bets all their lives. Once you realize their personalities, you've got your answer."

"Sure," grumbled Louise. "Obvious to you."

***

### Announcement: Find the Pot of Gold!

Can you find the pot of gold hidden somewhere on the grounds of Lilac Inn? It's actually a jar of tupelo honey from guest Louise Owens, who presented the honey tasting on Thursday. Tupelo honey is considered among the best-tasting of honeys. Winner can claim the jar of honey plus a gift certificate to May's Gift Shoppe in town. Thanks to Louise for coming up with the challenge and donating the honey.

*Will and Julie Harris, Owner/Managers*
*Lilac Inn Resort and Restaurant*

# 27. Later Friday Morning

Julie came around her desk and gave Nancy a big hug. Then she hugged Louise. "I'm so sorry I doubted you," she said. "You came through spectacularly. Harvey and Malcolm ought to be ashamed of themselves. We also now know who the thief of the housekeeping supplies was, and we'll be getting all our stuff back.

Will turned to leave, but Nancy said, "Wait. You can help us clear up another mystery."

"Me?" said Will.

"Yes," Nancy said. "Everybody come with me."

She marched them out of the office, through the lobby, and stopped as she saw Aysha and Cole reading in the wicker chairs on the veranda. The two kids were throwing the Frisbee for Tilly to catch and bring back.

Aysha glanced up at the group staring at them. "The kids aren't too noisy, are they?" she asked. "I can take them on a hike away from here."

"They're fine," said Nancy, "but we'd like the four of you to join us on a short walk to the barn."

"What?" Will looked at Nancy with horror. "No. That barn is private."

"Not any more," said Julie, taking his arm. "Do what Nancy says. "Your invention is scaring people. It's time you shared what you've been working on."

"But. . ." Will sputtered, backing away.

"It's important," said Nancy, "and will clear up another mystery that's been a problem for you."

"Do what she says," Julie repeated.

Aysha and Cole put their books aside and called the kids. "They haven't gotten into any trouble, have they?" asked Aysha.

"No. The opposite," assured Nancy.

The group, eight of them, strolled to the barn. They arrived at the huge barn door and looked at Nancy expectantly. "All right," said Cole. "Now what?"

Nancy turned to Will. "I want you to take out your machine and fly it."

"He's got a flying machine?" asked Kimberly.

"That's a plane, stupid," said Kai. "You've got a plane in there?"

Will glared daggers at Nancy. "You better have a good reason for this."

"I do," she said.

Julie pushed him forward. "Go ahead. Let's see it."

He turned his back to the onlookers, unlocked the barn door, and slid it open. "All of you stay out here," he cautioned. "I don't want any accidents."

He disappeared into the gloom inside. Nancy and the others waited outside. After a few minutes, they heard a motor start up, then a whirr. The propeller, Nancy thought.

Kai and Kimberly tried to peer into the barn, but they were held back by their parents. They watched as Will, sitting on something like a bicycle seat in a contraption that resembled a dragonfly, drove it out of the barn, bouncing on the ruts, and steered it toward the meadow.

The two kids stared in awe.

Nancy ran alongside and shouted instructions to him. He nodded. She stepped back and he pushed on the throttle. The contraption moved forward and gradually picked up speed. In a minute, it was airborne. Will flew it about half a mile, then circled to return. He'd switched on red lights that glowed from both sides of the engine.

Kai and Kimberly screamed. "The Mothman! That's the Mothman!" They took cover behind their parents as Will landed the plane, taxied it forward, and stopped. He turned off the motor and climbed out. "You satisfied now?" he snarled at Nancy. "I wasn't ready to show it."

Nancy put her hands on her hips. "Yes, but you've been trying it out in the evenings and early mornings when we've been asleep or at breakfast or supper."

"I didn't want anyone to see it."

"But Kai and Kimberly don't always come in to dinner on time. Sometimes they'd eat and run out. Same with breakfast," said Nancy.

"That's right," Aysha said. "And they get dressed and run outside before we even wake up."

"They'd heard the Mothman stories," added Nancy, "so of course they thought your strange flying contraption, which doesn't look like any plane we'd see at the airport, was the Mothman. They've been telling everyone about it."

"Someone in town must have seen it, too," said Julie, "maybe while they were hiking in the woods. That's why the Mothman and Green Monster stories have sprung up again."

Will groaned. "Oh, no. I never thought of that. It doesn't

look anything like one of those so-called monsters."

"A sandhill crane doesn't look anything like a huge moth and a falling meteor doesn't resemble a flying saucer," Julie added, "but people see what they want to see and spread stories, anyway."

Nancy leaned down to shake the hands of Kai and Kimberly. "Thank you, kids, for helping us clear up a mystery."

Cole walked to the strange contraption and inspected it. "Incredible! And this thing actually flies," he said. "Why would anyone risk his life in it?"

"It's perfectly safe," Will said. He took over and proudly began explaining how it worked to Cole and the kids.

Nancy, Louise, and Julie walked back to the veranda.

"I can't believe it, Nancy," said Julie. "You solved the Mothman mystery, too!"

"I told you she was good," said Louise. "Nancy, you came through again with blue ribbons."

Nancy shook her head. "Will showed me what he was working on shortly after we'd arrived. Once I heard the kids describe what they'd seen and thought about it, it wasn't hard to make the connection."

"I am relieved." Julie's face glowed. "I've been so worried about all the strange things going on around here. Even Patty's murder but it can't have anything to do with us or the inn. I'll be glad when they catch the murderer. Then maybe I'll finally get a good night's sleep." She reached down to pet Tilly, who had hidden in the shrubbery when she saw Will take out his plane. "And next week, we're almost fully booked. I won't have to worry about stolen supplies, jewelry thieves, or the Mothman. I'll actually be able to enjoy Lilac Inn."

"Good," Louise said. "You and Will work so hard around here, you ought to be able to enjoy it."

Nancy agreed, but she was thinking about Patty Hovermale, aka Madam Nuri, and her murder. There was still one more mystery to solve. Even if it didn't happen at Lilac Inn, there was a connection. She was sure of it.

***

**Announcement Posted on Lobby Schedule Board**
**See the Mothman Meteor!**

We invite our guests to a demonstration at 2 p.m. this afternoon of Lilac Inn owner Will Harris's unique ultralight plane. In honor of the Mothman and the Green Monster legends, he is calling it the Mothman Meteor.

Join us behind the barn at the edge of the meadow for the demonstration. Afterwards, see Will land the machine so you can take a closer look, and he will answer your questions.

Lemonade and cookies will be served.

*Will and Julie Harris, Owner/Managers*
*Lilac Inn Resort and Restaurant*

# 28. Friday Lunch

Nancy saw Harvey standing by the reception desk as she and Louise entered the lobby. Louise ignored him and Nancy kept her eyes looking ahead to the group waiting for the dining room to open for lunch.

"Wait, Nancy," Harvey called out as she passed. He must have been waiting for her. He stepped closer to her and seeing no way to avoid talking to him, she stopped.

"I see George ahead," said Louise. She glared at Harvey. "I'm not talking to this riffraff. I'll see you in the dining room." She walked on.

Harvey shuffled a blue cap nervously from hand to hand and cleared his throat. "Nancy, I'd appreciate it if you and your friends will keep our little game quiet around Whisperwood." He searched her face. "Please. We didn't mean to get so carried away here." He cleared his throat again. "At least I didn't. I assure you it won't happen again."

Nancy's eyes narrowed, and she crossed her arms. "I'll talk to the other 90s Club members," she said, "but if I hear of any jewel thefts around Whisperwood, you'll be the prime suspect. You need to understand that."

"We meant nothing by it," insisted Harvey. "It was only a game."

"Not to Cole and not to Sarah." Nancy said. "Or Julie and Will. And expensive jewelry, stolen and missing, might have something to do with Patty's murder. Have you talked to the police yet?"

Harvey gasped. "We had nothing to do with that. We never went near her place. Don't even know where it is." He raised his hands as if to ward away such an evil idea. "Anyway, you and the Harrises have our addresses if they must contact us. I don't see why they would. Everything was returned exactly the way it was."

"Maybe, but the jewelry will be checked to make sure." Nancy turned to leave. "You've shown us neither you nor your brother can be trusted."

Malcolm emerged from the elevator and walked toward them. "Harvey, come on," he said. "Let's go."

Nancy saw Louise wave at her as the dining room doors opened, and the guests straggled in for lunch. "Don't think I'll forget this," she said to Harvey.

"All right." He sighed and with one last look at Nancy, he joined Malcolm, and they strolled into the dining room as if they had nothing to hide. "Thank you, Nancy," Harvey called back to her, holding up crossed fingers. Malcolm held his head high with a tight smile on his face.

Nancy caught up with Louise, and they walked through the dining room to the verandah to take their usual table next to the rail. They were perusing the menu when Fitz came bounding in a few minutes later, then George, who looked fluorescent in a neon orange T-shirt. Louise pulled sunglasses out of her shirt pocket and put them on as she often did in response to George's sartorial tastes. She pointedly looked him up and down. "Very nice, George," she said sarcastically. She looked up to see Ingunn at her elbow. They gave their orders, then Ingunn grabbed up the menus and bounced to the next table.

Louise watched her maneuver before turning to the others. "Now that we're all here," she began, "I can report Nancy did it again," Louise smiled fondly at her friend. "She caught the jewelry thieves."

Fitz glanced at Nancy's wrists. "This didn't get you tied up like in our last case, did it?"

"Not at all," Nancy grinned. "Piece of cake."

"I'm glad someone had a good day," grumbled George. "I think my clubs are crooked or the ball's dented or something. Anyway, tell us."

"We found out something else. You're not gonna believe what happened this morning." Louise waved her hands in excitement. "Tell 'em, Nancy."

Nancy told them. "I saw both those brothers in the dining room, and the idea struck me."

"You mean it was Harvey and Malcolm?" George gaped at Nancy.

"Obvious, once you think about it," said Fitz. "They were always trying to best each other. Stealing jewelry was another game to them."

"None of us caught on," said Louise, "but Nancy."

Nancy held up a hand. "They're asking us not to say anything."

Louise glared at the two men, engrossed in reading the menu at a far table by themselves. Her eyes sparked. "They have a lot of nerve."

Nancy glanced at Harvey and Malcolm. Harvey kept his head down and eyes glued to the menu as if he felt daggers aimed his way. Malcolm played with bravado, gaily laughing with Ann and Lula at the next table. Then Ingunn showed up with their lunch plates. Nancy paused to let her finish distributing the plates and move on.

"We should keep Harvey and Malcolm's little game quiet," said Nancy. "They aren't being charged with the thefts, so they would have grounds to sue us if we accused them publicly."

Louise was having none of it. "Four of us heard them admit it!" she said.

"Yes. That's our defense, but after all, they returned the jewelry," Nancy added. "If they try that kind of stunt again, though, we'll nail them."

Louise nodded. "You bet we will."

Fitz reached for Nancy's hand and squeezed it. The gesture felt warm and intimate, and she smiled at him as he turned serious. "I'm glad Harvey and Malcolm weren't the murderers, but they could have become violent when you accused them. I'd hate to see you hurt again."

"I'd hate to see me hurt again, too," said Nancy. "I don't want any of us hurt, especially now that Louise's wrist is okay."

Fitz leaned back and fiddled with the fork beside his plate. "We've done what we came for, and more. The thief of the hotel supplies is exposed and dead. We knew nothing about the jewelry thefts, but those thieves are exposed now, too."

Louise flapped her napkin. "But wait. Nancy solved another mystery here, too. Tell them, Nancy."

"With Kai and Kimberly's help," Nancy said. "It was a matter of putting two and two together."

"Oh, yeah. The Mothman mystery." said Fitz. "Seeing

whatever it was in the sky almost made me a believer."

Nancy related the story of the Green Monster and the Mothman and Will's invention. "The kids saw his contraption in the air one morning and thought it was the Mothman."

"It had red lights on each side that looked like eyes," added Louise. "That's what made it so spooky. Freaked me out, and I knew it was an invention."

"Probably a few of the people who live in the area spotted it and started spreading rumors," said Nancy. "Now Will's decided to make an event out of showing his contraption. He's demonstrating it to the guests this afternoon. He says it's his improvement on an ultralight airplane."

"Nancy suggested he demonstrate it." Louise smiled at her friend. "Now that he's gotten used to showing it, he's getting enthusiastic. He's planning to ask other ultralight pilots in the state to fly in for the day. Should be fun."

"Great for the business," said George.

"Should help squelch all those rumors about flying saucers, too," said Fitz.

"Three mysteries are solved so far," said Nancy, eyes sparkling. "One to go."

Fitz cocked an eyebrow at Nancy. "Why not let the police solve Patty's murder? Killers are dangerous."

"As we know only too well," said Louise.

Nancy glanced at Fitz. She knew he wanted to protect her, keep her safe, but it wasn't in her nature to give up the chase. She shook her head. "We're on the site," Nancy said. "The murderer is one of us here at the hotel. I'm sure that's true. No one else outside the hotel has shown any interest in Patty except possibly Horace the Potter."

"That we know of," reminded Fitz.

"True. We don't know what she did when she was home," said Nancy, "but she didn't have a car, and she seems to have been a recluse when she wasn't at the inn." Nancy paused and looked at Fitz. "Were you able to talk to Sam?"

Fitz pushed his chair away from the table. "I did. I dropped by, acting real casual. No one else was in there, so I bought a wrist brace and chatted him up. He didn't know anything though. I don't even think he ever met her. Why would he? He's stuck in that shop most of the time unless he's giving lessons or a demo."

Nancy nodded. "Good. I'm sure you're right about Sam. He goes home right after work, too. She mostly came around in the evenings."

"Follow the money," said George. "Who gets her property?"

"Horace seems to think he's in line for it," put in Louise. "He's probably already sniffing around to find out if there's anything to get. Nancy's right. We're in the best position to nose around among the guests here."

"That may be so," said Fitz slowly, "but we need to stay together. I don't want any of us getting hurt."

Louise glanced at her wrist. "Me neither. Anyway, despite what we think, we should keep the staff in the picture, too. Patty was almost staff and could have an enemy among anyone at the hotel."

Nancy agreed, but the uncomfortable feeling that someone was watching her crept over her. She casually scanned the dining area, mentally checking off the guests who sat around the tables. She didn't recognize several people, who must have dropped by for lunch. She dismissed them but then caught Sarah's intense stare directly at her. Gary was immersed in the menu. Nancy turned quickly away. That stare disturbed her. What did she mean by it?

The sound of a spoon tapping on a glass turned her attention to Julie, standing by the door. Then she stepped to the center of the room and again tapped on a glass with a knife for attention. All eyes turned her way. She held up her hand and waved. "I want to remind you of the demonstration this afternoon of my husband's ultralight plane, the Mothman Meteor. I hope you'll all come to see it. It will be in the meadow behind the barn." She gave the glass and knife to a server and after a brief smile at the guests, she disappeared down the hall.

"What's our next move, Detective Lady?" asked George.

"We only have the rest of today and tomorrow morning. We'll have to work fast. I've already checked out the other guests and the staff on my various databases. No one has anything more than a few traffic tickets on their record. I checked out Patty and her husband, too. They also seemed to be exemplary folks. Nothing showed up of a criminal nature. Both of them had career-related websites and Google references to their previous jobs, but nothing criminal or questionable. The only possible motive we've turned up was when Horace asked who inherited her property."

"Not much of a motive," said Fitz. "That property is practically worthless."

"We need to get a better handle on who Patty was and how people felt about her," said Louise.

Nancy nodded. "All of us can quietly do a little probing about Patty with the people here. Be subtle. Don't give the impression we're investigating her murder. We are nosy parkers, simply curious about the murder victim. We don't want the murderer to feel threatened by any of us. That's what gets us into trouble, and we end up tied to our chairs."

"All in favor of not being tied up, say aye." Louise raised her hand and winked at George.

"Aye," said the others in chorus, clinking their iced tea glasses.

"Okay," Nancy said. "Any other ideas?"

No one spoke. Finally, Nancy looked at her watch and rose. "Louise, you and I should go back to Horace, buy another piece of pottery, and see if we can learn anything more."

"Okay. Sounds good." Louise grinned and rubbed her hands.

"Meanwhile," Nancy began.

"Act casual," put in Louise, "but keep our ears open." Louise stood. "Let's meet in an hour. I have a couple of things to do."

"Right." Nancy headed for the door, but Sarah followed her out.

"Nancy, wait." Sarah caught up to her. "I need to talk to you." She glanced nervously behind her. "In private."

"I'm waiting for Louise," Nancy said. "We're going to drive down the road a bit. Explore."

"Good. I'll join you till she comes." Sarah stepped alongside.

As they strolled side by side on the mulched path toward the bird blind, Nancy kept silent, waiting for Sarah to unburden herself.

The woods closed around them. No one followed, and only the crows and blue jays broke the silence. "I'm scared and worried, Nancy," Sarah began. "Weird things have been happening here. My necklace and Cole's ring stolen and then returned. Patty's murder. I want to leave immediately, but Gary refuses because the hotel won't refund our money, and anyway we leave tomorrow. Gary insists the murder has nothing to do with the hotel."

"That's right," said Nancy. "Patty wasn't employed by the hotel." *What did Sarah want?* Nancy surreptitiously checked Sarah's shirt and slacks for the sign of a weapon. She didn't see any, and Sarah was overweight and not athletic, but it would be better to stay where others could see them. Nancy casually backtracked out of the woods and led Sarah to a bench in view of the verandah. "Let's sit here," she said.

"Patty was always hanging around the hotel." Sarah clenched her hands together. "Do you have any idea why she was murdered?"

"She was murdered in her home, not at the hotel," said Nancy, "and she didn't work for the hotel. They simply allowed her to provide a little entertainment for the guests."

"But she lived so close. An easy walk for anyone here," insisted Sarah. "Did the police ever find the weapon?"

"I don't know," said Nancy, wondering what Sarah really wanted to know. She was fishing for something. "Did you know where she lived?"

Sarah brushed the question aside. "Everybody did. Her house, if you could call it that, was only a city block away. Over there." She pointed to a patch of woods encroaching on the dining end of the verandah. "There's a path to it through the woods. You can almost see the house from here, but it's all gray rotting wood because the paint is pretty much worn off."

Nancy disagreed. Hardly anyone knew where Patty lived. Guests wouldn't know unless they asked, but why would they? Nancy peered through the woods but couldn't see Patty's house, then she glanced at Sarah. "Sounds like you've been there."

"I have," said Sarah, "but it's not what you think. I only went there for a private reading." She shuddered. "Her shack, and it was a shack, Nancy. It was horrible. She even had an outhouse. An outhouse! I can't imagine it."

"She ran into hard times," said Nancy.

"I guess so, but her place was full of stuff. Not junk, really, rolls of toilet paper and paper napkins, towels, sheets, all kinds of stuff, all new and in their original packaging. Where did she get all that?"

"The police are investigating," Nancy said. "I'm sure they'll find out what she's been doing."

"You know what was really weird," added Sarah. "She had a pile of "Wanted" flyers and police magazines on her desk. What was she doing with those? She kept flaunting them at me as if I would be interested. I'm not."

Now there was a motive for murder, Nancy thought. She'd heard about this hobby of Patty's before from someone. Patty's husband was a writer. No telling what he was delving into. "Maybe her husband was working on a mystery novel," Nancy said. "He probably had those flyers for research purposes."

Sarah nodded. "That could be. But people said you were a private detective," countered Sarah. "Aren't you investigating, too?"

Of course she was investigating. It was in her blood.

But not with the police. She was simply helping Julie and Will. Would it help or hurt to imply that she was looking into the murder? Nancy decided on caution.

"I'm here on a vacation with my friends, not to investigate a murder that has nothing to do with me. Or you. The police will catch the culprit, and you'll find the hotel is not involved." She made it firm. "I'm sure we're perfectly safe here."

"Oh, do you really think so?" Sarah breathed. "I'm so relieved."

She didn't sound relieved. Nancy didn't think she believed a word of it. In fact, if Nancy had to pinpoint the right word, she'd say that Sarah was worried and suspicious. Suspicious of Nancy and her motives. Why would that be unless she were guilty? Was she guilty?

"So you aren't involved at all?" Sarah asked.

Nancy sidestepped the question. "Did you know Patty? Had you met her before?"

"Oh, no. Never met her before." Sarah spoke quickly as if to push the idea away. "Knew nothing about her, but she was a fortuneteller. I was curious that's all. Wondered what she'd have to say about my future. We'd all like to know that, wouldn't we?" She gulped.

"I guess so," said Nancy. "How come you went to her house? I thought she met people in their rooms at the hotel."

"Yes, that's right," Sarah said. "She did, but she said some things I wanted her to clarify for me. That's why I went to her house. I wanted a little more than she gave me, that's all. She really was insightful, you know, and she knew things, things she couldn't have known. I was curious and wanted to talk to her alone, without Gary hovering about."

"What kind of things?" asked Nancy. Patty made several odd remarks to the hotel guests. Remarks that suggested she knew something unsavory about their past. Sarah was one of her targets, Nancy remembered.

"Nothing important," Sarah said quickly. "It was just odd, that's all."

Nancy doubted that. It was important enough for Sarah to follow up with Patty who needed only to scatter vague hints like seeds and then watch for which ones took root. A guilty person would provide fertile soil. Nancy's husband Bill, the magician, had pointed out how fortunetellers worked, especially if they were also con artists. Patty talked about frauds and fakes. Could that have been a veiled threat for blackmail? Had Sarah gone to Patty's cabin to pay blackmail or confront Patty? Maybe murder her?

"One thing is bothering me," said Sarah. She stared at the ground and bit her lips. "I'm worried about it even though I know Gary wouldn't do anything to harm Patty. Neither would I."

"What is that?" asked Nancy, realizing they had finally arrived at the real reason Sarah wanted to talk to her.

Sarah lowered her voice. "I'm telling you because I think it might have something to do with the murder."

Nancy waited.

"You see, Gary kept a gun in the glove compartment of his car. Just in case," Sarah said. "But several days ago, I noticed the gun was gone. I don't know what happened to it, but somebody stole that gun, and I'm very afraid that person used it on Patty."

Nancy kept her face blank, but this news was a bombshell. "Did you tell the police?" she asked.

"Of course not. They'd arrest him for the murder. I'm sure he didn't have anything to do with it. Someone stole the gun and used it to kill Patty." She suddenly seemed to notice the woods behind her. "I want to go back now," she said in a little girl voice. "But not alone. Come back with me, Nancy."

"All right." They walked back to the hotel. Nancy didn't say much. She was processing Sarah's words. Why did she tell Nancy about the gun? Was she trying to protect Gary? Or herself? Nancy remembered Sarah sitting back and letting Gary do the paddling on the canoe trip. In fact, now that she thought about it, he was always doing little things for her. How wealthy was Gary? Nancy suspected Sarah had plans for that money.

Did Sarah expect Nancy to tell the police about the gun? If she did, would the police settle on Gary and not look further for the culprit? They must be searching for the gun. If they found it, then they'd trace it to Gary—or not, if it wasn't his gun. Gary could have sold it weeks ago and not told Sarah.

At the verandah, Sarah left Nancy to join Gary sitting in a rocking chair. Nancy walked past them to Julie's office and tapped on the door. Julie opened it. "Good. I'm glad to see you, Nancy." Julie stepped aside to let Nancy enter, then closed the door behind her.

"The police have been here interviewing everyone again," she said, worry in her voice. "I told them what I could, but that wasn't much. They'd like to talk to you, too. I hope our guests will want to come back after all this." She twisted her hands together. "I don't know why the police are focusing on us."

Nancy nodded. "You told me a little about Patty's background. Do you know anything more? Do you have any ideas about why she was murdered or who would do such a thing?"

"I've been asking those questions myself, and I can't come up with anything. Why? Why? Why?"

"Did Patty have any particular friends on staff?"

Julie thought a moment. "Missy Crain. You know our housekeeper, Carola Crain is Missy's mother. Missy and Patty got along well." She nodded to herself. "Yes, Missy Crain. I used to see them laughing together in the swing out on the lawn. They were good pals."

"Do you mind if I talk to Missy?" Nancy asked. "It would take her away from her job for awhile."

"If you can clear up the mystery, go right ahead." Julie frowned. "I don't know how much more of this I can take. We had two cancellations today."

"People change plans. Doesn't necessarily have to do with the murder."

"The murder didn't help our business. A couple of guests asked me about refunds if they left early."

"The 90s Club is on the job along with the police. You won't have any more problems with either thefts of the supplies or the jewelry," said Nancy. "And there's nothing to say that Patty's murder had anything to do with Lilac Inn."

Julie grimaced. "I know that, and you know that, but all the guests hear is that there's been a murder nearby, and the victim was someone they all knew, someone who was a regular here." She picked up the phone. "I'll get Missy for you. You can talk to her in the office. I've got errands to run."

Missy showed up ten minutes later, visibly concerned. "I didn't do anything wrong, did I?" she asked. "Where's Ms. Julie?"

Nancy shook her head. "Everything's fine," she said. "Julie said you could take time off to talk with me."

Missy smiled and took a deep breath as she sat in the chair facing Nancy. "That's all right, then. I was worried. What do you want to know?"

"You knew Patty Hovermale pretty well, didn't you?"

Missy held up her hands as if to say "whoa." Then she said, "Wait a minute. This isn't about the murder, is it? I don't know anything about that."

"Of course you don't," soothed Nancy. "But you did know her better than the others, didn't you?"

"I guess I did. She was nice. I like—liked—talking with her." She smiled at the memory. "Had more to say than most of the people around here."

"I liked her, too. She was an interesting person."

"Yes, she was."

"What did you talk about?" asked Nancy.

"She was a widow, you know," said Missy. "She missed her husband. He must have been quite a guy. They both worked for NSA." She laughed. "You know, No Such Agency, NSA. National Security Agency. She joked about that and explained it to me." Missy stared down at her hands, then shook herself and continued. "I'll miss her. I'll never live an exciting life like she did. She was an actress, too. Amateur theater. When they moved out here that's what she planned to do. Her Madam Nuri act was part of it. Her husband wanted to write novels. Then he died, and that changed everything for her."

Nancy nodded. She knew what that was like. She'd been widowed twice, and sometimes, even now, the sadness from loss overwhelmed her. Especially at holidays. She stopped herself from gazing into that abyss and noticed Missy watching her curiously. "Patty lived in a terrible shack," Nancy said to continue the conversation.

"Yeah, but they had plans, you know, to build a custom house on the property. She showed me their plans once. You can probably find them over there if you look."

So she hadn't been poor, at least then. She must have had money. If Horace inherited her property, did he think he might find hidden money on it? "Can you tell me anything else about her? Did she mention any close relatives?" asked Nancy. "Maybe someone who might be next of kin?"

Missy shook her head. "No. That never came up. Why would it? She was basically a good person. Even in her fortunetelling, she tried to be constructive and positive, planting good seeds, not bad. She didn't want to hurt anyone. I know that's true, but she may have gone off base sometimes, exaggerated, you know. If she didn't take to somebody, she might not be so nice."

Quite a different point of view. Patty as kind and good, not the blackmailer making threats. Who was the real Patty? Had poverty changed her? Made her rationalize blackmail? It could be turned into a simple business transaction if you twisted it enough. You pay me, and I'll keep your secret.

"I see." Nancy stood and Missy followed her lead. "Thank you, Missy. I appreciate your talking to me about this. If you think of anything else that might help, please let me know."

"You and the police," said Missy grimly. "We all want this guy caught."

***

**Notice to Guests: Make Check-Out Easy**

Later this afternoon, we'll slide your bill for the week under your door. Please check it carefully so any concerns can be resolved before you leave. We hope you had an enjoyable stay. We look forward to seeing you again! For your next stay, we'll offer you a 10 percent discount.

*Will and Julie Harris, Owner/Managers*
*Lilac Inn Resort and Restaurant*

# 29. Friday Afternoon

After the meeting with Missy, Nancy and Louise headed off to see Horace Hovermale. The drive was toward town and took only a few minutes. They found the sign advertising his art studio and turned into the rutted, overgrown parking area.

The cottage with its row of large, north-facing windows stared blankly at them. The place looked deserted. Was he home? Nancy pulled the bell rope hanging by the door and heard the loud, clear tones.

No one responded at once, but Nancy and Louise waited, then tried again. This time the door opened, and Horace Hovermale peered out at them. He hadn't shaved and seemed to be wearing the same paint-stained jeans.

"Come on in," the man said. He held out his hand. "I'm Horace Hovermale. You folks here to see my studio?"

Nancy stepped forward. "We were here yesterday and bought one of your beautiful bowls. Came back to take another look."

"Of course. I remember you." He turned and gestured for them to follow. "Welcome back." He hesitated. "You're staying at Lilac Inn. Were you able to talk to the owners about displaying my work?"

Nancy shook her head. "Not yet. They have enough on

their hands right now."

"Oh yes. The murder." He led them back to his studio, muttering, "Terrible thing. Terrible thing."

"You're related to Patty Hovermale," said Louise leaning against the counter. "Do you have any ideas about who would murder her? Or why?" Louise didn't bother with tact and diplomacy.

"Not a clue." He stepped behind a counter and waved a hand. "Help yourselves." His pottery filled the shelves, so much so that Nancy wondered if he made any sales at all. She pretended to admire the bowls and saucers and mugs as she let Louise try to draw the man out.

"I only saw Randall once after they moved out here," said Horace. "Then he died, and she drew into herself. Never once invited me over. Ashamed of the place, I wouldn't wonder."

"I hear it was a wreck," Louise said. "Probably not worth much. More of a problem, I'd guess, to whoever inherits it."

"Is that what they're saying over at the inn?" asked Horace, glaring at Louise. "Trying to cut down the value of it, are they?"

"We hear the orchard's a bust and the house she lived in is a shack," commented Nancy, setting down a small tray. "No electricity. Outhouse. Only a few acres. Not much value there."

"So what? Those people over at the inn needn't think they're going to get it for a song." Horace thrust out his jaw. "And you can go and tell them that."

"I guess whoever owns it now will make that decision," said Nancy, inspecting a small bowl. "Patty may not have made a will."

"Maybe not," said Horace, "but I'm the closest kin she has. I ought to get the property. Next of kin or not. She owes it to me."

"Why is that?" asked Louise.

"I loaned her a lot of money, enough to fix up that place if that's what she wanted. Which I guess she didn't. She owes me. Course neither of us thought she was going to get herself murdered." He wiped his hands on his jeans. "I didn't kill her, either, if that's what you're thinking."

"Nobody but you seems to have a motive," said Louise.

Nancy watched his expression. Was he acting shocked or had Louise scored a point?

"I'd never. . .the sheriff can't think. . .I'd never hurt her." Horace gaped at them.

"The sheriff will probably be by to question you once they find the connection," said Louise.

"You're right." He chewed his lip, thinking. Then he looked at them. "Do you ladies really want to buy something or are you here snooping?"

"I'd like this mug," said Nancy. "It matches the one I bought yesterday."

"Okay, then." Horace took the money. "Now you ladies get out of here. I got some thinking to do."

Louise followed Nancy out the door. As they drove back to the resort, Louise said, "We found out what we wanted to know."

Nancy glanced at Louise with a smile. "We sure did." She paused before adding, "But I don't think he had anything to do with Patty's murder."

Louise nodded. "Neither do I."

***

**Notice to Guests**

This area has many fine artists who open their studios to visitors on the weekends.

If you see an "Open Studio" sign on your way home, stop by, look at their wares, and chat with them. They have interesting stories to share.

*Julie and Will Harris, Owner/Managers*
*Lilac Inn Resort and Restaurant*

# 30. Friday Evening

Despite Julie's fears, none of the guests, even Sarah, expressed anxiety over Patty's death at the early evening happy hour. The intern Bridie mingled with the group offering cocktail sausages and asparagus wrapped with bacon. Missy stood behind the bar, serving wine, beer, and soft drinks. Nancy and Louise looked for George and Fitz, but neither had arrived yet.

If the conversation was a bit more subdued than on previous nights, no one mentioned it, and no one brought up Patty's death. Nancy listened for hints of dissatisfaction or fear but heard only pleasant chatter about their day's activities.

She stood next to the wall and watched the friendly group, all comfortable with each other near the end of their week's stay. One of these people gathered in this room could be a murderer. Who was it? Nancy felt the pressure of time running out. Tomorrow, all of them would disperse, moving on to other destinations or returning home. Harvey and Malcolm had not shown up. Nancy hoped they were sequestered in their rooms suffering from remorse.

Her gaze drifted from one guest to the other. She was inclined to rule out Cole and Aysha, who seemed so wholeheartedly involved with their children. On the other hand, they said they were military. What kind of military? What did that mean exactly? They worked at Fort Meade, where the National Security Agency was located. Patty worked for NSA. Were Cole or Aysha actually on a military assignment here? Did they know Patty? Nancy could imagine a scenario in which Patty was a spy, and Aysha and Cole were sent here to assassinate her. She was sure she'd seen a movie like that, but it didn't seem likely in this bucolic setting.

The children were an excellent cover-up for a covert operation. Would Cole or Aysha endanger the kids? Nancy couldn't imagine that, but if they were here on assignment to kill Patty, she couldn't see any danger for the kids.

Which one of the others had a guilty secret that led to murder? Did anyone else have a possible connection to Patty or her husband? Patty said someone at the hotel was a faker. Who did she mean?

Kaye Anderson, immersed in a broken love affair, had brightened up with Lew Cookson's attention. She seemed submissive, vulnerable, and feminine, a born victim for a bragging macho bully like Lew. Kaye was probably doomed to another disappointment come Saturday when everyone went back to their real lives. But Nancy had seen a darker side to Kaye, a side full of secrets. Would she turn into a tiger if she saw a threat to her relationship with Lew?

Lew. What a specimen. He had an explosive temper and responded to threats with aggression. He expected deference and attention from women. Patty was attractive and wore fetching clothes, but she still grieved for her husband and showed no romantic interest in any of the men at the hotel. Had he confronted Patty in her cabin? Tried to rape her? Did he carry a gun with him? Or was it Patty's gun, and he grabbed it out of her hands? Maybe he stole Gary's gun. Where was it? Or had Sarah planted the idea in an attempt to protect Gary or herself? Right now, Lew was the most likely murderer on her list.

Evan Lester, independent loner, walked in, laughing with Marilyn. He was an entomologist and a birder. He seemed mild-mannered and uninterested in the people at the inn. Could he be hiding a secret that Patty discovered? Nancy pondered this possibility, but in the absence of any sign of emotion from Evan, other than the connection he'd found with Marilyn, she relegated him to the bottom of the list.

All subject to change.

Ann Bashaw and Lula Beall. Impossible to consider them separately. They were pleasant people. Ann was logical and a problem-solver. Stable. She probably did well at her job. Lula was calm, warm, and easy-going. The canoe trip had shown another side of them as they bickered incessantly down the river, but nothing came to anger and a fight. Would Ann really kill if provoked hard enough? Lula seemed to think so.

Sarah and Gary Lochowsky, the middle-aged newly-weds. Gary seemed to be conventional and conservative and genuinely in love with Sarah. Could he have some secret that Patty discovered? A secret that might damage his relationship or his business? There was the question of the gun, which may be the murder weapon.

Sarah could have used a false ID. Easy enough to obtain, especially if you were involved in criminal activities. As a fortuneteller, Patty had made several cryptic remarks to Sarah. They sounded threatening but could have been part of her act, although alienating potential clients didn't seem like a productive business strategy to Nancy.

Marilyn Goldfarb's credentials had been easy to find on the Internet. She had to be resourceful, reliable and disciplined to maintain that stressful job. She never stayed at a job long, though. Was that how she managed the stress?

Among the staff, Nancy felt she could rule out the interns from overseas. Carola Crain, Missy Crain, and Chef Tom were possibilities. They were local, and all of them could have had some interactions with Patty. Missy certainly did. They could even have helped her steal supplies and sell them. How could Patty be a threat to them?

And that was the question with all the suspects. How could Patty have been a threat to any of them? So big a threat that one of them killed her.

Julie and Will could be suspects as well, Nancy supposed, but Julie was committed to making Lilac Inn a success. Why would she threaten it? Unless Patty presented a threat, but what kind of threat? Will worked hard around the inn, but he also disappeared for hours now and then, probably to work on his plane but not necessarily. He also found the body, which might seem suspicious if this were a movie.

Fitz strolled in, picked up a glass of wine, and maneuvered his way through the crowd to Nancy's side. "Warm out there. Turtle heads been popping up all day in the pond," he said. "Swimming to logs along the shore to sun themselves. Couple of wood ducks—beautiful birds."

"Sounds like you're enjoying yourself," said Nancy, smiling at his exuberance.

"I am." He sipped the wine. "Much as I like Whisper-wood, it doesn't have the variety of birds I see here." He winked at Nancy and glanced around for any onlookers before kissing her on the cheek. "Even with Louise's native plant campaign."

"Don't tell her about it," Nancy said, blushing.

Fitz pretended to shudder. "Oh, I won't. Between us, don't you know?"

The dining room doors opened, and the guests began to disperse toward them, heading for dinner. Fitz scanned the lobby as Louise and George ambled in from the verandah.

"Shucks," said George. "Missed Happy Hour."

"Come on, George," grumbled Louise. "You don't need all those fattening goodies."

"The hell I don't." He eyed a tray placed on a side table and stepped toward it to pick up the sole radish nestled in a bedraggled leaf of lettuce. "All gone, dagnabbit." He popped the radish into his mouth.

"Anyway, it's dinner time." Louise pulled him over to Nancy and Fitz. "Let's go in," she said.

After dinner, they met in Louise's room. Nancy agreed that her own room was too messy for a meeting. Having grown up motherless with a housekeeper, she never paid attention to such details as neatness and basic homemaking tasks. She barely knew how to cook, so living at Whisper-wood with its lovely dining room and excellent meals was a blessing. That along with the gym and pool kept her healthy, and she didn't hoard so whatever the mess was, it was current.

They all knew Louise's room would have chairs free of clothes and the desk swept clean of litter. Although small, the room contained a loveseat, a desk chair, and an armchair. Four comfortable places to sit.

Louise turned to Nancy. "I don't have the faintest idea who killed Patty," she said. "Our best bet would have been Horace, who probably inherits her property, but it's not much unless there is money hidden somewhere, which I doubt, and I don't believe he's guilty."

George nodded. "Neither do I."

Nancy grimaced. "I don't either, so let's start with why she might have been murdered."

"She knew something," said Fitz. "And she was stony then. Broke, don't you know?"

"Blackmail," breathed Louise. "She knew something about someone at the hotel and tried to blackmail them."

"Good," said Nancy. "That's a real possibility. Was she the kind of person to try blackmail?"

George roused himself. "She lived in a shack. She didn't mind telling bogus fortunes and pretending to be a medium. She could delude herself into thinking blackmail was some kind of tit for tat bargain."

"Yeah," added Louise. "I can see her doing that. Rationalizing it as a legitimate exchange."

Nancy gazed at the carpet. She could imagine Patty, desperately poor, seeking a way out, thinking one of the wealthy patrons of the hotel could easily spare money in exchange for guaranteed silence from Patty. "So who might have a guilty secret?" she asked.

The four looked at each other. "We all have met with the guests. Let's go through the list one by one. I've racked my brain on it, but you might have some other insights." Nancy pulled the list out of her purse. She started with the first on her list, Aysha and Cole.

"They're too wholesome," said Louise. "Can't see them being blackmail victims. Either of them."

"Neither can I," put in George.

Nancy went through the list of names. "The Smithson brothers could have killed Patty, but they readily admitted to the thefts and returned the jewelry. They were game-players and heavily into betting but made no secret of any of it except the thefts. They said they planned to return the jewelry all along."

"Maybe," said Louise. "But maybe Patty saw them steal the jewelry and threatened them with blackmail."

"And," added George, "they returned the jewelry so they could deny whatever she said."

Fitz spoke up in his Jamaican lilt. "Did either of them have another dark secret?"

Nancy nodded. "They could have. Any of the guests could have. How would they react to a blackmailer?"

"Lew would bully and fight a blackmailer," said George, "and I could see him attacking a woman, beating and raping her, but not shooting her."

"Kaye would fall apart," said Louise, "and be easily victimized. Can't stand that type of woman, but would she have the money to pay? I could see her running to Lew for help."

"Evan was a loner," added Fitz. "I don't think he'd care what anyone thought."

Nancy nodded as she studied the list. "Ann Bashaw had an executive-level job she could lose if the secret was dangerous enough." Then there was Lula. Pleasant, amiable, accommodating Lula. What if a secret threatened her relationship with Ann? They treated each other as equals. Ann seemed like the dominant one, but Lula was no pushover. How would either of them react to a blackmailer?

"Marilyn Goldfarb is a straight shooter. Kind of blunt," put in Louise. "She'd be more likely to try to counsel Patty. Help her find a better solution. She probably has had enough experience with dubious people not to be threatened by them."

Nancy thought of the dead baby robin. Why had Marilyn changed jobs so often?

George looked up. "Gary Lochowsky is in insurance, isn't he? He could lose his position and income if a dirty secret came out." He snapped his fingers. "That's not all. Sarah could lose her husband and comfortable lifestyle."

George was right. Nancy could not find much background on Sarah, married name or unmarried name. She could have an unsavory past as an embezzler, call girl, jailbird, or some other kind of criminal. She could be the fraud Patty talked about at the séance on Monday.

They mulled over the possibilities in silence for a couple of minutes until Nancy asked, "Any suggestions or comments?"

"All that about how they'd react is speculation," put in George. "We don't really know any of it for sure."

"I know." Nancy leaned back in her chair.

"So why else would someone want to kill Patty?" asked Fitz.

They stared glumly at the floor. Louise stirred. "Maybe her property was really valuable and she wouldn't sell."

Fitz glanced at her. "I say, have you seen her property? Not more than five acres with a shack and a dying apple tree orchard on it. Land prices in this area are depressed, and I doubt her property has oil, gold, or even coal on it."

"Maybe Will found out about her stealing the hotel supplies and killed her to stop the thefts," suggested George. "He was the one to find her, after all."

"I don't think so," said Nancy. "If he knew she was the thief, he could easily reclaim the goods and stop her access to the resort."

"Well," grumbled George, "you asked for ideas. We're brainstorming here."

"I don't think we're getting anywhere," Louise said. "We need proof, not speculation."

"She's the first person murdered in this county for years," said Fitz quietly. "I know, because I've read back issues of the local weekly. The last person killed here was five years ago. A local man thought he could goad a neighbor into shooting him, then he would sue the shooter for all he's got. He thought he'd receive a flesh wound, but he ended up dead instead."

"What an idiot," said Louise.

"Since the guests all came from somewhere else," added George, "we can't rule out a serial killer."

"Going through those back issues is the kind of thing I usually do, too," Nancy smiled at Fitz, "but I've been reading the local histories instead."

"Local history." Louise cut into Nancy's comment. "Maybe Patty called up a ghost who shot her with a ghost gun."

"Okay. Time to quit." George glanced at his watch. "It's late. We're getting nowhere. I'm going to bed." He stepped to the door. "Today is Friday. We leave tomorrow.

If we don't come up with the murderer tomorrow morning, leave it to the local sheriff. We did our job. The hotel thefts have stopped. We found the jewelry thieves and debunked the Mothman stories. We've done good here." He opened the door and walked out. "See you tomorrow."

Fitz yawned and was the next to leave. Louise reached over and tapped Nancy's arm. "Sarah acts like a spoiled prima donna, but what else do we know about her? What did she do before she married Gary? That's what we need to find out, Nancy."

Nancy resolved to chat with Sarah again at breakfast.

***

### Thank You to Our Guests

We hope you had a wonderful time here at Lilac Inn and that we'll see you again soon. Please let us know what you liked—and what needs improvement—by filling in the quick survey we slid under your door while you were at dinner. We'll give you a special parting gift when you turn it in at the front desk. Also, please check your itemized bill for any errors. We cannot be responsible for correcting mistakes after you leave the property. Have a safe trip home!

Until we meet again, happy trails! Don't forget the 10 percent discount on your next visit!

*Will and Julie Harris, Owner/Managers*
*Lilac Inn Resort and Restaurant*

# 31. Saturday Morning
# LAST DAY

Nancy rose early to hang around the lobby and wait for Gary and Sarah to show up. Ann and Lula were the first to appear. "Care to join us, Nancy?" asked Ann.

Nancy shook her head. "Waiting for Louise," she said.

Kaye came in next, her eyes sparkling and a wide smile on her face. Lew followed behind "We're off to tour Charleston," Kaye said, reaching over to take Lew's hand. "It's on our way back to D.C."

"Capitol has a gold dome, how about that?" added Lew, and they paraded past Nancy into the dining room. Kaye stopped. "You go on and get a table," she said to Lew. "I want to say something to Nancy."

He nodded, glanced at Nancy, and walked on. Kaye smiled at Nancy. "I know you think it's a mistake for me to spend time with Lew," she said.

Nancy demurred, remembering Lew's heartfelt sigh that night when he thought he was alone.

"His wife is leaving him," Kaye said. "He's going through a bad time. He needs company right now."

"Of course," Nancy said. She may have misgivings, but she knew how black and devastating the night can be. "Have a good time," she said.

"We will." Kaye stepped forward, gave Nancy a quick hug, then waved as she walked to the table where Lew sat waiting.

Louise came next, her eyes widening when she saw Nancy. "What's up?"

Nancy pulled her away from the dining room entrance. "I want to join Sarah and Gary for breakfast today. Stay with me and act busy until they come."

"You think they might've done it?" asked Louise, watching the elevator.

"I can't find much about Sarah on the Net. Maybe we can coax something out of her at a casual breakfast."

Louise nodded. "I see. Hope they come soon." She stepped to the dining room door to read the posted menu.

Marilyn walked out of the elevator next. "Louise! I'm so glad I met you. I still haven't thanked you properly for the tour you graciously provided of the social services in this area. I really appreciate that, but it doesn't make me want to move here." She laughed. "I found out I'm a big city girl."

Louise beamed. "It was fun for me, too. I guess this area isn't for everyone."

"I guess not," Marilyn glanced into the dining room. "Care to join me?"

Louise looked at Nancy. She wanted to spend time with Marilyn, and Nancy didn't have the heart to insist Louise stick with the original plan. "Go ahead," Nancy said and then to forestall Marilyn from insisting Nancy join them, she added, "I'm waiting for Sarah and Gary."

Louise gave Nancy a long look, nodded, and followed Marilyn into the dining room for breakfast.

Nancy studied the posted menu. Perusing it was a good ploy. She watched the elevator as it opened. This time, it discharged Sarah and Gary. "Show time," whispered Nancy to herself. She turned to gaze out over the dining tables as the couple approached. Turning casually, she nodded at them. "Mind if I sit with you?" she asked. "I was looking for company."

"Of course," said Sarah. "Join us."

They found a table on the verandah next to the rail. Nancy took her customary seat facing the dining room.

Gary leaned back and patted his stomach. "I'm gonna miss these five-star meals," he said.

Sarah glanced at him, shaking her head. "I'm glad we're going home. I shudder to think how many pounds I've gained." She looked up as the server arrived and took their orders.

Nancy smiled winsomely at Gary. "I hear you're in the insurance business," she ventured.

"That's right. Homeowners, automobile, whatever. If it's insurance, we do it." He pulled out a card case. "Take my card. Anything you want to know about insurance, call me."

"Thank you," Nancy said, tucking the card into her pants pocket. "What about you?" she asked, looking at Sarah.

"I worked in the office. Love blossomed." She giggled and snuggled closer to Gary. He put his hand on top of hers.

"It sure did. After my first wife died, I didn't know what to do with myself." He gazed fondly at Sarah. "This little lady was a real help during that tough time."

"I'm sure." Nancy was busy reassessing Sarah and

Gary Lochowsky. Sarah didn't have a mysterious past, only a banal one. Unless she used poison on Gary's wife. "Did you both come from that town? What was it again?"

"Cleveland," Sarah and Gary said at once. "I was born there," said Gary. "Went off to college, came back and stayed." He stopped as the server arrived with their plates.

"I was born in Chicago," added Sarah. "Went through a bunch of jobs then moved to Cleveland to try something different. Now that was a good move." She smiled at Gary and blew him a kiss.

"Sure was, honeybun," said Gary, winking at her.

*Who moves to Cleveland on a whim?* The Internet search showed she'd been from Canton. Maybe she had to get out of the Canton area. Did she leave on the run or for some other dubious reason?

"Hard to pick up and move," Nancy commented.

Sarah shrugged. "Nothing to keep me in Chicago."

"What kind of work did you do?" Nancy asked.

"Clerical. Bookkeeping." Sarah laughed. "Easy to pick up that kind of job."

Nancy glanced at Louise, chatting happily with Marilyn at another table. Bookkeeping. That was interesting. She remembered working on a case once involving an itinerant bookkeeper who wormed her way into the confidence of her employer, embezzled the company, and then moved on, using new credentials, new IDs, new hair color, each time. Nancy tracked her down, though, and she'd been convicted. That was years ago, but new crooks cropped up all the time.

Gary shoved his chair back. "Got to go. We have to pack and clear out of the room, and I want to make my tee time." He nodded apologetically to Nancy. "I'll get in nine holes anyway before we have to leave."

"I plan to sit on the verandah and read until he's done," said Sarah. She stood and smiled at Nancy. "Pleasure meeting you. Maybe we'll see you again sometime."

"Thanks for the company," Nancy said.

Sarah took Gary's arm, and they walked out together toward the elevator, passing Marilyn on the way. She blew a kiss to Nancy. "Got some packing to do," she said. "It's been great."

Louise walked to Nancy and whispered, "I saw all that lovey dovey stuff between Sarah and Gary. Made me want to puke. Did it seem as phony to you as it did to me?" Louise had a low tolerance for what she termed as "mush."

Nancy raised an eyebrow at her and shrugged. "Go figure."

"So do you think either of them did it?" pursued Louise.

Nancy gazed at the elevator. "I don't know." Maybe she had been too hasty in her Internet search. A lot of unsavory activities could easily fall below the radar and never appear on the Internet or a police blotter. Sarah's background was sketchy at best. Nancy considered Missy's account of Sarah's visit to Patty. Sarah had left Patty's place teary and angry. A recipe for murder?

Maybe it was time to heat the pot. Nancy turned to Louise. "George is out on the links again, isn't he?"

Louise sighed. "Who would have thought? Here I am, a golf widow, and I'm not even married."

"I'll find Fitz. When Sarah and Gary come down to check out, I'll ask Julie to bring them into her office. Can you hang around the lobby and join us in the office?

"Oh boy." Louise rubbed her hands. "Is this going to be one of those unmask the villain sessions?"

"Maybe," said Nancy.

In thirty minutes, the small group was assembled in Julie's office. She brought in extra chairs so everyone could sit comfortably in the space. A coffee pot and hot water for tea sat on a small credenza next to the door along with cups, sugar, and cream. Tilly the dog lay at Julie's feet, watching and emitting periodic low growls.

"So why are we here?" asked Sarah. She sat upright and tense, gripping her handbag in her lap. Gary sat next to her, eying all of them as if waiting for a timeshare spiel. Louise and Fitz leaned back in their chairs, looking at Nancy.

Nancy deliberately slowed her pace, taking a cup, filling it with hot water and a tea bag. Adding sugar, stirring, removing the tea bag. She could hear the impatient rustling in the chairs behind her. Then she turned and took a sip of tea. She wasn't sure how to proceed, but moving slow should ramp up the tension.

"Why are we here?" repeated Sarah. "We have things to do."

"Thank you for coming," said Nancy. "I'm sure we all want to get to the bottom of the problems here at Lilac Inn, particularly Patty's murder."

"We had nothing to do with that!" Sarah's voice rose.

"I've been checking on Patty and the residents here," said Nancy. "You were the last to see Patty alive. You went over there late Tuesday evening. One of the staff saw you."

"I couldn't have been the last person to see her alive," argued Sarah. "I didn't kill her."

"You were seen leaving her place angry and upset." Nancy took a deep breath. "And you had access to a gun."

"What?" said Gary. "She most certainly did not."

"I told you. It was stolen days ago, way before Patty's death." Sarah's face turned red. "I only went over there for a private reading. When she finished, I went home. Simple as that. I may have been upset at some of the things she said, but I didn't kill her."

"I'm sure Missy has already talked to the police," Nancy said, "but I'm also going to tell them and suggest they look into your background carefully. I think they'll find you have a lot to hide."

Sarah glanced at Gary and bit her lip as she stared down at her hands twisting together in her lap. Finally, she said, "I'm a nice person. Really, I am." She looked at Gary. "You know I'm nice, and I work hard, and I never gave the company any reason to not trust me, did I?"

Gary shook his head. "It's all right, honey. I love you. I know you're a good person."

Sarah took a deep breath and kept her eyes on his face. "I got into some trouble a long time ago. That's it. Nothing to do with Patty or my life now. Nothing of interest to the police. There's absolutely no reason to tell the police anything about me. I had nothing to do with the murder." She began to cry.

Nancy snuck a look at Gary's face. He was staring at Sarah thoughtfully. He sighed and turned to Nancy. "Leave her alone. I'm the one you're looking for."

Sarah glanced at him through her tears in astonishment. "You?"

"Tell us about it," said Nancy softly.

Gary spoke directly to Sarah. "I knew you were in trouble, honey. I could tell by your face and then when you crept out of our room Tuesday night, I decided to follow you." He wiped a hand across his eyes. "I wasn't jealous, baby, but I had to know what was bothering you." His eyes swept the room, hovering briefly on Nancy's face, then Julie's. "I listened outside the shack which was full of holes. Can't imagine anyone living in that kind of hovel." He shrugged.

"I couldn't hear all she said to you but enough to know she was blackmailing you." Sarah started to speak, but he held up his hand. "There's no use dealing with blackmailers. They'll never go away. They'll keep on bleeding you and bleeding you until there's nothing left. I couldn't let that happen."

"She didn't want much money," Sarah cried. "Only a little to get her back to civilization. I could have given her that."

"Only the beginning, honey. Only the beginning." Gary sighed again. "So after you came back to the hotel, I went to my car, retrieved my gun from the, uh, trunk of the car— that's why you didn't see it in the glove compartment. I wasn't going to shoot her. Only threaten her with it, but the damn thing has a hair trigger, and it went off by accident." He shrugged. "Of course, no one's going to believe that."

Sarah turned to him and took his hands in hers. "We'll get the best lawyer we can find," she said. "It was an accident."

He looked at her. "I love you, honey. I didn't want you hurt." He glanced at Nancy. "Now you don't have to have the police check into her past. Leave her alone. She had nothing to do with it."

"What did you do with the gun?" asked Nancy.

He laughed "What do you think? Maybe I dropped it into the deepest part of the river we canoed in on Wednesday. Whatever I did with it, nobody'll ever find it."

Nancy glanced at the others. Louise's eyes were narrowed as they darted from Gary to Sarah and back again. Did she believe Gary's story? Fitz had his chin in his hand as if he, too, were appraising the situation. Julie's face had cleared, the worry gone. After a few minutes, she reached for the phone. "I'm calling the police."

Nancy watched the touching scene, but she was already having misgivings. Gary was doing his best to protect Sarah. If Sarah recognized what he was doing, would she let him confess to a murder he didn't commit?

"We'll wait here," said Gary. Sarah had pulled her chair closer to his, and they sat together, holding hands.

"I'm so sorry. . ." began Sarah through her tears. "You deserved better than me, and now. . ." she gulped, and the tears started again.

"Buck up, honey," said Gary, putting his arm around her. "I'll feel better getting all this out in the open." He looked at Julie. "Can I use your phone? I guess I'm gonna need a good lawyer."

Sarah's cries became louder. Nancy felt the gnawing in her stomach. This scene wasn't right. *I've made a mistake.*

"Shush, shush, my little darling," said Gary. "It's good that it's all come out. I don't care what you've done. We'll get through this. Remember that we Lochowskys don't pay blackmailers."

Nancy reached over and patted their clasped hands. "I'm sure you will," she said. They aren't guilty, she thought, but continued to play out the scene as her mind raced through the list of suspects. "You're right. It is good." She looked at Julie. "Otherwise, all the staff here would be under a cloud of uncertainty, each person wondering if the other person was a murderer."

She turned to Julie. "The police will be here soon, so we'll leave and let you all take care of it." She opened the door and stepped out. Fitz and Louise followed.

They walked to the dining room, picked up another cup of coffee or, in Nancy's case, tea, and found chairs on the verandah. Since the week's guests were packing up and getting ready to leave, no one else sat there.

"Is he protecting Sarah?" asked Louise, "Playing gallant hero?"

"I was wondering that, too," said Fitz. "Or were they accomplices?"

"I don't think either one of them did it," said Nancy, "I made a mistake."

"What?" Louise stopped to stare at Nancy. "Gary confessed."

"I was wondering about that confession," said Fitz.

Nancy nodded. "Sarah was the most likely person for blackmail, and I knew she'd met with Patty the night before her murder and came away angry. I could find out very little about her on the Internet, which seemed as if she'd either done nothing criminal or changed her name to hide it, but changing her name didn't necessarily have to be for criminal reasons. Of course, she was a newlywed and changed her name when she married, but there was nothing under her previous name either. It was all a bit suspicious."

"I would have voted for Lew myself,' said Louise. "Of

all the blustering. . ."

Fitz laughed. "We know, Louise."

Louise gazed off at the golf course. "I wonder if George would murder someone for me."

"What are you going to do about this problem?" asked Fitz. "They shouldn't have to be arrested and tried for a crime they didn't commit."

"I don't know," said Nancy. "Yet."

***

### A Treat on Your Trip Home

On your trip home, stop at Horace Hovermale's art studio, which is several miles down the road towards town. He is a fine artist and potter and today only, he is offering Lilac Inn guests a 20 percent discount on any purchases. We will be proudly carrying his art and pottery in our gift shop and restaurant in the future. Also, don't forget that we're offering a 10 percent discount to returning guests. Please have a safe trip home. We hope to see you again soon!

*Will and Julie Harris, Owner/Managers*
*Lilac Inn Resort and Restaurant*

# 32.  Later Saturday Morning

Nancy and Louise sat in the wicker chairs on the verandah and watched the sheriff's car arrive, lights flashing.

"Subtle," said Louise. "No one would ever know."

Nancy didn't respond. She didn't feel like talking. Sarah and Gary. Newlyweds on a belated honeymoon that turned ugly, and now their life together was blighted, maybe destroyed. She hoped Gary had a good lawyer.

She watched Fitz walk back from the bird blind and trot up the steps. He leaned down and kissed her cheek. "Still brooding?" he whispered.

"I don't think they did it," said Nancy. Out of the corner of her eye, she saw Louise take in the kiss and realization dawn. Thank goodness she didn't say anything. Nancy sighed. "I'm so sorry about Sarah and Gary."

Louise snorted. "I'm not. I think they're guilty, and I'm glad they were caught. They almost ruined Lilac Inn with their shenanigans. I wouldn't be surprised if Sarah was going to pull the same stunt on Gary, given time."

Louise was probably right, Nancy thought. Patty's murder gave Sarah a powerful hold on Gary if he hadn't confessed, and she learned he'd done it. It was still a sad ending to the week.

Nancy sat silently a long time, mulling over the events

of the week. She didn't like sending Sarah or Gary to jail. Especially since she was questioning what happened. Gary thought Sarah had killed Patty. That was obvious. So he was protecting her by claiming to be the murderer himself. And Sarah seemed to believe that Gary had killed Patty to protect her. Why wouldn't she? He'd been super protective of her all week. But if Gary didn't do it, and Sarah didn't do it, who did?

Nancy sat back in the wicker chair and thought. An inspiration suddenly struck. She saw Louise on the lawn chatting with Marilyn. "Louise!" she called. "Can I talk to you for a minute?"

Louise waved to Marilyn and climbed the verandah steps. "What's up?"

"I want to use your expertise," Nancy said, heading for the lobby elevator.

Louise followed Nancy to her room. Inside, Nancy opened her laptop and typed in a name in the search window. A long list of entries appeared. Nancy selected one. "Do you know anyone here?" she asked.

Louise scanned the entry. "Not here," she said, "but I saw another place." She backtracked and selected a different entry. "This one. I know several of the people here."

"Call them," said Nancy. "I have some questions for you to ask."

***

An hour later, Nancy, Louise, Fitz, Julie, Will, and Marilyn sat in Julie's office.

"I've made a mistake," Nancy said. "Sarah and Gary had nothing to do with Patty's murder."

Every face in the group looked astonished but Louise's and one other's. Nancy watched her and noticed the clenched teeth and the hands that gripped the chair arms. "It all seemed right. Sarah did have something to hide, and Patty knew it. Sarah probably thought about how she could get rid of Patty but in terms of paying her off, not murder. Gary assumed Sarah had killed her. He'd missed the gun and thought his wife had taken it. We've all seen how protective he has been toward her this week. Of course he'd step in and claim to have killed Patty."

"I'm really sorry about this," said Louise, "but the game's up, Marilyn.

"Me?" Marilyn blustered. "I didn't kill anyone. Why would I kill someone I barely knew?"

"She was like that little bird, wasn't she?" said Nancy. "A pathetic creature you thought needed to be taken out of its misery." She shook her head. "But Patty was blackmailing you, too, wasn't she?"

"We found out about your mercy killings in New York," said Louise. "I have friends in the agency you worked for, and I checked with several others. You've left quite a trail."

"You're crazy," Marilyn shouted. "They don't know what they're talking about."

Louise turned to the others. "The trouble is no one wanted to ask questions. People died when Marilyn worked with them. She usually used their own medicines to kill them or some other subtle ploy. Hard to prove anything against her, so they quietly let her go to find another job and the same thing would happen. Again and again. Not enough to do more than raise eyebrows but leaving her coworkers uneasy."

"I knew Marilyn had jumped from job to job," added

Nancy. "I just didn't connect that with the way serial medical killers work."

Marilyn stood and her eyes darted from Nancy to Louise to the others in the room. "Those people all died of natural causes," she said. "I can't help it if I happen to be there when they died. None of it was my fault." She edged toward the door, but Will stood in front of it, blocking her way.

"I think the authorities will be looking closely into all those cases," Nancy said. "They are on to you." She glanced at Julie who was biting her lips, staring at her lap and shaking her head. "Patty was getting her life back in order," Julie said quietly. "Her husband's death unhinged her for a while, but she was getting better. I could see it in her."

"Serial killers in the medical field can rack up hundreds of deaths before they're caught," said Louise. "If there's any suspicion, they are let go to move on to some other place. When the new place calls for references, they get a standard response with no hint of wrongdoing or problems. No one wants to get sued."

"I still didn't kill Patty." Marilyn folded her arms and glowered. "No one's proved I did anything wrong ever."

"I called the sheriff before this meeting. He is hunting the grounds for the gun you stole out of Gary's car," said Nancy. "I think you hid it on the grounds near the house. They'll find it, and it will have your fingerprints on it. I know you didn't have it on the canoe trip. You didn't carry anything with you big enough to hide it, so you didn't throw it in the river."

"You shouldn't have changed your MO," said Louise. "That's what did you in. They'd never have gotten you if you'd just used pills or maybe a poison mushroom or two."

Will stepped out of the office. He was gone a moment before poking his head in. "The sheriff's here. Paddy wagon's out front. Here he is." Will stepped aside.

The officer stepped in and nodded at Nancy. "We got it," he said, glancing around the room. He looked at Marilyn. "This here the person we want?"

"That's right, Officer," said Nancy. "Here's a list of names who can corroborate what we've been saying."

He took the list and nodded at Marilyn. "We've got places to go, ma'am." She stood and stared at the floor quietly as she was handcuffed and walked out.

"I can't believe it," said Julie. "What a week!"

***

### Special Gift Cards to Nancy and Louise

*Dear Nancy and Louise,*
*Both of you are welcome to dine in our restaurant and stay in our luxury suites at our inn at no charge. We ask that you call ahead for reservations because we anticipate that we will be very, very busy and the restaurant and rooms will book up fast.*

*Thank you for all your help!*

*Julie and Will*

# 33. Saturday at Lunch

Nancy, Fitz, and Louise followed the sheriff out of the office. In the lobby, Louise banged her cane on the floor. "Think of it," she said. "We came to solve one crime, the theft of housekeeping supplies at Lilac Inn, and ended up helping solve a case of jewelry theft, squelch the Mothman rumors, and uncover a murderer. I think all that's worth four more notches on my bedpost." She grinned. "That makes seven so far."

Fitz laughed and Nancy smiled as George walked in. "What's so funny?" he asked.

"Never mind, George," said Louise. "My suitcases are packed, but I'd like to have lunch here and then say goodbye to Julie before leaving."

"Good plan," said Nancy. "The dining room just opened."

They trooped through the lobby to the dining room, bypassing a pile of suitcases at the reception desk. Harvey and Malcolm stood next to them with their wallets out. Malcolm turned and spotted Nancy as she passed.

"Don't worry," he grumbled to her. "We're checking out. You won't have us to kick around any more."

Harvey fiddled with the keys in his pocket. "Don't forget, Nancy. I'll make it up to you."

"What did he mean?" asked Louise as they took their regular places in the dining room next to the rail on the verandah.

"He promised no games at Whisperwood." Nancy unfolded her napkin. "And I'm holding him to it."

Fitz laughed. "Maybe you should hold out for a diamond necklace."

Nancy shook her head.

Ingunn, the Norwegian intern, arrived with water and champagne glasses. "From Chef Pierre," she said. "And all of us. Thank you. We worry that we will be accused, but now everything okay." She glanced at the entrance where a group of people in shorts, T-shirts, and sunscreen waited. "And so we have all new guests, you see?" She pointed to Chef Pierre in the doorway to the kitchen, flaunting a thumb's up sign toward their table.

As one, the 90s Club—Nancy, Fitz, George, and Louise—stood and applauded the chef and the staff.

Later, as they left the dining room, Julie and Will met them in the lobby. "We don't know how to thank all of you," said Julie. "Now we can get back on an even track, and right on time, too."

"Season's starting," added Will with a grin. "Almost fully booked."

"You don't say." George beamed at them, his face glowing almost as much as the neon green polo shirt he wore.

Julie threw her arms around Louise to hug her, then hugged Nancy, Fitz, and George in turn. "Come back, anytime. Lunch, dinner, even a week's stay, will be on us."

"And call on us, if you have any more burglaries, murders, or Mothmen," said Fitz, chuckling. "We're the 90s

Club, no job too hard."

The goodbyes were said all around. The elevator opened, and Daquon walked out with their suitcases stacked on a cart, nodded to them, and headed to the cars in the parking area. The foursome followed him.

Fitz and Nancy strolled slowly behind Louise and George, who were holding hands.

"We have a lot to discuss, don't we," said Fitz.

Nancy looked up at him, eyes glowing, a shy smile on her face. "Yes, we do," she said.

*** 

*The Whisperwood Breeze:*
**Travel Notes from Our Residents**
Nancy Dickenson, Louise Owens, Fitzhugh Connelly, and George Burroughs recently returned from a week's stay at a fabulous new resort only an hour's drive from Whisperwood. They highly recommend Lilac Inn, near Flatwoods and the Wildlife Management Area, for a relaxing stay with birding, hiking, canoeing, golfing, tennis and other outdoor activities. All agree that the restaurant, with both outdoor and indoor seating, is superb and worth a visit for that alone.
*Newsletter, Whisperwood Retirement Village.*

# Acknowledgements

In each of the 90s Club mysteries I use some elements from the Nancy Drew book of the borrowed title and include hidden references in the story. It's up to the reader to guess what those might be.

In driving through West Virginia, my husband Rog and I came across billboards advertising the "Green Monster Festival." We asked in the next town what the festival was about. Who was the Green Monster? We found out the festivals had been discontinued, but no one could tell us about the Green Monster. I looked it up on the Internet and learned about the Green Monster and the Mothman there. My description of these two bits of West Virginia lore are accurate and fit well into the mysteries plaguing Lilac Inn.

My husband Rog and I owned a farm for twelve years outside the spa resort town of Berkeley Springs, West Virginia. Our farm had a second house that we turned into a vacation retreat for visitors to the town. I was a member of Travel Berkeley Springs and chair of the Ecotourism Committee. Our farm became an ecotourism site. We were also beekeepers and as part of our ecotourism activities, we gave honey tastings, using honeys given to me by friends who traveled around the world as well as our own delicious pine pollen honey. I enjoyed recapturing some of these memories in this book.

My 90s Club series portrays 90-year-olds as able, alert, and active like many of today's 90-year-olds. They present a positive role model for the perennial decades, one badly needed to counter the pervasive negative stereotypes that ridicule, stifle, and emotionally cripple the aging.

I want to thank all those who helped me in writing this book. My critique group partners, Millie Mack, author of the Millie Mack mysteries, and Janis Wilson, author of *Goulston Street: The Quest for Jack the Ripper*, spent hours on chapter after chapter offering comments and suggestions. Maureen Klovers provided invaluable help in fine-tuning the plot. Meg Magee and Penny Clifton, author of *Murder Among the Mannequins*, each gave the manuscript a careful editing eye. Sisters in Crime and the Maryland Writers' Association continue to provide inspiration, insights, and information. Most of all, I am indebted to my husband Rog who backs me every step of the way and provides ideas and suggestions to keep me going.

*Eileen Haavik McIntire*

**If you liked this book
please put a review on
Amazon.com**

# *Enjoy these other 90s Club Mysteries*

### The 90s Club & the Hidden Staircase

Nancy Dickenson and the 90s Club at Whisperwood Retirement Village discover a simmering brew of thefts, murders, and exploitation bubbling beneath Whisperwood's luxurious lifestyle. The menace grows and even Nancy's kitty cat Malone takes part, turning the murderer's confidence into terror. "A 'must' for readers of cozy mysteries." *(Midwest Book Review)*

### The 90s Club & the Whispering Statue

The 90s Club heads south to Fort Lauderdale to rescue one friend and find another. Once again, murder and mayhem stalk the 90s Club as they race to save their friends' lives and, ultimately, their own. "A fun read. . .nostalgia and. . .social commentary, wrapped up in an engaging mystery novel." *(Foreword Reviews)*

### The 90s Club & the Secret of the Old Clock

Nancy seeks an antique clock's secret as she and the 90s Club discover swindlers are targeting the residents at Whisperwood Retirement Village. The 90s Club pursues a killer and the con men, but the killer is no fool and attacks first. This time, the killer swears, Nancy will not escape. "An impressively well crafted and thoroughly entertaining mystery. . ." *(Midwest Book Review)*

# *Historical Novels by*
# *Eileen Haavik McIntire*

## Shadow of the Rock

Two women, 200 years apart, seek their past and their future in parallel stories that merge in an ancient cemetery in Gibraltar.

Setting sail for America in 1781, Rachel Levy and her father are captured by Barbary pirates and brought to Morocco for sale. Without money or resources, Rachel and Moses must use their wits to find a way to freedom.

Two hundred years later, Sara Miller discovers her grandmother's buried past and is sent on a quest to find her great-uncle lost in the Holocaust.

"A riveting tale of time and humanity, highly recommended. (*Midwest Book Review*) "A bold adventure." (*Foreword Reviews*)

## In Rembrandt's Shadow

In 1616 Spanish Netherlands, Saul Levi Morteira rescues a family from the ravages of the Inquisition and takes

them to egalitarian, tolerant Amsterdam. In gratitude, the family commissions Rembrandt to paint a portrait of Saul as a gift.

Four centuries later, Sara Miller and Josh Davila dig up a Rembrandt painting, hidden since the Holocaust, and risk their lives seeking the rightful owner.

# Suspense by
# Eileen Haavik McIntire

## The Two-Sided Set-Up

Melanie Fletcher flits from one bad relationship to the next, then she meets the man of her dreams and marries him. She soon realizes he's an abuser and a criminal, but

she has a secret, a private "room of her own," a boat adequate for living aboard. She escapes the brute she married, taking incriminating documents with her, and sails back to her home to confront the demon who set her up for bad choices—her abusive, obstinate, drunk of a dad. Now she's in for more surprises as he sets her up for the fight of her life. Who can she trust? Who will help her? Where will she hide when the man she married tracks her to the small backwater town and tries to reclaim her and the documents she stole? He will never let her go alive.

## From Kirkus Reviews -

"McIntire's latest novel is a fast-paced and multilayered thriller with well-developed characters and colorful settings. . . Most of the action is set in Virginia, and McIntire does a fine job of capturing the rhythm of its small-town life, from the friendliness of local business to the calm of quiet nights on the water. An engaging tale for aficionados of psychological suspense."